DETROIT PUBLIC LIBRARY

P9-EFJ-196

ENDORSEMENTS FOR PAT SIMMONS

I am so loving Guilty by Association! *Girl, you went all out!!!! When I thought there could not be a man to compare to Parke, you created "Kidd"! WOW is all I can say. . . . No, I take that back, WOW! WOW! WOW! The love . . . WOW! The relationship blossoming . . . WOW! The man . . . WOW!*

—DARLENE MITCHELL, VIRGINIA GUILTY CAPTAIN

Life and a last name is all that Kevin "Kidd" Jamieson received from his father, but that doesn't stop his father's family from seeking him out. In Pat Simmons' latest book, Guilty by Association, *we meet Kevin Jamieson, a man with a chip the size of the Grand Canyon on his shoulders. The resounding message is* love *and the ultimate love comes from God. I love this series and can't wait for the installment that will be about Kidd's bad boy brother, Ace.*

CHASE BRANCH LIBRARY
17731 W. SEVEN MILE RD.
DETROIT, MI 48235
578-8002

—JERSEY GIRL MIA DANIEL, NEW JERSEY GUILTY CAPTAIN

Each book keeps getting better and better. I enjoyed Guilty by Association *from cover to cover.*

—YOLANDA HARRIS, PRESIDENT GLORY GIRLS BOOK CLUB
AND ST. LOUIS GUILTY CAPTAIN

—*Crowning Glory* . . . voted best Christian fiction for 2011 by O.O.S.A. Online Book Club and the Romance Slam Jam Committee

—*Not Guilty of Love* nominated for African-American Literary Festival in Norfolk, VA

—*Still Guilty* voted best Inspirational Romance of the Year (2010) by Romance Slam Jam/Emma Rodgers Awards committee

OCT 2012

CHASE BRANCH LIBRARY
17731 W. SEVEN MILE RD.
DETROIT, MI 48235
678-8002

THE JAMIESON LEGACY

free from guilt

PAT SIMMONS

guilt

MOODY PUBLISHERS

CHICAGO

© 2012 by
PAT SIMMONS

All rights reserved. No part of this book may be reproduced in any form without permission in writing from the publisher, except in the case of brief quotations embodied in critical articles or reviews.

Scriptures taken from the *Holy Bible, New International Version*®, NIV®. Copyright © 1973, 1978, 1984, 2011 by Biblica, Inc.™ Used by permission of Zondervan. All rights reserved worldwide. www.zondervan.com.

Edited by Kathryn Hall
Interior design: Ragont Design
Cover design: Faceout Studio
Cover image: iStock #6823112 / Shutterstock #43055743 and #44351440
            123RF #8822479
Author photo: Naum Furman

Library of Congress Cataloging-in-Publication Data

Simmons, Pat
    Free from guilt / Pat Siimmons.
      p. cm.
    ISBN 978-0-8024-0389-6
    1. Man-woman relationships—Fiction. 2. African Americans—Fiction.
3. Saint Louis (Mo.)—Fiction. I. Title.
PS3619.I56125F74 2012
813'.6—dc23

                                            2012023827

1 3 5 7 9 10 8 6 4 2

Printed in the United States of America

"For though we live in the world, we do not wage war as the world does. The weapons we fight with are not the weapons of the world. On the contrary, they have divine power to demolish strongholds. We demolish arguments and every pretension that sets itself up against the knowledge of God, and we take captive every thought to make it obedient to Christ."
—2 Corinthians 10:3–5

C ameron Daniel Jamieson wasn't going down like his brothers and cousins in the romance department. No woman in the world would get him to a prayer altar as a prerequisite for the wedding altar.

Absolutely, he wanted to get married, and he somewhat was on the prowl for a wife. His criterion was she had to be the one his heart refused to let get away. Furthermore, he had a major stipulation. Cameron didn't believe in mixing religion with politics—at the workplace or in relationships—and definitely not outside of the church walls. That was nonnegotiable.

He did a quick sweep of his relatives gathered in the dressing room of the small St. Louis, Missouri, church. Cameron noted the common thread among the men. Their wives had dug their stilettos into the ground, refusing a diamond ring, unless their Jamieson men humbled themselves to Christ first. How ridiculous was that? Yet that's exactly what happened to them.

His cousin Aaron "Ace" and Ace's wife, Talise Jamieson, were moments away from renewing their wedding vows in an elaborate ceremony. A few months earlier, the couple had married a mere three weeks before their precious daughter was born.

This was a happy ending to their tumultuous courtship. Cameron paused in his thinking. He guessed there were always exceptions to any rule. Maybe, if it wasn't for Jesus intervening in the couple's troubled relationship, he wouldn't be standing there about to witness the affirmation of their bliss.

Nonetheless, Cameron took credit for introducing Talise and Ace, even though they eventually split on bad terms. Later, when he learned that a future illegitimate Jamieson child was at stake, Cameron didn't hesitate to intervene in his cousin's business. He refused to lose any connections to his ancestral tree.

Once Ace got his act together and proposed, Talise had two stipulations to her holdout of saying yes. First, she didn't want to be pregnant in a wedding dress. Second, her sister, who was serving in the Persian Gulf, had to be present. Today Talise had her wishes fulfilled. Women and their demands could really put a strain on a brother.

Oddly, the "groom" was nervously pacing the floor.

"Chill, dude. You're already married. It's not like Talise is going to leave you standing at the altar," Cameron taunted his cousin, who was more like a third brother to him.

"Today is all about my baby. You have no idea how important this is to her. Everything has to be perfect," Ace replied. With a thoughtful pause, he stared down at Talise's wedding rings and his band. Now cupped in his palm, those precious jewels had been on their fingers a day earlier.

At that moment, Ace's s cell phone rang and ended the discussion. When he answered, the photographer snapped a picture. Eavesdropping on the one-sided conversation, Cameron sensed something wasn't going as planned.

"She did what? You've got to be kidding me!" Ace roared. After listening a few minutes longer, his voice softened. "It'll be okay, love," he consoled. Then exhaling, he finished the conversation, "I'll see you in a few. I love you, babe."

"Something is not okay. What's going on?" Cameron, along with the other groomsmen, was ready to spring into action.

"It's Talise's stepmother, Donna," Ace responded. With a quick glance around the room, he checked to see if his father-in-law had returned from the men's room.

"She's in the bridal chamber giving Tay all kinds of grief. Among other things, she's complaining about why she had to wear pink instead of white. You'd think it was her wedding day. If that's not enough, the woman's harping on why we couldn't renew our vows in Talise's hometown of Richmond. Her parents still live there, but my wife hasn't lived there in years."

Cameron knew Ace didn't hold his tongue if anyone upset his wife. This was supposed to be a joyful occasion.

"The final straw was when Donna demanded to be escorted down the aisle as part of the wedding party. Thank God, Grandma BB stepped in and put the woman in her place."

"Yikes." Cameron stuffed his hands in his pockets. It was a known fact that Talise did not refer to Donna as her stepmother. After the death of her mother, the best Talise could manage was to claim the woman as her father's new wife.

"Yikes is right. Grandma BB shoved Donna out the door with a warning. Unless Donna wanted to go home with a limp, she'd better not even try to put her big toe in the center aisle."

Cameron barked out a laugh. He would never get use to the antics of Mrs. Beatrice Tilly Beacon, better known as Grandma BB.

Ace shook his head. "We'd better keep an eye on her, or Grandma BB will be fighting in church."

"Stranger things have happened," Cameron mumbled, recalling the notorious behavior of the woman who claimed to be seventysomething years old. Interestingly enough, she vehemently maintained her status as part of the family–even though she didn't have a drop of Jamieson blood.

The childless widow took her role as grandma seriously.

The photographer snapped a few more shots and walked out just as Talise's father entered the room. "Wait until you see her. She's beautiful and happy." Frederick grinned and shook hands with Ace. "Keep her that way and there won't be any problems."

After that statement, Parke, Cameron's oldest brother, suggested they pray. Linking hands, the men bowed their heads.

"Father, in the Name of Jesus, we come before Your throne of grace. We worship You today for this opportunity to witness the love between husband and wife. I ask that You bless my cousin's marriage and bless his life in this Christian journey. Most of all, Father, bless their precious daughter."

Parke paused, before adding, "And, Lord Jesus, please bless every married man and their households represented here today. Help us never to fail You as the strong Christian men You created us to be, in the Name of Jesus. Amen."

A series of Amens echoed around the circle. One by one, the men patted Ace on the back. Frederick, the proud father-in-law, had the first honor.

Ace tilted his head. "Ah, it appears there's one man standing in this room who isn't hitched. Cameron, you're the lone ranger."

"Not for long. Even the Bible says it's not good for man to be alone. With thirty-two knocking on my door, who am I to argue with God?"

"You argue with us about God all the time," Parke reminded him. "Why stop now?"

"Trust me," Cameron said with a wink. "I don't need God's help on this. I'm fully capable of choosing my own woman. Her body and beauty have to attract me, her intellect has to mesmerize me, her ambition must impress me, and a strong sense of family ties will keep me."

"She's taken." The sentiment floated around the room, as each Jamieson claimed they had already married that woman.

Cameron confidently asserted, "There's one more, and she won't get away."

Chapter One

Gabrielle Dupree, and her sidekick since college, Denise Rayford, quickly squeezed into the church pew. The processional was about to start any minute. It had been one delay after another to get there. Their flight from the East Coast was late, their rental car wasn't ready, and then they made a wrong turn. It was amazing they'd made it on time.

Talise and Gabrielle had become extremely close when they worked together at an airline in Boston. Before she relocated to St. Louis, Talise had come to depend on Gabrielle as her confidant for friendship, advice, and prayer.

As a result, Gabrielle wouldn't have missed Talise's big day for anything. Denise, on the other hand, had her own agenda for attending the ceremony. Her sole purpose was to verify if she was related to the wedding party. It was a long, complicated story that still confused her.

If Gabrielle could have rearranged her work schedule to be there days earlier, she would have been a bridesmaid along with the others. Still, Talise wanted to include her in the wedding pictures and ordered her to wear pink.

About two hundred guests packed the sanctuary. Besides the many floral arrangements positioned throughout, silver and pink satin bows adorned the ends of each pew. Suddenly, the lights dimmed and candles flickered.

Romantic was the only word Gabrielle could utter to describe the setting. Minutes later, a minister led a group of five, tall, buffed, and jaw-dropping handsome groomsmen to the altar. She had to exhale over the awesome spectacle. Particularly noting the one with a shaved head and a goatee, Gabrielle thought, *Wow, bald never looked so good on a man.*

With a laser-like focus on the back of the church, the groom stood erect by the minister.

Denise nudged her. Gabrielle was breathless with awe. "The darker ones are almost carbon copies of my brother."

"Really?" Gabrielle said casually. "I have no complaints about God's handiwork. They are all fine. My girl has good taste," Gabrielle whispered to her friend, whom she had dubbed the "wedding crasher."

Denise was under the impression Talise's husband and brother-in-law could be her half brothers—all because of the last name Jamieson. There must be thousands of Jamiesons in the world. Still, Denise was on a mission to track down and unite the eleven children her deceased father, Samuel, had spawned in his younger years.

"But are you sure?" Gabrielle looked around to see if anyone nearby was eavesdropping. She had never met any of Denise's brothers, only her older sister.

"Now what?"

Frowning, Gabrielle leaned closer. "What do you mean, 'now what'? You're the one who masterminded this scheme."

"I know. When you said your friend was marrying Aaron Jamieson from Boston, I cross-referenced his name with the information I've gathered. There were too many coincidences for me to ignore. But how do you approach someone who is possibly your sibling and say, 'We have the same no-good daddy. I thought we should meet and get to know each other'?"

This was all Gabrielle's fault. Somewhat regretfully, she had mentioned an invitation to a Jamieson wedding. When Denise asked her if she was taking a date along, Gabrielle responded no. She had yet to understand why there was an unspoken rule about attending nuptials alone. Yet she didn't think having one of her brothers to escort her was necessary. All of that gave Denise a perfect opportunity to invite herself.

Gabrielle glanced around at some of the guests. Many were coupled off. A few seemed to be in hushed intimate conversations. Love was thick in the air. She sighed. It had been a while since a man who put the Lord first in his life had come her way. Being the romantic that she was, Gabrielle believed just witnessing the ceremony would renew her hope that true love was still possible for single Black Christian women.

As the music shifted to the wedding march, guests turned their attention to the back of the church where the double doors slowly opened. As though she were the main attraction, an elderly woman stood smiling and then slightly bowed her head. With what appeared to be a death grip on her usher's arm, the woman began her slow, unsteady walk. Watching her proudly holding her chin high, one would have thought it was a runway performance.

Murmurs increased with her every step. As the distinguished matron neared her pew, Gabrielle blinked. Although elegantly dressed, she raised a brow at the woman's peculiar choice of footwear. Two-tone burgundy-and-white Stacy Adams shoes seemed to swallow up her delicate feet. The shoestrings were replaced with pink satin ribbons that complemented her rose-colored evening gown. *Eccentric* was the only word to describe her.

"Who dressed her?" Denise whispered.

"I think she did. I believe that's Grandma BB. Talise told me about her. The woman is a force to be reckoned with."

"I'll remember that if she's related on the Jamieson side."

Next, as a memorial to Talise's deceased mother, a female usher slowly walked down the aisle, carrying a single white candle with a pink bow around the base. She paused at the altar and then proceeded to light a large candelabrum nearby.

Waiting in the wings was Talise's mother-in-law. Sandra stood regally in a pink satin dress that wrapped around her slender but shapely figure. No one would believe she was in her mid-fifties.

Watching her walk down the aisle, Gabrielle hoped she had a body like Sandra's when she hit fifty. Plus legs like Tina Turner's. Talise told her it was a long story why her mother-in-law had never married.

Oohs and *ahhs* could be heard as Sandra moved in step with the music, cradling Talise and Ace's infant daughter in her arms. Ten-week-old Lauren was also adorned in a long, pink satin dress and bonnet. She looked more like a porcelain doll than a baby.

"Wow." Gabrielle sighed, as she followed the graceful glide. Her eyes misted in happiness that her friend had found the love of her life, even if Ace had to beg for her forgiveness. Talise called him a jerk during most of her pregnancy.

"Do you think I should say something?" Denise asked, breaking into her reverie.

"Huh?" Gabrielle blinked, not appreciating the interruption of her thoughts. "What? I don't know. This is a festive occasion. If they don't already know about you, then I don't think now is the time. Saying something that might dampen the mood, I'm sure, will not go over well. You're only supposed to be an observer, remember? Not an interloper."

Denise placed her finger to her lips. "*Shhh*. I'm trying to get caught up, surrounded by all this love."

After the five bridesmaids and the flower girl made their entrances, two musicians rose to their feet and blew their trumpets. Throughout the chapel, the guests also stood. Beaming with a proud look, Talise's father escorted his ecstatic daughter down the aisle. From the expression on her face, one would never know that she had been married already for more than two months.

But Gabrielle had witnessed firsthand Talise's heartaches that came before the bliss. Standing on the sidelines, she had cheered the couple on. She was a true believer that love would find its way. Unfortunately, it hadn't made it to her yet.

With Talise's move to St. Louis, Gabrielle felt the void. As close friends, they had become inseparable. Often complimented on their beauty, there was no competition between them. Now staring at Talise in yards of tulle and satin, Gabrielle doubted if she would ever duplicate that spectacular look if God blessed her with a mate.

Turning her attention to Ace's face, Gabrielle sighed at the tender loving way the man was looking at Talise. Her mind captured another wow moment to pen in her handbook of romance. It was one of those silly notions she had started as a teenager when she began writing fanciful ideas in a spiral notebook.

Gabrielle loved weddings. It didn't matter if she was a guest or part of the bridal party. It was the atmosphere, the romance, the gaiety, the peace-on-earth feeling that always engulfed her.

She withheld a chuckle. Gabrielle was the only girl in a family of three brothers, and none of them were married. Since her brothers welcomed her to the thirties club last month—she wondered what her siblings were waiting on. For her, it was definitely the perfect God-fearing man.

Her main requirement in a mate was that he had to be a practicing Christian man, not a Sunday morning pew warmer . . . Add to that description, the love of her life must be highly romantic . . . Okay, for her future children's sake, she definitely needed to add good looks.

Ace's eyes sparkled as he locked on Talise's every movement. Even when Lauren whimpered in his mother's arms, he never took his attention away from his bride. When Talise was close enough, Ace stepped forward and reached for her hand. Lovingly, he escorted her to the altar.

Admittedly, Talise's pregnancy was the reason behind their hasty nuptials a couple of months ago. The couple's initial vows had taken place in a pastor's office back in Boston. However, there was no doubt in Gabrielle's mind that Ace loved her friend. God blessed them in a mighty way after they repented for their sins and followed the Lord's complete plan for their salvation. From now on, they had the power to live godly.

Unexpectedly, Ace knelt before Talise and looked up into her glowing face. Gabrielle thought she would faint from his public display of seduction and admiration. She strained to hear every word of their renewed vows.

"Baby, you gave me everything when I met you. You're beautiful, you love God, and you love me. I promise to cherish you—"

"Hey," Denise whispered, nudging her again, "he even sounds a little like—"

Gritting her teeth, Gabrielle shushed Denise. Bringing her along was definitely a bad idea.

Ace finished his vows, stood to his feet, and slipped on Talise's rings. Then he reached into his pocket and pulled out a tiny box with a pink strip of ribbon inside. Walking over to his mother, he knelt and tied it around his daughter's tiny wrist. Gabrielle couldn't see it all, but the gesture was purely tender and romantic.

"Whoa, I am so itching to ask them."

Annoyed, Gabrielle squinted at Denise. "And I am so itching to put you back on a plane for the East Coast. With all this love in the air, again, now is not a good time. I can swing by the drugstore and get you a bottle of Benadryl. Not only will it stop the itch, the antihistamine should knock you out."

—⚏—

Cameron smirked at the conclusion of the ceremony. Once again, another Jamieson had reached a happy ending. He didn't know Ace had that much romance bottled up inside of him. It was mind boggling to witness the way his cousin wooed the woman who was already his wife.

The ushers asked that everyone wait in the foyer to congratulate the couple. The photographer would be taking wedding party pictures within the chapel for a time.

As Cameron gazed around the sanctuary, a flash of beauty assaulted him. Holding his breath, Cameron locked in on his target—a woman gathering her things from a pew—a vision of pure loveliness.

Who was she and who had invited her? He dare not lust in church, but the woman was a striking temptress. From her body language, he deciphered that she and another woman were involved in some type of disagreement. *About what?* he wondered.

Cameron noted that she was also wearing pink. The gorgeous creature could definitely be mistaken as part of the bridal party. Mentally, he scratched out the word *striking* from his assessment. *Exquisite* was a better description. As she stepped out of the pew, he couldn't keep his eyes off her legs. Kudos on their lusciousness.

Her hair was coal black, her face was medium brown with dark brows and eyes that could hold a man captive . . . and her smile . . . there was absolutely nothing unattractive about her.

Evidently, other men thought so, too, as Cameron spied them admiring her. He snickered, knowing how this scenario was going to play out. Hopefully, she was planning on attending the reception. If so, no other man would get within three feet of her. Cameron would make sure of that.

Glancing over his shoulder, the photographer was shooting Ace, Talise, and Lauren. After verifying that his presence wasn't needed yet, he turned back to check the woman's hands. Her ring finger was waiting for a proposal.

Yes!

How was she still available? Never mind, she was, and that's all that mattered. He folded his arms as his nephews ran circles around him. Cameron was about to make his move and introduce himself when the object of his attention started heading his way.

Unfortunately, disappointment took over when he discovered that he wasn't the main attraction. Cameron watched her bypass him and connect with Talise. The two screamed their delight at seeing each other. Side by side they could pass as sisters or close relatives.

"Gabrielle, I'm so glad you could make it!" They wrapped each other in a tight, lingering hug.

Gabrielle. Hmm, an angel in disguise? Or, naughty as sin? Before the evening was over, Cameron would have his answer.

"It was so beautiful," Gabrielle gushed. They chatted on until the photographer broke up their reunion and Cameron's assessment.

The patient photographer instructed everyone to get into position for group pictures which, surprisingly, included Gabrielle. Good, she wouldn't be able to escape.

After countless poses and flashes, the photographer advised that he had a special request from the bride and groom. Sitting gracefully in a chair, Sandra held in each arm, her two granddaughters, Kidd's and Ace's babies, who were less than a month apart. No doubt, the cousins would be heartbreakers in the future. That tender moment would forever be ingrained in Cameron's mind.

Family. He would always have a soft spot for kinfolks. His brothers and cousins dubbed him the "family man" because of his thirst to track down his ancestors. Ironically, it was now apparent that Cameron was the only one without a family—no wife or children.

"Okay, people," announced Eva. Talise's sister-in-law was the self-appointed wedding organizer. Clapping her hands to get their attention, Eva instructed, "The photos are complete for now. Our guests have formed a line outside the door leading to the Hummer limo that's waiting for us. The sparklers are lit and everyone's waiting to cheer the happy couple on, so let's go."

Sandra's two sons lifted their daughters from her arms. Members of the wedding party paired up and followed the happy bride and groom through the church's double doors. Everybody, that is, except Cameron. He had his eye on Gabrielle, who seemed to be engaged in another hushed conversation with the woman he'd seen her with earlier. What was their story?

Gabrielle hadn't noticed him throughout the picture taking, but Cameron planned to make a lasting impression. Before he could put a plan into action, to his surprise, her friend practically dragged her toward his way. Lucky him. Stuffing his hand in his pocket, Cameron held back. Lifting a brow, he waited.

"Excuse me. My name is Giselle Rayford, but I go by Denise. And, this is Gabrielle Dupree . . ."

"The G-Gs," he commented, as his gaze strayed to Gabrielle and lingered on her face. "I'm Cameron Jamieson." He shook Gabrielle's hand first, immediately noticing her soft touch.

"Yes, we got that a lot when we were in college, so I started to use my middle name," Denise interjected.

"What college?" he asked, shrugging off his cousin Ace, who was waving for him to come on. He motioned one moment with his finger but would take more time if needed. He could apologize to Ace and Talise later.

"Howard University," Denise answered proudly.

"Hmm. Founded in 1867. It still remains a thriving HBCU today," Cameron rolled out the tidbit. "Impressive list of alumni: Debbie Allen, former U.S. Supreme Court Justice Thurgood Marshall, Andrew Young, Vernon Jordan, the first African-American mayor of New York City, David Dinkins . . . I graduated with a double engineering degree from MIT in Boston, and recently completed my doctorate."

"Gabrielle lives in Boston," Denise said, appearing in awe of his knowledge.

Could his luck get any better?

On the other hand, her friend didn't seem fazed, as Gabrielle added, "Yes, we take pride in the success of every alumni."

Did she just politely dismiss him? Cameron grinned and tried again. "Of course, I'm just trying to impress the lovely ladies. So you're the Gabrielle who worked at the airport with Talise. Did you actually graduate from Howard?" Immediately, he frowned.

That didn't come out right either. Cameron always spoke his mind and got it right the first time, so why was he backpedaling with Gabrielle? Personally, he had nothing against a ticket agent position, but that job didn't require a degree.

Degrees opened doors. That's why he now had three. He was looking for a woman who was well-rounded, and that included reaching for the highest opportunities.

"Do you mind if I have a word with you?" Denise asked before he could further put his foot in his mouth.

"Only if Gabrielle accompanies you," Cameron answered Denise, never taking his eyes off her friend. "I hope you're coming to the reception. Trust me, you will have my undivided attention." He walked away toward the waiting limo outside.

Chapter Two

*F*irst impressions rule. Why did all good-looking men seem to be pompous? Cameron Jamieson was the epitome of cocky. There was no way that arrogant man could be the same one Talise raved about. Especially considering she had been pregnant and couldn't stand any Jamieson. Period.

The way her friend described him, Cameron was thoughtful and sweet in addition to being all things masculine. At the least, Gabrielle would give him credit on the last point.

"If he's related to you, I don't like him. He might as well have the word *pride* tattooed on his forehead," Gabrielle chided, watching him swagger out the door. To make matters worse, she was mad that she couldn't keep her eyes off him.

Denise, who barely could keep quiet throughout the ceremony, had no comment. Once the ceremony was over, Gabrielle couldn't talk her friend out of holding her peace. At her first opportunity, Denise was determined to say something. Of all the Jamiesons standing at the altar, she randomly chose to approach Cameron. Gabrielle wanted to wring her best friend's neck when she dragged her along.

"Was it my imagination, or did he turn up his nose at my profession?"

When Denise shrugged, Gabrielle vented silently. Her friend was burning to mention her maiden name was Jamieson to anyone who would listen. If there had been a puppy in the wedding party, Denise would probably hold it captive too. Why couldn't she take an indirect approach and talk to Talise in a few months?

Lord, please don't let us cause a scene. Gabrielle inwardly groaned as she gathered her purse, program, and shawl off the front pew and prepared to leave. This was her punishment for bringing an uninvited guest. Never, ever again.

Once they were outside the church, Gabrielle took in the joyful sight. Guests had formed a Soul Train line on both sides of the pathway. Most were serenading the couple—off key—to R&B singer Brian McKnight's "Love of My Life." Fortunately, the crooners got the words right since they were printed on the back of the wedding programs. The singing continued as the silver stretch Hummer limo pulled away from the curb—another wow moment for her handbook.

"That was classy," Gabrielle declared, as they fell in step with the crowd. Everyone began dispersing to their respective vehicles. Crossing the street, she deactivated the alarm on her rental car. In her opinion, everything had been perfect until Cameron opened his mouth.

"And those Jamieson men are so good-looking," Denise said, after getting inside the Ford Taurus.

"No argument there." After strapping in her seat belt and adjusting the rearview mirror, Gabrielle activated the GPS. In seconds, they had directions to the reception venue in downtown St. Louis.

Gabrielle didn't hold back her thoughts. "I wish you would reconsider talking to them. Why spoil their happiness by revisiting the sins of your father? There's a time and place for that and, believe me, this isn't either."

"Gabrielle, I do plan to use sensitivity, but I've traveled farther than you have from Hartford."

"Hartford is barely an hour from Boston," Gabrielle reminded her. "Since I gave you a buddy voucher, the flight cost you nothing. So you'll get no sympathy from me, sister."

"But who knows when I'm going to see these people again?"

"I can always get you a free ticket, you know that. Have you ever heard of exchanging numbers or 'friending' them on Facebook?"

When Denise didn't respond, Gabrielle prayed her friend was considering the possible fallout of bringing up dirty family laundry.

They rode in silence much of the way. Despite the British woman's precise directions on her GPS, Gabrielle made a wrong turn. Finally, she got back on track, and they arrived fifteen minutes later than expected.

Pulling into the valet parking lot, Gabrielle handed over the keys and they got out. While Gabrielle smoothed the wrinkles from her dress, Denise fussed with straightening hers around her hips.

Where some women might consider Denise a bit on the "healthy side," Gabrielle would describe her friend as a gorgeous, full-figured diva with curves. She had the height and waist to complement her hips. Regardless of Denise's size, she was able to snag a husband before Gabrielle. And Denise was still in love with her college sweetheart. Something must have worked for her.

As they began their short stroll down Washington Street, Gabrielle could see the Gateway Arch in the backdrop. It reminded her of a rainbow over the city. If they didn't know where Personal Touch Banquet Hall was located, the steady stream of guests entering the building was the biggest hint.

"I know you don't understand my zeal for tracking down my half siblings," Denise resumed the conversation. She explained, "But I learned that time waits for no man. When my half sister in Oklahoma first contacted me several years ago to let me know that my father had died, I had attitude up to here." She lifted her hand above her head.

"We didn't even know my dad had remarried or where he was. He just walked away and we never heard from him again. I felt betrayed. I was hurt and didn't want anything to do with her or her sister. My brothers and sister felt the same way, so we ignored their existence. Years went by with no further contact, and then my oldest brother died."

Gabrielle didn't interrupt. She knew about Denise's loss but not about any half siblings until recently.

As they walked closer to the entrance, Gabrielle peered through the large windows. Adorning the tables, she could see inviting splashes of colorful flowers cascading from towering vases. The chandeliers were eye catching as the servers busily catered to the beehive of guests.

"I remember that. I'm sorry."

Taking a deep breath, Denise stopped in her tracks and faced Gabrielle. She sniffed and continued. "A couple of years after his death, I reflected on that call from my half sister. I felt bad about how I had treated her. I thought about her missed opportunity to meet my brother."

Stepping aside, Denise cleared the pathway for other guests to go inside. "When I tried to track her down, I learned she had died several months earlier. It was too late. The window of opportunity to make it right had closed."

Gasping, Gabrielle reached for Denise's hand and squeezed. She had to blink to keep her eyes from misting. She took a deep breath and recalled verse 14 in James 4: *"You do not even know what will happen tomorrow. What is your life? You are a mist that appears for a little while and then vanishes."*

"You never shared that story with me before. I'm sorry." She hugged Denise and then released her. "Did you repent?" When Denise nodded, Gabrielle smiled. "Do you believe God forgave you?"

"Yes."

"Then you're free from guilt."

Denise nodded in agreement. "I guess that's why I'm so eager to find those missing links. We're all family. Whether we care to associate with each other or not, we still need to know each other."

Gabrielle tried to put herself in her friend's shoes. As far as she knew, her parents didn't have any "love children." Neither did her brothers sire any offspring.

Although she couldn't relate to Denise's quest to know an extended family, Gabrielle could empathize with missed opportunities. How many untold blessings had passed her by because she bucked the career path Dr. and Mrs. Bernard Dupree had set out for their only daughter? Then there were some decisions where she didn't seek God's guidance. Not to mention the men she turned away.

"As long as it is day, we must do the works of him who sent me. Night is coming, when no one can work," God spoke from John 9:4 and convicted her spirit.

If God had laid it upon Denise's heart to locate her remaining siblings, then Gabrielle wanted to be a blessing and have her back. She looped her arm through Denise's.

"Come on. Let's go see if ugly men are related to you."

"Yes!" Denise pumped a fist in the air. "Girl, don't be bad-mouthing my kinfolks."

Laughing, they strolled through the grand entrance. A woman greeter asked them the name of their party. She courteously directed them to the ballroom on the right. Music from another function across the spacious, marble-floor lobby briefly distracted Gabrielle.

Inside the room reserved for the Jamiesons, there were definitely more people present than those who attended the ceremony. Denise craned her neck. "Do you see him?"

Gabrielle scanned the room. Sure enough, the handsome hunk was holding court with a group of adoring female fans. She twisted her lips in annoyance and pointed. "Yep, Adonis is over there."

As if he sensed their presence or attraction, Cameron glanced their way. Excusing himself, he walked toward them. With each step, heads turned until finally he invaded their space. His cologne tickled her nose.

25

Quickly appraising him, Gabrielle surmised that Cameron was used to being the center of attention. This gorgeous, six-foot-plus man standing before her believed Talise when she told him about her pregnancy—even when Ace didn't. The same man had also planned to set up a trust fund for their baby before Ace came to his senses. Maybe that was what endeared Cameron to Talise.

During the scene at the church, Gabrielle didn't miss his condescending and confused expressions about her job. It was as if all Howard University graduates had to become politicians or performers. Not everyone would take the literary world by storm, like Toni Morrison, and be recognized for their achievements.

What he didn't know was Gabrielle's position was in middle management within the company, not a ticket agent. She wore many hats, including handling the workload of three people.

But things were about to change. It was time to explore a challenging new career, even if she did have to forfeit her travel vouchers. Gabrielle had always been smart with her money. She could cover her own expenses and fly twice a year to exotic places for vacations, if she so desired.

Gabrielle had already started interviewing for top-level positions outside of the industry and the city. Acting as her personal headhunter, Talise was even trying to lure her to St. Louis. In the end, God would always have the final say in Gabrielle's life: personal, business, and spiritual. So far, the Lord wasn't talking.

"Ladies," Cameron greeted them with a sultry grin. The silky hair of his goatee outlined perfectly inviting lips. His dimple was barely noticeable to the eye. So how did she see it? No doubt, he had the power to make any woman lust after him, including Gabrielle. She definitely needed to remember that and keep her distance.

However, Cameron had other plans as he steered them in another direction. "Why don't we pick up where we left off? Did you already find your seats?"

Guests were preassigned seats, so Cameron strolled from table to table, checking the names on the tent cards. When he located Gabrielle's name, he pulled out three chairs. Once they were seated, he sat between them.

After winking at Gabrielle, Cameron turned his attention to Denise. "You look somewhat familiar. Who is it you remind me of?" he asked, with a puzzled look.

His comment seemed to paint a smile on Denise's face.

"So what would you like to ask me?"

All of a sudden, Denise seemed uncomfortable as she glanced around the room. "I was hoping for a bit more privacy."

Lifting his jet-black silky brow, Cameron looked between them. He nodded suspiciously and stood.

"It's getting pretty packed in here. Why don't we go out into the lobby? I'm sure there's some secluded alcove where we can chat."

Leaving the reception, they canvassed the lobby area. "Ah, I see something," Cameron noted. There was an unoccupied corner near the elevator bank. He walked ahead to the vacant group seating area. Folding his arms, he eyed anyone who even looked like they wanted those seats.

Gabrielle didn't want to be present for the conversation, or anywhere near this man, for that matter. But she promised her support. She and Denise settled on an oversized loveseat. Cameron chose the ottoman and faced them. Resting his elbows on his knees and leaning closer, he linked his hands and glanced from one woman to the other.

True to his word, he gave them his full attention, even when a few people called out his name. Cameron didn't blink, as he waved them away. "Ladies," he said with a nod, "I'm all yours."

When Denise hesitated, Gabrielle reached for her hand and squeezed. Cameron squinted at the gesture.

Taking a deep breath, Denise slowly exhaled. "We might be related."

Gabrielle cringed. Did her friend have to be so direct? She could have warmed up to it. They waited for Cameron's perplexed reaction. Nevertheless, Denise's bluntness didn't seem to faze him.

"Both of you?" Swallowing, he stared at Gabrielle. Disappointment was evident.

"No, just me." Denise patted her chest, trying to steer his attention back to her.

Cameron nodded and relaxed. "Go on. Please explain."

"Well, it's a long story."

Gabrielle took that as a cue for privacy. She cleared her throat and touched Denise's arm. "Hey, I'm going to the ladies' room. Take your time."

Before she could stand, Cameron did. While making a speedy escape, Gabrielle mistakenly glanced over her shoulder. He was still watching her. She guessed he was waiting for her to get out of hearing range.

To allow them a chance to talk, she took her time heading for the ladies' room. Guests were mingling throughout the lobby, causing her to exchange smiles with the passersby. Gabrielle continued to pray silently. *Jesus, please bless my friend. If they are related, please let Talise's new family receive Denise in the spirit of love.*

Inside the restroom, she spent a few minutes chatting with some ladies while fussing with her hair and makeup. Gabrielle wanted to stall as long as possible. She hoped the conversation between Denise and Cameron was going well.

Well, I guess I can't put it off any longer, she thought, as she strolled out of the restroom. All of a sudden, she caught the scent of alcohol. The next thing she knew, a man was blocking her path.

"Dance with me, pretty lady," the stranger demanded. The suit and tie he was wearing didn't quite mask his uncouth manners. She couldn't help but notice the guy's face had the markings of a rough life.

"No, thank you," Gabrielle graciously declined and tried to walk around him, but he matched her step. Her heart pumped with fear. Surely, this man wouldn't try something in a public place, would he? "I'm really not interested," she addressed him.

When his thick, grimy hand quickly encircled her wrist, Gabrielle tried to jerk free, but couldn't. She didn't want to make a scene, but she only had two choices: scream for help or make him sorry he stopped her.

The latter sounded better. Using her free hand, she fumbled inside her purse, which hung from her shoulder. Gabrielle was itching to try out her new can of Mace, and this guy seemed like a good candidate to test it. She would only use enough to deter him.

Pulling it out, she aimed for his face and fired. In that instant, a bulky figure blocked her path, and the drunken man released his hold. Too late, Gabrielle was already spraying. Then she recognized her rescuer from the back of his head—it was Cameron.

"Oops!" she said, stopping immediately.

"The lady's not interested. You want a dance partner, I'm it." His voice was low, but threatening.

"Man, you ain't no lady," the guy said, becoming indignant.

"But I can dance. Do you want to see my fancy footwork?"

Gabrielle rolled her eyes. No way, Cameron could not think he was Muhammad Ali's protégé. Just then, a gentleman who appeared to be on security duty approached them. The woman introduced as Grandma BB was making her way to the scene too. In describing her character, Talise once mentioned to Gabrielle that Grandma BB had a way of sniffing out mischief.

"Is there a problem?" the security detail asked.

Instantly, Cameron took control of the situation and explained to the officer what he had observed from a distance. Gabrielle reassured everyone that she was all right. While the guard proceeded to defuse the incident, Gabrielle went in search of someone who worked at the facility. She had to act quickly to put together an antidote before a stinging sensation penetrated Cameron's skin.

Stepping inside an entrance to the nearest banquet room, she said, "Excuse me," to the first server she encountered. "Can I get a glass of milk, please—a big one? Hurry, please."

Then she raced back to the ladies' room. Luckily, it was stocked with fluffy white terrycloth hand towels rather than paper towels. Grabbing one, she dampened it with cold water. As she rushed out, the staffer was coming from the opposite direction, searching for her.

Curiously, the young man handed her the glass and watched as she held the towel over a potted planter and poured milk on it. "Thanks. I really appreciate this," she said and left him standing there in wonder.

As security escorted the drunkard in another direction, Grandma BB gave the offender a swift kick with one of her Stacy Adams. He twirled around and snarled at her.

Grandma BB batted her lashes. "I'd love to dance." Then she turned to Gabrielle. "You're my hero. I saw everything and was coming to your rescue. We'll talk later about recruiting you for my team."

"Okay." Gabrielle had no idea what the old woman meant. Walking up behind Cameron, she gently touched his arm and applied the compress to the back of his neck. His shoulders tensed as he jerked instinctively. When he began to relax, Gabrielle knew the concoction was taking some of the sting away.

Reaching around, he covered her hand with his. As if they were performing a tango, Cameron slowly guided her to face him.

She cringed as she removed the towel, not knowing how he would respond. "Sorry, you got in my way." She apologized profusely. "I'm so glad it wasn't your face or eyes. Is there anything else I can get for you?"

"For foiling my attempt at rescuing you, I'll recover more speedily if you go out with me."

He was smooth. Gabrielle wasn't expecting that. She wrinkled her nose. "Even if I'm armed and dangerous?"

"I don't scare easily." Cameron pressed. His stare was so intense that he seemed dangerous to her better judgment. "We already have something in common besides loving Ace and Talise."

As far as Gabrielle was concerned, that's where their interest ended. "And what is that?"

"We're both from Boston, remember? So is that a yes or no?"

"Maybe." Gabrielle couldn't believe her mouth said that. Her answer should have been a flat-out no.

"I hope you don't play poker because your expression is so readable. You're thinking of every excuse to say no, aren't you?"

It was eerie that he could so easily challenge her, and she thought about lying just to make a point. But he wasn't worth a moment of sin. "And when I come up with a real good one, I'll let you know." Ending her spiel with a smile, Gabrielle turned to walk away.

Cameron grunted. "Ooh. This stuff is really starting to sting." He winced. "You may need to call an ambulance before I suffer nerve damage."

"You're lying."

"And how do you know that?"

"It's in your eyes, your smirk, and your fake mannerism. Maybe you're the one who shouldn't play poker."

Gabrielle tried to act unaffected, but his subtle cologne was intoxicating, and she had to get away before it sucked her in more. "Ah, but just in case I'm wrong—"

"You are wrong about me."

She ignored him. "I meant about the pepper spray. I'll go and get you another towel."

This time, Gabrielle escaped before she would succumb to the Jamieson charm.

Chapter Three

*C*ameron masked his pain as he stared into Gabrielle's clear brown eyes. Beautifully thick lashes encircled them. Her concerned expression was endearing and seductive. Whatever potion she nursed him with helped, but the evidence still lingered.

Their chemistry was undeniable as he watched her walk away. Very few women turned him down. Yet, she basically did. Cameron snickered. It was definitely a struggle for her to do it.

Still, this was a wedding reception, not a back alley. Weddings were supposed to be about love and happiness, not pepper spray and lost loved ones.

He knew Denise wasn't lying. It had nothing to do with her facial similarities to Ace and his brother Kidd. Because his family had uncovered many relatives while researching the Jamieson tree, everyone was very much aware of Ace's other siblings. However, getting in contact with them was a sticky issue.

Ace was a free spirit, and when Cameron tracked him down using genealogy research, his cousin accepted him at face value. On the other hand, Kidd wasn't interested in knowing *any* Jamiesons. Even after

Kidd embraced his salvation a few years back, he still had the most hatred for Samuel Jamieson. His father's philandering ways resulted in almost a dozen children. According to Denise, only nine remained out of eleven.

When Kidd finally agreed to learn about his father, the Jamieson clan easily uncovered information about Samuel. Unfortunately, that research included his obituary. His death years earlier denied Kidd the opportunity to confront his father and clear the air between them.

Cameron was in Boston when his brothers broke the news to Kidd and he was distraught after reading Samuel's death notice online:

Samuel Jamieson was the son of Kingston III and Hulda Robertson. He was united in holy matrimony to Eillian Ivy and to this union seven children were born: Saul, Jayson, Mayson, Zaki, Benjamin, Giselle Rayford (Jacob), and Lacey Jamieson of Hartford, Conn.

Years later, Samuel was united in holy matrimony to Zenita Pope, and to this union two daughters were born: Suzette and Queen of Tulsa, Okla. He was also the father of Kevin and Aaron Jamieson of Boston, Mass.

Along with the rest of the family, Cameron was taken by surprise over the disturbing report. Anyone who knew Cameron was aware of how protective he was of his own. His number one priority was keeping the peace in his family.

But what about Denise? He could identify with her quest. Yet, at the moment, he couldn't care less about a Jamieson missing link.

Cameron wanted to know more about Gabrielle besides her education. He thought about restraining her before she hurried away, but with that can of Mace in her purse, he didn't want to become the intended target. At the same time, he couldn't just let her go. Before she left tonight, he would corner her in a nonthreatening manner and press her to say yes to a date.

Holding the cold towel on the back of his neck, Cameron accepted that Gabrielle was probably hiding out in the ladies' room. Or maybe she was somewhere telling Denise about her incident. So he returned to the reception, ignoring the guests' questionable stares and curiosity about what happened to him. The only one he had to avoid was the photographer.

Since his two sisters-in-law had abandoned their seats at the bridal table, Cameron flopped in the chair between his brothers, Parke and Malcolm.

They stopped talking and gave him a curious stare. Finally, Parke asked, "Bro, what happened to you?"

"I got sprayed with Mace."

Parke smirked. "That's a first. What did you do?" He didn't look one ounce concerned.

Cameron grunted. "Man, I tried to protect a woman who apparently didn't need protecting. She was 'armed and dangerous'," he said, using her exact phrase. Suddenly, his heart pounded as if it sensed her presence. Cameron couldn't tear his eyes away from her. He was speechless.

Effortlessly, Gabrielle garnished attention with each step as she wove her way through a throng of guests. She moved with determination in her advancement toward him. Needless to say, Cameron liked the way she walked.

"Well, if that's her, it appears she's coming to finish you off." Parke snickered. "Death by beauty. What a way to go, Cam."

"Hello," Gabrielle greeted the two men, capping it off with a dazzling smile. They nodded in return. "Excuse me. He's my patient." She pointed and stepped behind Cameron.

Delicately, she removed the towel Cameron still held on the back of his head. "Here's a fresh one. It should help to extract some more of the oil in the pepper spray."

Gabrielle's ministration was gentle. He wanted to close his eyes and moan from her pampering, but it ended too soon. Plus, with his brothers having front row seats, he had an unwelcome audience. No doubt

34

about it, Cameron needed to get her alone, without any distractions. He was convinced he could win Gabrielle over. Positively.

"I'm sorry again. I really am." She paused and said to him, before taking off. "Well, I'd better get back to Denise."

He watched her retreating, gorgeous figure. Cameron didn't realize he was in a trance until Parke nudged him.

"Breathe, dude."

"Huh?" Reluctantly, he shook his head and then frowned at the interruption.

His brother Malcolm interjected, "So do you want to tell us about her?"

"Not yet. It's her friend and . . . our cousin Denise I need to tell you about."

The mention of an unknown family member put his brothers on alert. "Do we have a cousin named Denise?" Parke asked.

Cameron imagined Parke was mentally scanning their genealogy Rolodex for that name. "That's her middle name. She's a Jamieson, Giselle Jamieson." Before landing the clincher, he hesitated slightly, "Shall we say, the groom's half sister?"

"Yikes." Parke responded and gritted his teeth. "Samuel's first family that lived in Hartford?"

"Yes, and from what Denise told me, her oldest brother is deceased. He was killed in a car accident a few years after Samuel died. He was drunk at the time."

Malcolm whistled. "Man."

"Although I think her timing is off, Denise is here now and you two need to deal with her," Cameron said.

"What do you mean, us two?" Parke frowned, as if to intimidate Cameron like he did when they were younger. "You're the lead genealogist in the family. I'm surprised you're not recording her information on your iPhone for the archives. Plus, you're closer to Ace than we are. More importantly, we need you to run interference with Kidd."

Chuckling, Cameron stood. "You're on your own, big brother. Right now, I'm in need of first aid. I was wounded, remember? Come on, I'll introduce you."

When the three made it to the table where their newly discovered cousin was chatting away with another woman, Cameron kept his eyes on Gabrielle the entire time. Sitting across the table, she was preoccupied with a group of men vying for her attention.

"Excuse me, Denise. These are my older brothers, Parke and Malcolm. You three should talk and work out the details."

Assuming they would take it from there, Cameron stalked over to the other side of the table to address his competitors. Gabrielle finally glanced up and acknowledged him. The snapshot of her smile arrested his heart and caused him to stumble. But his recovery was swift. Besides her striking beauty, there was something about her that attracted him to her.

Clearing his throat, he made his presence known. Then, extending his hand to each of the men, he introduced himself. "Cameron Jamieson, the groom's cousin and best friend. And you are?" Without waiting for an answer, he dismissed them one by one.

"You don't mind if I steal her, do you?" It wasn't a question as he reached for her hand and slightly tugged her away from the male admirers.

Frowning, she followed willingly. "What's the matter? Is it still stinging?"

"Actually, I feel better. You should have been a nurse. I'm curious about what you did." Cameron looked around for two nearby seats that had been abandoned. Without releasing her hand, he pulled out one for her before he took the other.

"I should've been a lot of things." She shrugged. "I would never intentionally hurt someone without knowing the antidote to help them."

"What? That defeats the purpose."

"That man was drunk, but forceful. The only thing I wanted was to subdue him. I admit that the Mace was overkill. I should have called for security to handle him or ask someone nearby to intervene."

As far as Cameron was concerned, if he got a man down, the brother was down for the count. Before the conversation could advance, Talise took to the microphone and started singing "Single Ladies." Cameron huffed. He was not getting a break with trying to hold Gabrielle's attention.

The women in the room jumped to their feet, singing along and lifting their hands in the air.

"It's time for the bouquet toss, ladies," Talise announced.

Women seemed to come from every direction toward the dance floor. Gabrielle sat back and crossed her legs. It didn't appear as though she was going to budge.

Relaxing in his seat, Cameron crossed his ankle over his knee. That was a good sign. He smirked in satisfaction. "Aren't you going up there?"

"Nope."

"Really? Why not? Are you married or engaged?" While waiting for her to answer, Cameron mentally summed up her status. Without a ring, Gabrielle Dupree was fair game. Let the best man win her heart.

"Neither. I'm sitting this one out. I think Talise has her mind set on who she'll aim the flowers toward."

"Who?"

"Her mother-in-law."

Sandra? Cameron swallowed. He forgot all about Ace's mother. How would she factor in if the extended families were to meet? How would she feel about coming face-to-face with the other two women who bore children by the same man?

Refocus, idiot, he heard his heart say.

"So you don't want Talise to be your matchmaker, huh? She may have someone special in mind. As a matter of fact, I happen to be acquainted with this real nice guy who knows how to treat a lady."

"I already have a matchmaker," she said, trying to ignore him.

That got his attention. "Yeah, who?"

"The Lord Jesus Christ. I'm waiting on Him," she said smugly.

Oh. Cameron wanted to laugh, but Gabrielle didn't blink. *God?* She couldn't be serious. Whenever people say they were waiting on the Lord, he always felt it was a cop-out for them not to aggressively work for what they wanted.

"God gave me a free will to pick and choose who and what I want. I plan to exercise that right."

Disappointment registered on her face. "That's too bad, because I'll take a recommendation from the Lord any day. I happen to believe that Jesus gives the best of the best—and I want the best."

"I'm not trying to sound cocky—"

"Then don't," Gabrielle cut him off.

Cameron wasn't expecting that. He had never come up against a strong-willed woman who didn't appreciate his attention. Okay, there were a few. If the theory held true that opposites attract, then there was no hope to pursue her. But he was too curious to let it go.

"What is it about me that you don't find appealing?"

Evading another one of his bothersome questions, Gabrielle stood. "You know, I've changed my mind. Maybe I will get in on the bouquet toss." She grinned sarcastically. "After all, I should take the initiative to meet my mate. Excuse me."

Frowning, Cameron rubbed his shaved head. Confused and insulted is how he felt. He possessed three degrees, carried a distinguished title, and was rather good-looking, so he had been told. Yet he was dumbfounded on how to get this woman to consent to one date with him.

I'm so happy for you and Ace. You've truly been blessed with one of God's best men. For me, the ceremony was the most romantic scene since I watched *Jumping the Broom*. And you know how many times I saw that movie at the theatre, on DVD, and on cable." Gabrielle practically gushed at Talise, as she gently rocked her sleeping goddaughter in her arms.

It was Monday afternoon and all of the guests had returned home, except Gabrielle. During an extended stay, she was enjoying some quiet time, lounging in the nursery of her friend's new home.

Talise laughed. "Yes, I know. Look out, Jane Austen, Gabrielle Dupree is about to form a *Jumping the Broom* club."

Sticking out her tongue, Gabrielle said with a grin, "I just might."

Talise had ordered Gabrielle to stay with her until Gabrielle returned to Boston on Tuesday afternoon. On Sunday, Denise had reluctantly flown back home to her family in Connecticut. Although she had been ecstatic about meeting both of her half brothers, Denise was disheartened that she didn't get a chance to meet Kidd. Somehow, he had managed to avoid an introduction at the reception.

Gabrielle did introduce her to Talise and Ace, who promised to rectify Kidd's evasion at a future time. "Hopefully, it will be in the near future," she commented, while expressing her disappointment.

As the girl chat continued, Talise attempted to snoop into Gabrielle's personal life. They were waiting for Gabrielle's big brother, Drexel, to drive down from Springfield, Illinois, to spend the evening with her. Drexel, professionally known as Judge Dupree, would then turn around and drive the two-hour trip back. He was scheduled to appear in court the next day to preside over pending cases.

Cleverly, Gabrielle turned the conversation back to Talise's romantic story. "Girl, I am so in love with that man," Talise declared, as she shook her head. "It's just God. I couldn't see me forgiving Ace after the way he deserted me."

"It was all a big misunderstanding." Gabrielle summed up her friend's romance with a deep sigh. "Sometimes God allows us to get to the lowest point in our lives and then He pulls us up. Praise the Lord for happy endings."

"Yes, praise Jesus for joy." Talise lifted her hands in the air. "Besides his mom and Cameron, you were about the only one who had faith in Ace. My roommate was ready to strangle him, my daddy wanted to shoot him in the leg, and my sister wanted to have a one-on-one prayer meeting with him."

"I remember." Just then, Lauren made a sucking sound with her lips. Gabriele glanced down and smiled at the sleeping infant. "She's so beautiful."

Talise beamed. "Yep, Mr. Jamieson and I did good."

"Yes, you two did. Oh, and I can't believe you really did aim that bouquet at your mother-in-law. It landed right in her hands."

"I know. How amazing was that? I saw a few of the guys checking Sandra out too." She squinted. "But maybe I should have thrown it to you. That might have been even more interesting. I noticed you had an entourage snooping behind you, including my cousin-in-law."

"Oh, no, we are not going there," Gabrielle warned. "Back to your mother-in-law, Sandra is beautiful and graceful. I'm surprised she's never been married. She is to be commended for rearing her sons single-handedly. Wow."

"I know, but you taught me that God doesn't have a limit on blessings. I have so much respect for her. Without even knowing if I was carrying Ace's child, she reached out to me. Then, when that minister from her church was interested in me, she kept her peace. I don't know if I could have done that. What a Christian role model." Talise became quiet for a moment and then perked up. "Now, I've got to get you hitched."

"Ha! Get in line. You, my parents, and my brothers . . . but God has the best track record. I'm waiting for His candidate before I tie the knot."

Gabrielle hoped that would put an end to Talise's scheming for the moment. In an attempt to further divert her friend's attention, she took an interest in checking out the colorful nursery. Bright cartoon murals against soft pink walls accented the white juvenile furniture. But the pile of stuffed animals filling up an entire corner seemed like overkill for one child.

As much as she wanted to dismiss her interest in Cameron, the subject of finding the right man continued to gnaw away at Gabrielle. Having an opportunity to share her desires with her close friend, she couldn't resist expressing her thoughts. So Gabrielle picked the subject back up, "Besides being a man who's willing to submit to God, he has to be romantic."

"If Cameron is anything like Ace, then you've got a winner in that area."

"I don't need a word from the Lord to know your arrogant cousin-in-law is not the one for me," Gabrielle pushed back.

"Why not?" Talise pouted. "Cameron is fine, he's highly educated—"

"And arrogant. His education credentials were practically the second thing that spilled out of his mouth. Like all those degrees impress me. My parents have a few plaques of mine hanging on their walls too, but that shouldn't be the centerpiece of a conversation. Humph."

Gabrielle gently played with the baby's fingers. "Where some women want a man with a high-paying job, I want a man who knows Jesus. Unfortunately, it seems like that pool of available candidates is shrinking." She sighed deeply.

"I know." Talise shrugged. "But I still say that Cameron might be a good candidate. I've heard the Jamiesons have been working on him for years, and I've learned firsthand how persuasive they can be. He happens to be the last holdout. What you call arrogant, I call confident. He's a good guy and he loves family. Besides, he has a good job," Talise defended before she summed up his biggest dilemma. "As his oldest brother puts it, Cameron has too much worldly sense to understand the simplicity of God's plan of salvation."

Gabrielle interjected, "The Bible says, 'For the wisdom of this world is foolishness in God's sight.'" She felt genuine pity for the man.

Talise grinned. "I miss how you whip out those Scriptures. Okay, tell me where that one is located."

"Not only read your Bible, Talise, study it. That's 1 Corinthians 3:19." Gabrielle adjusted the baby in her arms. Pushing back, she caused the rocking chair to sway. "The bottom line with any man is—looks fade and companies go out of business—but God's Word never changes. He wants to save us from our self-righteous selves. That sounds like a simple formula that even a double-, triple-, or quadruple-degreed man could understand."

As a nursery rhyme played gently in the background, they sat quietly, lost in their own thoughts. A few minutes later, Ace tapped on the door before opening it. "Mrs. Jamieson, do you want me to take over babysitting duties while you and Gabrielle have lunch?"

Talise shook her head and whispered, "She's asleep. Plus, Gabrielle's brother is coming to get her."

"I can still hold her. I'm on a conference call the rest of the afternoon, so I have to get my time in when I can," he whispered back. Stepping farther in the room, he brushed a kiss in Talise's hair. Gabrielle stood and handed over Lauren to him.

Gabrielle smiled as she watched Ace gently cradle his daughter in his arms and sit in the rocker. The women quietly left the room. Exhaling, Gabrielle patted her chest. "I see why you love that man. But you might want to tell him that since he's the father, he doesn't get babysitting pay for watching his own child."

They laughed.

"The same God who blessed you with him—" Gabrielle tilted her head toward the door— "has a godly man for me too."

"Amen to that, sister."

The doorbell rang. Talise hurried to answer it before it disturbed Lauren. She opened it and stepped back. "Hey, Cameron." She glanced over her shoulder at Gabrielle, who rolled her eyes.

Talise accepted a hug from Cameron before asking, "Aren't you flying out later?"

"Yep." He walked in the house, standing larger than life. The tux was gone, but his rugged handsomeness remained even in an oxford shirt and jeans. His eyes landed on Gabrielle and sparkled.

"I came to claim lunch with Gabrielle before I leave."

Before Talise could close the door, Gabrielle's brother cleared the doorway. Gabrielle softened her scream and raced for his arms. "Drexel, look at you!" She hugged him.

After one more squeeze, she made the introductions. "Talise, this is my big brother, Judge Drexel Dupree," she said proudly.

"Don't mind her." He extended his hand to Talise.

"And this is her cousin, Cameron."

Drexel eyed him before offering a handshake. "I was right behind," he said with a nod. "Sorry, man, you'll have to take a rain check on lunch with my sister. You have to make reservations early with her."

"Noted." Cameron shook his hand. Then, stuffing both hands in his pockets, he said casually, "But since I'm flying out, I hope you don't mind if I invite myself along."

Gabrielle and Talise gasped at his nerve. Evidently, his family had no problem with self-confidence.

"I do mind," Drexel said with finality. "Let's go, sis."

Gabrielle nodded and grabbed her jacket and purse from the hall closet. "Ready. Oh, Cameron, since I won't see you again before you take off, have a safe trip back home. And again, sorry about that pepper spray."

"Pepper spray?" Drexel nostrils flared. He kept his eyes trained on Cameron as he questioned her. "What did he do that you needed to defend yourself?"

Before Cameron could open his mouth, Gabrielle saved him the trouble. "He was my rescuer who happened to get in the line of fire. We were at the reception and a drunkard became persistent with wanting me to dance with him."

Drexel nodded his thanks to Cameron, who obviously seemed to have developed an attitude. *Men and their hormones.* Gabrielle sighed.

"Let me add a footnote to that story," Cameron interjected. "Jamieson men don't assault women, we care for them."

With a spur of the moment thought, Gabrielle decided she'd better check on his neck one last time. Walking behind Cameron, she stood on her toes and examined it with a light touch of the area.

"There. Your skin is as perfect as before," she concluded, as Cameron covered her hand and guided her around to face him. For them, it was a déjà vu moment, this time with her brother and Talise as their audience. Gabrielle blushed from embarrassment.

His piercing eyes sucked her into his trance, as he whispered, "What time does your flight leave tomorrow?"

"Two in the afternoon, it was the only nonstop I could get."

"Good thing I just changed my flight," Gabrielle thought she heard Cameron say, as she walked out the door with Drexel.

Chapter Five

*Y*ou changed your flight?" Ace asked, appearing from nowhere. Confusion registered on his face.

Cameron cursed under his breath as he pivoted on his heel. "Yep."

It was enough that Talise and Drexel had witnessed his portrayal of seduction. He didn't need Ace in the mix.

As the two men made their way into the living room, Ace asked, "And when did you do this?" He eyed his cousin suspiciously, waiting for an answer. Ace had tried to convince Cameron to stay a while longer. Folding his arms, he seemed prepared to listen to whatever reason his cousin wanted to give. This one could be the truth or a lie, considering Cameron had given one excuse after another for why he had to get back to Boston that afternoon.

Whipping out his iPhone, Cameron pulled up the link to the airline. "I'm doing it right now."

Ace smirked, then barked out a laugh. Talise slapped him on the arm and hurried back to the nursery to check on Lauren. As Cameron snarled, his cousin laughed harder until he dropped on a nearby chair.

Ignoring him, Cameron completed his transaction. "There. Tomorrow afternoon at two . . . and it's a nonstop."

"I'm sure that wasn't cheap. You know I'm aware of those last-minute flights to see my wife and child."

"You were an idiot back then, but I plan to finish what I started."

"As long as you don't become an idiot this time, Professor Jamieson. Well, you'd better up your game because, from what Tay tells me, big brother is watching you. And I would say literally," Ace replied half-jokingly.

Cameron massaged his goatee. The judge was going to be an obstacle to Gabrielle, but not a roadblock. He estimated her brother to be six-three or four. Drexel wasn't buff like him—okay, maybe a little. But Drexel could stand to lose some inches around the mid-section. Anyway, the man appeared polished, from his signature clothing and shoes, to the smell of his high-priced cologne. Not too worry. Cameron could easily exceed or match his bank account.

What really irked him was Gabrielle had barely acknowledged him as she smothered her brother with all the affection. Women were just more emotional. He loved Malcolm and Parke too, but they had some kind of unspoken rule on how long brothers' hugs should last.

Cameron considered a conniving thought. He could always bring up the pepper spray incident again to garner her sympathy. But he didn't play games. Honestly, he didn't know if he could resort to that tactic again.

When the duo were on their way out, Cameron followed the brother and sister outside and stood on the porch. Watching them descend the steps, he didn't know if Drexel purposely tried to bait him, or if it was a personal conversation between siblings. Either way, Cameron's ears were keen when they needed to be.

"I can't believe one of those Boston men hasn't snapped you up," Drexel had said. "Move to Springfield and I can introduce you to some movers and shakers."

"The pickings are slim in Beantown," Gabrielle had the nerve to say.

What? Cameron was ready to follow them in his car and show her that whether he was a native of St. Louis or a transplanted Bostonian, he could make Gabrielle eat her words.

He hadn't figured out the how-to yet, but he would. Whether it was her rejection that propelled him or her beauty, Gabrielle had some unexplained pull on him.

At the wedding, she had been stunning in her flirty pink dress and stilettos, which showcased perfectly manicured toes. Today, her attire was casual in denim and shorter heels. She was still gorgeous.

Cameron could see why she and Talise were friends. They were both classy women. Although he was no stranger to sassy women, Gabrielle was a mystery. If only he could get her off to himself, he could solve it. Hopefully, the flight back home would do the trick.

As luck would have it, Cameron finally met a woman who piqued his interest, but it was only after he'd already decided to move back home. He had only two months before he would officially report to St. Louis's prestigious Washington University as chairperson of the School of Engineering.

Evidently, Gabrielle wasn't impressed with his professional status, so he would have to go after her from another direction. He was searching for a companion, but he didn't want God to be an issue that stood between them.

Talise walked into the living room with the baby. She didn't question the smirk on her husband's face.

"Cameron, you're welcome to stay for lunch. Ace made chicken quesadillas. They're not too spicy."

He snorted. "Ace can't cook."

"You would be surprised at what my husband can do." She lifted a brow, as if taunting him to ask. "I also made a Greek salad."

All of a sudden, he was becoming an outcast in his own family.

Married relatives were starting to make him nauseous. God knows he wanted a wife. Women had no idea the criteria a man searched for in securing a life partner. Physical attraction was only part of it, the feeling of completion with that special someone sealed the deal.

Chapter Six

*Y*ou may be sorry that you pepper sprayed Cameron when he got in the line of fire," were Drexel's first words, as he settled behind the wheel of his Benz. "But I don't think you should have any remorse. There's something about him I don't like, including the smell of his cologne."

Actually, Gabrielle liked the scent. The musk tickled her nose. She'd been thinking it would have made a wonderful birthday gift for Drexel. Scratch that now.

Clicking her seat belt, Gabrielle wasn't surprised by her oldest brother's assessment. He was a circuit court judge in Springfield, and a good one. Even before he entered the political sector, Drexel was known for giving his opinion and then reaching a verdict without a jury.

"Yes, he does have a knack of rubbing people the wrong way. But I guess I can't really bad-mouth the man after he came to my defense," Gabrielle responded.

"I can, and I did. My advice is to stay away from him when you return to Boston. Cameron's definitely not the type of man to take home to Mom and Dad." Drexel punched in places to eat on his GPS.

Shifting the subject, he remarked, "I heard this Crown Candy Kitchen is a St. Louis landmark."

"Before I satisfy my sweet tooth, I'd rather have some real food." Gabrielle's stomach growled to prove her point. They could have eaten at the Jamieson's, but Drexel wanted to spend some alone time with his baby sister.

"That's the name of the diner, but my colleagues say it serves great food."

"Then let's go." Relaxing, Gabrielle noted the scenery as he wove throughout Talise's neighborhood and onto the main street. So far, she liked St. Louis. That reality began to set in as she reflected on job offers from two of the city's major employers, Nestle Purina and Brown Shoe Company.

Her mind switched to Cameron. Why was she continuously avoiding his question about going out to dinner? Could it be her lips were ready to say no, but her heart cautiously said not so fast? She smiled, reliving his act of chivalry at the reception. It was definitely a "wow" moment for her handbook. At the time, Gabrielle had no idea he was paying any attention to what was going on with her. That endeared him to her.

"Sis, I've been talking to you." Drexel pulled her back to the present. "What's got you smiling?"

She glanced at her brother and knew he wasn't going to like her answer. "Cameron, actually. I didn't like him at first, but there's something mysterious about him that makes me want to solve the hidden clues."

"You're not going to listen to me, are you? There is no mystery. He wants one thing from you and God wants another. Take my counsel, please, and stay away from him. Give the Lord what He wants, your body as a living sacrifice, holy and pleasing to God, and—"

Gabrielle finished with verse two of Romans 12, "*Do not conform to the pattern of this world, but be transformed by the renewing of your mind. Then you will be able to test and approve what God's will is—His good, pleasing, and perfect will.'* I know the Scripture, Drexel."

"I'm just a concerned brother." As the oldest, Drexel took his role seriously growing up.

"And a loving one too." Gabrielle sighed as the St. Louis Arch came into view. The voice of the GPS guided them off Interstate 70. The neighborhood wasn't far from downtown and was a mix of old and restored buildings. Nothing appeared new.

She was surprised to see that Crown Candy was a corner establishment with a metal green awning and old lettering. It wasn't a huge restaurant. The place reminded her of a drugstore from days gone by. Locating a parking space, Drexel's Benz seemed out of place.

Gabrielle waited for him to get out and come around to assist her. It was etiquette her father had drilled into all three of her siblings. He said that if Gabrielle's brothers didn't treat her like a lady, how would she know what to expect from other men?

Gabrielle didn't escape her mother's favorite lecture either. Veronica Dupree often reminded her daughter, "Carry yourself like a lady. If you expect chivalry, then the right man will shower you with it."

That was one of the many life lessons her parents instilled in her. She had listened to 99 percent of their wisdom when interacting with her suitors.

Thanking Drexel for his assistance, she missed the pamper treatment that her brothers showered on her. Whoever snagged them would have jewels. Now, if only God would send a prince her way. It seemed like she'd been waiting all her life for him to come along.

When they walked inside the diner, it was a throwback to an era before her time. The vintage setting was personally appealing, though, considering that she loved to visit ancient ruins when she traveled.

As they waited for seating, Gabrielle scanned the memorabilia, which included several nostalgic Coca-Cola posters displayed on the walls. Her interest was piqued when she read that two Macedonian immigrants opened the business one hundred years ago. She was further impressed to read that Crown Candy was considered one of the oldest remaining places with an operating soda fountain.

"Wow," she said, taking it all in.

Drexel leaned over her shoulder and grinned. "I know. I thought you would like it."

Turning around, she gave her brother a hug. He knew how much she enjoyed visiting foreign countries and cultures. While Drexel preferred American soil, she and her brother Philip were considered the family's world travelers. Since he was an evangelist, Philip seemed to be traveling out of the country more than living within the states.

Gabrielle's interest in international travel developed during her sophomore year at Howard University. To date, she had visited ten different countries, but Greece and Macedonia would always be her favorites. There was never enough time to see everything. Those countries were not only beautiful, they held biblical significance.

Once they were shown their seats and handed menus, she didn't waste any time scanning the food selection.

"A segment of *Man vs. Food* was taped here," Drexel told her, interrupting her decision-making process.

"You're just a wealth of information. This must be one of St. Louis's best-kept secrets."

"I'm sure there's more to the city. My colleagues split their time between St. Louis and Chicago for weekend getaways. Speaking of home and here, how's your job search coming?"

Before she could answer, the server asked if they wanted to sample the world-famous fountain sodas. Gabrielle decided to go for it, while Drexel declined and ordered the heart-stopping BLT.

Her jaw dropped. "Ooh, I'm going to tell Daddy," she taunted him. Dr. Bernard Dupree would gasp at the damage his eldest was about to suffer to his arteries.

"Hey, I'm enjoying some time with my sister. I can splurge every now and then."

"Don't put me in it." Turning to the server, she asked for the baked chicken.

Once they were alone again, her brother revisited the subject of her job decision. "Mom and Dad would love for you to return to Chi-town."

"I know, but the closest I may get could be St. Louis. I haven't told Talise yet, but three companies here have made me an offer with travel opportunities. I've already turned down one. Two are in the running. There are also companies in San Diego and Tucson that are trying to lure me. In both those cases, the pay is good, but the benefits are lacking. I'm almost certain I'll pass on them."

"If I didn't miss my baby sister, I'd be all for you moving to a warmer climate. However, it would be nice if you lived closer to your family in the Midwest."

As Chicago natives, her brother stayed in Illinois and attended college while she headed to the nation's capital. During freshman year, she debated with her parents about her choice of degree programs. In the end, Gabrielle graduated from Howard with a liberal arts degree and two minors. Then she moved to Dallas where she completed her MBA. After spending a few years in Boston, Gabrielle was becoming restless again. She felt it was time to take flight and relocate.

Gabrielle smiled at Drexel's heartfelt request. Suddenly, she began to miss home and her family. She would have to make a trip to see her parents soon. Maybe she was in a sentimental mood after witnessing Denise's excitement over connecting with siblings she had never met.

"I'll keep that in mind," she said while once again taking in her surroundings. Spying jars of jelly beans on a shelf, she would definitely have to get some before they left.

"I'll pray on it and see where God leads me."

"Well, I'm putting in my bid for St. Louis." He showed a handsome smile. Growing up, she had more girlfriends than she wanted because of her three good-looking brothers. On the downside, she had very few suitors because of them.

After their food arrived, they said grace and continued to chat about the family. Drexel confessed he was ready to settle down but was trusting in the Lord to find the right spiritual fit.

"Funny, at thirty years old, I want to be found. Maybe God needs to give my future husband a spiritual GPS." They laughed. "I'll accept whoever God sends."

Now Gabrielle was blaming Talise's bliss for her melancholy mood. Sharing in her good friend's wedding celebration caused her to suddenly want to fill the void in her own life. Perhaps she needed to hang out more with unmarried and unattached friends.

"I detest women throwing themselves at me. At thirty-seven, I'm so ready to cut to the chase and reach my destination in life. I probably need one of those God-promised spiritual blessing devices myself."

"You're a good catch. You have heartbreaking looks, a solid career—" Her words sounded identical to Cameron's résumé. On the other hand, knowing how much Drexel embraced Jesus, Gabrielle had no idea about the level of Cameron's commitment to the Lord. She never gave him more than three minutes—if that—to find out.

Checking her watch, Gabrielle couldn't believe how much time had passed. She and Drexel had been there for more than an hour, stuffing themselves and reminiscing.

"This really was nice, G. Seriously think about moving here, and we can do this more often. I'd better get you back to Talise's now, so I can get on the road before rush hour."

"Okay." She pouted. Their time together made her dread returning to Boston alone. At least she could look forward to her upcoming excursion to Northern Greece.

How ironic that Gabrielle ate at a historic place with a Macedonian connection. In less than two weeks, she would behold the art and culture of Macedonia. She was excited about being transported back to the places where the biblical churches began.

The ride back to Talise and Ace's house seemed shorter, as they good-naturedly argued about who pulled the best pranks on their parents and siblings.

Before Drexel dropped her off, they sat in the car and prayed for each other's safe travels back home. After their final goodbye hug, it seemed as if Drexel wanted to have the last word concerning her social life. "And remember, if you see that Cameron Jamieson coming your way, don't hesitate to use that can of pepper spray again."

—— ༘ ——

The next afternoon, Gabrielle sat in Lambert Airport waiting for her flight back to the fast-paced life of Boston. She sighed. Oddly, after one trip to St. Louis, she felt as if she was leaving home and going back to a strange land. If she accepted either job offer, her brothers would be within hours driving time. At the end of the day, the downside of giving up her present position and losing her travel vouchers wasn't enough to sway her to stay in Boston.

Her mind then reflected on how happy Talise seemed in her role as wife and mother. She thought about her friend's stepmother, Donna, whom she referred to only as her father's new wife. Throughout the festivities, the woman had been eerily quiet, almost like a scared puppy. Talise shared with Gabrielle that Grandma BB had an invisible muzzle on Donna's mouth, daring her to utter one sound and she would be limping back to Virginia.

"Donna believed her too," Talise regaled, and Gabrielle couldn't stop laughing.

"See, Grandma BB's a clown for the devil when she could be a servant for the Lord," Gabrielle recalled saying, as she and Talise struggled to keep a straight face.

Remembering the good time she had, Gabrielle would have to return for a longer visit. Next, her mind drifted to her brother. There was no way she could forget how much she enjoyed spending time with Drexel.

Still, she had a life back in Boston—at least for the time being. She did have other friends there. And, of course, there was the Spirit-led church she attended. Besides, if she got bored, she could catch a plane to Hartford and visit with Denise.

"Why am I giving myself a pep talk?"

Sighing, she shifted in her seat and focused on a plane landing when a deep voice stole her attention.

"Is this seat taken?"

"Ah, no." When she reached over to move her purse, at the same time, she looked up and sucked in her breath. Over the past three days, whenever she saw Ace's cousin, he seemed to become more handsome.

"Cameron," she greeted him cordially, as she swallowed and tried to maintain her composure.

While he was making himself comfortable, a whiff of his cologne tickled her nostrils. Boy, Gabrielle didn't care what Drexel said, she liked the smell of his brand. Turning back to gaze out the window, she hoped to be distracted by the activities on the tarmac.

Her mind raced. So they were on the same plane. Topping that off, she was stuck with him for one and a half hours before the flight even took off.

"How are you?"

"I'm well. Thanks."

"Looking forward to going home?" Cameron asked.

Humph. Home was where the heart was, and her heart no longer seemed to be in Boston. She shrugged and turned again to look out the window. This time she focused on a plane about to take off. Although she could feel his eyes on her, which made her nervous, Gabrielle was determined to stay in control.

After a moment of silence, Cameron called her name softly. When she faced him, his intensity unnerved her. "I don't believe in playing games, Gabrielle."

Coming from him, why did her name sound like a caress to her ears? It was an unusual feeling and she wondered about that.

"I'm almost thirty-two years old." Cameron leaned closer, inches from invading her personal space. "I'm attracted to you. I have only two months to prove to you I'm worthy of your consideration. Go out with me and I'll dispel every myth you have about me."

"You keep a schedule?" Gabrielle didn't conceal her offense. "Is that your cutoff time before you move on to another woman?"

"Unfortunately, I'm moving back home, and that's all the time we'll have in Boston."

We? Gabrielle tried to keep a straight face. The fact that he was moving to the exact place where she was seriously considering relocating intimidated her. She wanted to laugh and correct him that there was no "we."

It was like she couldn't escape him, not by going to the ladies' room or while being at Talise's house. Now, here he was at the airport. And, perhaps they would eventually share the same city? *God, is there a lesson to be learned with this man?* she silently asked.

"Stand firm and see the deliverance I will give you," God whispered back.

Gabrielle recognized the partial verse from 2 Chronicles 20:17, but that was in reference to a physical battle. What kind of tug-of-war should she prepare for with Cameron? When God didn't utter another whisper, she resolved that she had no choice. This was a time to stand still and keep her eyes wide open. *Jesus, help me not even to blink.*

"I know it's late in the day and I'm probably not the first one to compliment you, but I'll say it anyway. You're beautiful."

All Gabrielle could do was hold her breath and manage to smile. Actually, no one had said that to her today or since the wedding now that she thought about it. But it wasn't as if she expected it either. She exhaled.

During her lengthy airline career, Gabrielle had attracted many men of stature and from many nationalities. She had turned down marriage proposals, gifts, and other enticements. What she desired most was a man who could meet her on all levels. The prerequisite was his genuine humility before the Lord. Then too, Jesus must be satisfied with her choice. Subsequently, if God actually sent someone, He would have to be pleased with the man, right? She desperately tried to reason with herself.

"Thank you. But Cameron, I'm going to be honest with you. I don't see us as a good fit. Sorry."

He remained expressionless as she delivered the blow. Instantly, she felt bad. No one liked rejection, but he would need more than good looks to get her attention. As if the realization was beginning to sink in, Cameron turned away and watched passengers hurrying to make their flights. Was he contemplating a comeback?

"If you open your pretty brown eyes, you might see what I see—because I totally reject your assessment." Stretching out his legs, his mannerism seemed to parlay into a man about to conduct a seminar. "What attracts you to a man?"

Was he trying to dissect her heart or her mind? Even so, a small, small piece of her was flattered that he wasn't about to give up.

"Excuse me?"

"Let's analyze this notion. How do we make the pieces fit? Simple. We can prune, mold, or puff up their size. I'm a quick study and I'm learning that, with you, I have to repeat my questions more than once to get an answer." He winked.

That gesture softened his scolding.

"What qualities does a man need to snag your attention? In addition to my . . ." He cleared his throat. "I mean—the man's looks, employment, and education."

Gabrielle laughed. "You slipped."

"Never. I'm very calculated in my approach to you. I meant *I*, but I sense you feel less threatened if I keep it generalized. Trust me, before the next eight weeks have ended, it's going to be all personal—"

Swallowing, Gabrielle was once again tongue-tied.

When his cell phone played a tune, he mumbled choice words and snatched it out of its holder. "It's Ace," he informed her and stood. "Will you watch my jacket and carry-on?" She nodded and he walked away.

Gabrielle's heart shifted. The curse under Cameron's breath broke his spell. She was so caught up in his web that it took God to show her the truth. Unless He pruned Cameron, the man could never fit into her life.

Chapter Seven

*C*ameron had to do damage control fast. Of all times, why did a harmless slip of the tongue happen right now, in front of Gabrielle? He was sure that mistake would cost him and he would make his cousin pay for causing the setback. He cursed again; this time under his breath. In his book, a PG-rated swearword didn't make him a bad person. His good deeds canceled out his bad faults, didn't they?

Since he was becoming a pro at reading her expressions, when he returned to the seating area, Cameron knew he was back to square one.

Next to his parents, Gabrielle was now at the top of his list of people for whom he would rein in his tongue whenever he was around them. It was simply mind over matter.

He who can control his tongue can also control himself in every other way.

Cameron's mind froze as he considered the mental interruption. Those words had to come from somewhere. It was as if the airwaves carried them from God. When he had time, he would have to look that up in the Bible, which was somewhere in his condo. He vowed to check it out. With that settled, he resumed his damage control.

"I'm sorry, Gabrielle."

She turned to him with a disappointing stare. "What are you apologizing for, your profanity or for taking the call?" She lifted an arched brow in a challenge.

"Both."

"I accept . . ." she replied.

Forgiven. Whew, that was easy. Cameron returned her smile, as he admired her features. She was naturally pretty. If she wore makeup, he couldn't tell it.

"Thank you for helping me to make up my mind. For the past few days, I've been struggling over whether I should go out with you or stay as far away as possible. Cameron, I can't be with a man who lifts up praises to God and from the same mouth spews curse words."

He was dumbfounded. How could Gabrielle let a few misguided words stop her from possibly finding the best thing that ever happened to her?

"I'm not a perfect man, Gabrielle."

Her eyes misted. "That's a given, but are you trying to be?"

Please don't let her cry. Otherwise, he would come undone. Although he planned to give her a truthful answer, he had to be careful how he phrased it. "I'm as perfect as I . . ." he began. Patting his chest, he completed his defense. "Know how to be. Gabrielle, you are no ordinary woman. If any woman could show me the error of my ways, it would be you."

Her eyes brightened as they searched his; Cameron could tell she was judging him carefully to see if he was sincere. When she laid her hand on top of his, he trapped it. She didn't resist his gentle hold.

"We can be friends," she said softly.

"Oh, no. That's not going to work." Cameron had his share of female "friends" over the years. Their motive was hoping they would become more.

The chemistry between him and Gabrielle was different. It was building rapidly and too powerful for him to let get away. He had to find out what it was about her that made her so special.

With her, Cameron knew a friendship would be nothing but a farce. The fireworks hadn't been extinguished since he laid eyes on her, and he wasn't referring to the stinging from the Mace. Obviously, she was fighting the magnetism.

For the second time, Cameron stood and asked her to save his seat. There had to be somewhere in the airport where he could purchase some flowers. Romance 101 was now in session.

———⟶⟵———

Perfection was in God's eyes. Gabrielle knew that, but she wanted Cameron to be flawless for selfish reasons. Torn by her own superficial thoughts proved to be a disappointing exercise. Yet, overlooking the small mishaps could cause bigger issues to sneak up on her—then her world would come crashing down. That was the real danger.

With a troubled heart, she forced her eyes from admiring his gait until he disappeared down the terminal. Bowing her head, but keeping her eyes open, Gabrielle began to pray, *Jesus, I don't know what I'm doing here. God, I'm confused. I don't know what to pray.*

Pausing for a moment to listen for God's answer, she sensed the Holy Spirit was making intercessory requests on her behalf. Gabrielle could feel the internal utterings going forth. Before ending with Amen, she added, *God, I'm not afraid of the devil. But, I'm leery of the temptation Cameron invokes in me. Please help me, in the Name of Jesus. Amen.*

I have already prayed for you, Jesus spoke.

"Thank You," she whispered back.

Taking a deep breath, she looked at her surroundings. Gabrielle had never met a man like Cameron. Usually, men got the message when she didn't want to be bothered. They either moved on or felt she wasn't worth wearing down. Where her expressions might be an open book to

63

him, his expressions were unreadable. He calmly took her rejection and bounced back as if he hadn't heard a word she said.

Minutes went by. It was almost time to board and Cameron hadn't returned. Getting to her feet, Gabrielle wondered what she should do about his jacket and bag. Deciding to take them with her, she wormed her way through the passengers and stood in line under A20–25, the designated numbers to be called for boarding. When she turned around, Cameron was coming her way. Shaking her head, Gabrielle had to give it to him. The man's proud, confident stride would get any woman's attention.

Edging others out of his way, he presented her with a small bouquet of flowers.

"For you."

She was so busy watching his gait, she hadn't noticed what was in his hand. "Thank you." She looked up into his eyes as he towered over her.

Retrieving his belongings from her, he stepped back and looked at the number for his spot in line. Gabrielle didn't know when he booked this flight, but usually any last-minute passengers were given a C boarding, which was basically the last group to get on the plane. Judging from the crowd, it appeared the plane would be packed.

That was not the case with Cameron. Somehow, he had managed to snag a spot in group A, just ahead of her.

Instead of staying there, Cameron returned to her side and offered the man behind her his priority number. The gentleman eagerly accepted and moved up in line. Forgetting his earlier transgression, Gabrielle experienced another "wow" moment for her handbook of romance. The attractiveness of a determined man was very intriguing. Yet Cameron Jamieson could not be taken at face value, even if he did have a handsome face.

"So you're a business traveler," she stated, knowing those passengers received preferential seating and boarded first.

"Yep, between work and home, I rack up the miles. That will come to an end when I move back home where all my folks are, unless . . ." He paused and gave her the most considerate look. "Unless a very special lady misses me and wants me to come back and visit her. In the words of Michael Jackson's pop hit, 'I'll be there.' That is, on the next flight."

Somehow, Gabrielle believed him. When she shifted her carry-on to her other hand, Cameron took it from her. Smiling, she thanked him.

The crowded line moved along. In their confined space, Gabrielle racked her brain for a neutral topic. She was much more comfortable with him when he wasn't trying to hit on her.

"I'm so glad no one got upset with me for letting Denise come along. I didn't realize she was hurting so badly to find her relatives."

Cameron shook his head as he extended his hand for Gabrielle to walk ahead of him to have her ticket scanned. "Once you discover one ancestor, you begin to hunger and thirst for more."

Hunger and *thirst*, two words that were synonymous with righteousness in Matthew 5:6, she mentally recalled.

"Have you or your family members traced your roots?" he asked.

"No, honestly, I don't think there's an interest. We're content with knowing what we know." She shrugged. Stepping on the plane, she nodded at a flight attendant. With Cameron behind her, she assumed he would automatically commandeer the seat next to her.

He didn't and asked politely. "Do you mind if I sit with Gabrielle?"

Smiling, she patted the cushion. It was so refreshing to see him drop the "I am man" persona.

Recognizing a few faces of fellow employees, Gabrielle waved.

"I'm sure my brothers fed her so much information that it left her tipsy. We're constantly updating our family data on familytree.com. Researching ancestors is a group effort, and it could take generations to connect the dots. Now Denise will have access to documents and more information than she has time to read."

Cameron snickered. "She was floored to find out that she was an eleventh generation descendant of Prince Paki Kokumuo Jaja, who was the firstborn son of King Seif of the Diomande tribe. Royalty runs through our veins." He winked.

Gabrielle twisted her mouth in amusement. So much for a reprieve on Cameron's stuck-on-himself attitude. As far as she knew, the Duprees were simple people with Southern roots via Africa.

"You are a chosen people, a royal priesthood, a holy nation, God's special possession, that you may declare the praises of him who called you out of darkness into his wonderful light," Jesus whispered 1 Peter 2:9 to her spirit.

As the remaining passengers boarded the plane, seats became scarce. A pretty woman, who had evidently been heavy-handed with her perfume bottle, grabbed the aisle seat next to Cameron. When her skirt climbed up on her thighs, it appeared she had no shame to tame it.

Sniffing her flowers, Gabrielle hid her smile as she slyly watched Cameron try not to watch the woman's movements. Then she softly giggled.

Men preferred shapely legs, and the woman had them. As a matter of fact, Gabrielle would be shocked if he didn't try to sneak a peek. But, so far, he hadn't given in to the temptation.

Then Cameron's seatmate tugged on her skirt to no avail. The thing wasn't moving. Defeated, she clicked her belt. Next, she turned and extended her hand.

"Hi . . ." she introduced herself.

"Cameron." He nodded and briefly met her hand with his.

Calling for everyone's attention, the crew demonstrated the safety procedures, patrolled the aisles for a seat belt check, and prepared for takeoff. Within seconds, Cameron's seatmate resumed her conversation.

Gabrielle took that as her cue to look out the window. But something was wrong with her. All of a sudden, she craved Cameron's undivided attention to engage her in meaningless chit-chat.

It wasn't that a glimpse at the woman's legs had anything to do with her wish. Cameron didn't, because she watched him. Any seed of jealousy that the devil tried to plant, Gabrielle was on guard to rebuke it. She reminded herself that God had a man for her. And that man wouldn't have a wandering eye. That was the desire of her heart, so she relaxed . . . or tried to.

"So who do you work for?" Miss Chatterbox inquired.

"I teach at a school in Boston."

Gabrielle blinked. What? Cameron turned down the opportunity to bombast his credentials. Was he suddenly not feeling well? What gives?

"Hmm. That's a noble profession. I wouldn't have pegged you for an educator. You have the air of a CEO."

Gabrielle rolled her eyes to keep from shaking her head. Talk about whipping it on thick. The woman needed to turn off her blender. She was adding layers to Cameron's already oversaturated ego.

"If my teachers in school looked like you, I never would have graduated."

Hmm. I don't doubt that. Gabrielle had enough of eavesdropping. Resting the bouquet on her lap, she dug into her purse for the romance novel she had started when she left Boston for St. Louis. Opening it to the page where her bookmark rested, she made her best attempt to get lost in the story:

Chapter Four

Xena had made bad choices with the men in her past, but this time, she was letting God do the picking. Bryson had a ready-made family, but he loved her and so did his two boys. That was all she wanted . . .

Engrossed, Gabrielle hadn't realized that Cameron was nudging her. When his warm breath tickled her ear, she giggled and then blushed. It wasn't because of him. Xena and Bryson were about to share their first kiss.

"What are you doing?" She faced him, a little annoyed at the interruption.

"How does Xena look?" he whispered.

"What?"

"You smile when you read, so I'm curious. Why are you fantasizing about romance when it could be your reality?"

"You know nothing about me," she snapped. Putting the bookmark back in place, she closed her book. Gabrielle arched her brow and looked at him, defiantly.

"I know enough to want to know more." He matched her lifted brow.

And so Cameron, the flirt, had returned. *Why doesn't he use his charm on the siren on the other side of him?* She wondered.

They stared at each other. The man had the perfect jawbone to pull off a goatee. His brown eyes were mesmerizing. Through peripheral vision, a manicured hand came out of nowhere and patted Cameron on his thigh. Gabrielle noticed his leg muscle tensed.

"I'm visiting my sister in Cambridge for a week," Miss Chatterbox said. "Why don't we exchange numbers? Maybe we can go out for drinks or something?"

She was daring—and rude. Did the woman not see that the man was speaking with her? They could have been a couple for all she knew, but the flirt threw out the invitation anyway. He wouldn't be all male not to bite.

"I hope you enjoy your stay. I stopped drinking years ago—well sort of. It's terrible on your liver, and the number of people killed every year from drunk drinking is staggering."

Just answer the question, Gabrielle thought. She was sure the woman was holding her breath too.

"Well, here's my number in case you think of something else to do." When she tried to give him her card, Cameron held up his hands, declining.

"I can't juggle more than one woman at a time. Actually, I'm trying to get the number from this gorgeous lady over here." He pointed to Gabrielle.

Gabrielle's jaw dropped as the woman leaned over. The stranger seemed to assess her presence for the first time, and then smirked. "Well, I don't play hard to get."

To each her own, Gabrielle wanted to reply. Where men were concerned, she didn't lose all common sense—not yet anyway.

"Sorry to decline again. Once I stake my claim, I take possession," he said with finality. Then, turning back to Gabrielle, Cameron whispered, "Open your book. I want to see how romantic this Bryson is after he kisses Xena."

"You're a complex man," Gabrielle mumbled. She blinked. "Who are you?" She wasn't kidding. He was proving to be as unpredictable as he was mysterious.

Cameron's nostrils flared as he made it obvious that he was inhaling her perfume. "Take a chance, Gabrielle, because what you see is what you really get."

"Yes, and what I've seen so far scares me."

Chapter Eight

*C*ameron enjoyed making Gabrielle speechless. As a matter of
fact, he'd like it even better if he could kiss her breathless. But
assuming her slap would leave a lasting imprint was enough to
deter him from trying it.

In actuality, he couldn't care less about reading her book, but
Gabrielle seemed enthralled nonetheless. That Bryson character had
nothing on him. Cameron snickered. The guy needed some Jamieson
in his blood to win the heroine over. If Gabrielle would just talk to him
without any distractions, he could convince her that she had met her
match.

Reading along with her, he randomly scanned sections until he
noticed that she wasn't turning the pages anymore. Her lids fluttered
until finally she began to doze. Cameron sighed with relief. Did people
actually get paid to write that fairy-tale stuff? He was surprised he
wasn't asleep himself.

The woman sitting on the other side of him was a character too.
While he attempted to be cordial, her boldness and lack of respect for
Gabrielle was a turnoff. The seductress didn't even take the time to find

out if Gabrielle was his lady, wife, or fiancée.

Mentally, Cameron backed up. If Gabrielle or any woman permanently belonged to him, she would have a rock on that third finger that could cut through glass.

As for a nice pair of legs, Gabrielle had literally stopped traffic at the ceremony with the pair God gave her. Cameron smirked again. Earlier he could feel her watching him, even though she acted uninterested when the woman's hem inched higher. Like he had informed her earlier, he didn't play games. What was going through Gabrielle's mind when his seatmate toyed with him?

Gabrielle didn't stir until the plane landed. She lifted her head from his shoulder, which he didn't have a problem with her using it as a resting place. Unfortunately, he did have issues with the woman who claimed his other shoulder as a pillow.

Blinking, Gabrielle gathered her bearings and eyed the other passenger, but didn't comment. When the plane came to a stop, she reached for her phone. Once it was powered up, her long fingers touched the keypad and sent a text.

Before the captain could turn off the unfasten seat belt light, many travelers stood. As Cameron gathered their things from the overhead bay, Gabrielle received a text. She smiled at the message. When he looked at her, she must have read his curious expression, but he had no right to ask.

"I sent texts to Talise and my brother, letting them know I had landed safely," she offered.

"Good idea."

Once they were in the terminal, Cameron stayed close to Gabrielle. "Am I going to have a problem with your brother?" he asked out of nowhere.

"Only if you create one. The Jamiesons aren't the only close-knit family," she replied as if she had issued a warning. When a woman called Gabrielle's name, she politely dismissed him to greet some of her coworkers.

He stood nearby. She would not get rid of him that easily. Cameron was in no hurry to get back to his condo. No one was waiting for him—not a cat, dog, bird, or goldfish.

When Gabrielle started toward the baggage claim area, Cameron's long stride easily matched her pace. "I really want to see you again."

Although he expected a flat-out no, her hesitation was encouraging. A few moments later, he soon learned the source of her indecisiveness. Evidently, Gabrielle wasn't paying him any attention as she watched for her luggage.

As she moved forward to retrieve her bag, he was swiftly by her side. Reaching for another bag, Gabrielle shook her head and pointed to a burgundy one. Cameron lifted it off the carousel with ease.

"Do you need a ride?" he asked, eying his luggage, which was making its way around. Grabbing his garment bag, he turned to her.

Adjusting the handle on her roller, she replied, "No, thank you. My car's at the employee lot." Her mannerism indicated she was about to say farewell. That wasn't acceptable.

This was his last opportunity. Stepping closer, Cameron invaded her space. He towered over her even in her heels. "One date, one chance, and one moment to woo you. After that, you can call the shots, but I hope you won't call it quits," he said sincerely, studying her expression. Her resistance was fading.

Jutting her chin, she wrinkled her nose. It was a cute gesture. She lifted her finger and stared up into his eyes. "One."

"Was that a question or a statement?" he whispered to make her draw closer. When she blinked, he smirked, just before slipping a long envelope from his inside jacket and handing it to her.

She looked at it before accepting it. "What's this?"

"Don't open it until you get home."

She gave him a faint smile. Gabrielle's eyes seemed to light up at the thrill of a mystery. Taking the liberty, Cameron brushed a kiss against her forehead, adjusted the garment bag over his arm, and strolled away. When he glanced over his shoulder to get one more mental snapshot, she was still staring.

"Gabrielle Dupree, you're going down, woman. You just might be the one, and if you turn out to be a perfect fit, then we're going to fall together," he mumbled confidently and continued on his way.

Chapter Nine

*H*e did what?" Talise repeated.

Minutes after entering her apartment from the airport, Gabrielle phoned her friend. It had only been seconds after opening the envelope from Cameron.

"Ace never gave me an envelope full of rose petals."

"Consider it done, babe," her husband said in the background.

"Stop eavesdropping," she fussed at him. But even to Gabrielle's ears, Talise didn't sound convincing.

Gabrielle heard the faint click of a door closing in the background.

"Do you have to tell your husband all my business? I may not want it to get back to Cameron that I'm even mentioning his name."

"Sorry. If I ask Ace not to say anything, he won't."

"I hope not." Relaxing, Gabrielle sat in her favorite living room chair. She hadn't told Talise about the note inside yet. "I can't figure him out. We were sitting at the gate waiting for our plane to arrive. The next thing I know, he asks me to watch his things and he disappears down the terminal. Then he returned with a bouquet. I thought that was a sweet gesture, but this completely caught me off guard."

Not wanting to spoil Talise's angelic image of Cameron, she omitted that the bouquet was an apology for his swearing.

"Isn't that what romance is about—spontaneity, surprises, and tenderness? I'd rather have that than be a woman who has to program her man to buy roses, when to call, how to plan a night out, yada yada yada. That seems like too much work. At least Cameron appears to be already programmed," Talise argued.

She read the note aloud. "The man asked me to be his valentine? He's a little late."

"Why limit love to one month? I think that's romantic. Mark that down in your handbook."

"Don't think I won't when I finish talking with you." Gabrielle giggled and took a deep breath. "But still . . . I've been courted by the best. Don't you think it's odd that out of all his brothers and cousins, he seems to be the only one detached from the notion of surrendering to Jesus? How can he be around what the Bible calls 'a cloud of witnesses' and act nonchalant about God's sovereignty?" Gabrielle gnawed on her lip, perplexed.

"I'm still a baby saint. Don't ask me. But tell me where that quote is in the Bible," Talise said eagerly.

Talise hadn't been a new convert for a year yet, but she had a hunger for God's Word. It was a good sign that her friend was in it for the long run.

"Hebrews 12:1: *Therefore, since we are surrounded by such a great cloud of witnesses, let us throw off everything that hinders and the sin that so easily entangles. And let us run with perseverance the race marked out for us.*'"

Jotting down the reference, Talise said, "Thanks. Ace and I can study together tonight. Sometimes we read aloud to Lauren. We hope it helps."

"The Bible says the promise is for you and your children, and as many as the Lord God will call," Gabrielle responded.

75

Contrary to Talise's accolades, Gabrielle couldn't recite all the Scriptures from all sixty-six books. Anticipating her friend's next query, she added, "Before you ask where, that's a paraphrase of Acts 2:39. And, by the way, God never breaks His promises."

"Okay, Bible teacher, back to my cousin-in-law. Maybe the right person hasn't persuaded him. I don't know. I mean of all people to witness to me about Christ, it was the mother of a man who I couldn't stand during most of my pregnancy. Go figure."

Gabrielle digested the simplicity of how God worked. "Yes, I do remember that, and you wound up marrying that man." Ace turned out not to be the monster Talise had pegged him.

"Call and accept the dinner invitation. Think of it as a free meal."

Gabrielle stared at Cameron's phone number again. "I'll pray on it." The thing her evangelist brother drilled into her head was to be aware of the spiritual devices of wickedness as well as physical temptation. They work hand in hand.

One look into Cameron's eyes could blur her determination to live like every day was her last until Jesus' return. Cameron was the poster boy of temptation until the next millennium. She sighed. Although Drexel had told her to stay away from him, her heart wasn't listening.

"I'll pray too. I hope he can win you over."

"You mean, you hope I can win *him* over to a complete surrender to Christ. When Jesus saves, He saves completely. We'll see. He'll have to wait until I come back from my vacation."

"I do miss jet-setting across the country at a moment's notice, but that was my life before my baby and my husband. Maybe I'll return to the airlines when Lauren gets older."

"Right, if you and Ace don't have any more babies."

"I won't complain," Talise said.

After a few more minutes of chatting, they disconnected. Gabrielle fingered the rose petals. "Lord, if I close my eyes to the outer man, will You show me what's in Cameron's heart?"

"Stand firm and see my deliverance," the Lord answered, citing Exodus 14:13.

———— ⁓⁓ ————

The next day at work, Gabrielle wished she was cloned. There was no time to think about Cameron or his dinner date. Forgoing paperwork in her office, she headed directly to a ticket counter to help the agent on duty, who was feverishly trying to handle the customers alone. Another employee had called in sick and they were short staffed. Gabrielle found a replacement, but she would fill in until that worker arrived.

A new crowd formed as soon as she gave the agent permission to take a long overdue break. Working solo, she assisted each passenger as efficiently and friendly as possible.

Looking to the next customer, she came face-to-face with Cameron. His smile was mesmerizing. Her heart fluttered as she welcomed his unexpected presence. His timing couldn't be better as the sick worker's replacement hurried in and a crowd huddled around the counter.

Gabrielle moved to the next terminal in hopes that the ticket agent on break would return any minute. Cameron slid to her side. "Has it been this busy all day?"

She nodded. "If you don't have a question about a flight, then I'm going to ask you to step aside."

"I understand." He checked his watch. "I'll wait." Cameron found a seat in the nearby gate area. The few times she glanced his way, he was watching her. That made her uncomfortable. Her brothers drilled in her head when a man scrutinized a woman, either he was mentally undressing her or thinking of naughty possibilities.

If she asked him what he was thinking, would he tell her the truth? Gabrielle cleared her head and concentrated on the steady flow of customers until the ticket agent finally returned.

The agent had begun to develop a habit of leaving early for breaks and returning late. Gabrielle didn't want to notate the infractions in the woman's personnel file, but that was her job. First, as her supervisor, Gabrielle would hear her out. "I'm going to need an explanation for your tardiness," she advised her.

"I have one, Miss Dupree." She confided that she was pregnant and trying to manage her shift as best she could without missing work. Her husband was recently laid off.

Nodding, Gabrielle had compassion because she remembered when Talise worked there and was pregnant. If God's grace was endless toward her, He expected her to pass it on. She would pray for the woman like she did for Talise and be more understanding of her long breaks.

She logged off the terminal and stepped away from the counter. Cameron quickly closed the book he was reading and stuffed it in his briefcase. Standing, he offered her the sexiest smile.

"Do you have time to grab a bite to eat with me?"

"Are you sure you want to be seen with a woman who looks like a ticket agent?" she asked him and then whispered, "I wouldn't want to ruin your image or anything."

"I deserve that dig, but I'm very sure I want to be seen with *you*, even if you wore overalls and carried a hammer." Then, with puppy dog eyes, he apologized. "I'm sorry for that condescending comment when we first met."

"Apology accepted . . . and for good measure, I'll even forget about it," Gabrielle said, as Cameron guided her away from the path of a hurried traveler.

"You are an angel. This does not replace the dinner you owe me."

Laughing, Gabrielle conceded. "Okay. How about Earl of Sandwich?"

"Lead the way, Miss Dupree."

"Where are you off to this time?" she asked, as they strolled down Terminal E. Cameron's attention didn't seem to stray when beautiful, fast-walking women passed them.

Brownie points. The man was definitely collecting them. Once they were in front of the restaurant, he insisted on paying and Gabrielle told him what she wanted. They chose a table, Cameron rested his briefcase in a chair and then headed toward the counter. Kicking off her shoes, she stretched her legs and wiggled her toes.

While looking down at her tired feet, something sticking out of Cameron's briefcase got her attention. It was a paperback. Nosy, Gabrielle inched it out far enough to read the title. Gabrielle's mouth dropped in shock. It was a romance novel.

What in the world is he doing reading this? she wondered. As she fingered it open, pages were marked up as if it were a textbook.

Cameron had scribbled notes throughout, such as "Never sleep with a woman on the first date." "You don't care about this woman, you cheated." "A text message saying 'I miss you,' okay that's doable."

Forget the book. His notes make for an interesting read, Gabrielle thought. She stifled a roar of laughter. Checking the counter, Cameron already had their orders. As he grabbed napkins and straws, Gabrielle hurriedly stuffed the book back before he caught her. She coaxed herself to keep a straight face.

"Here you go." He slid the tray in front of her. "Your All-American sandwich and a side salad."

Stifling a giggle, Gabrielle could barely thank him. He moved his briefcase over and sat in the space beside her. With the oddest expression, he frowned. "What's so funny?"

"Nothing." She shook her head and waved her hand in the air.

Clearing his throat, he waited. "Either you're going to laugh, cry, or bless our food." His eyes twinkled with mischief.

She patted the corners of her eyes and gathered deep breaths. Gabrielle could hardly compose herself enough to draw her mind in to pray. "Would you do the honors?"

Cameron didn't hesitate and wrapped his strong hand around hers. "Lord, in the Name of Jesus, we thank You for our food. We ask You to remove all impurities for our consumption and sanctify it. Thank You, in Jesus' Name. Amen."

Although his prayer had been over their food, she enjoyed listening to him just the same. For a brief time, they ate in silence. Then Gabrielle decided to begin her quizzing. "When I was at the ticket counter, why were you watching me?"

"You're a beautiful woman and I appreciate the finer things in life."

"Good answer, but while you were appreciating the finer things in life, what were you thinking?"

He practically choked. "Ah, I don't think you really want to know." He actually blushed.

"I don't ask questions without wanting to know the answers," she challenged him. "Tell me."

Stalling for a few seconds, Cameron avoided eye contact. Seemingly, he was uncomfortable. "I was thinking about making love to you."

Oh, my goodness. He told the truth and that scared her. It took a few seconds for her to recover from his blunt honesty, but she was ready with her own response. "You can't make love to me without loving me. Anything else is mere sex."

"I don't sleep with women on the first date or the second. I have to feel there's more to the relationship than hormones," he stated and took a sip of his iced tea.

Yeah, I know. I read your notes. "Cameron, you amaze me. I didn't know if you were going to be truthful or not. Now let me be blunt." She paused. "I'm not going to sleep with you or any other man. If any man loves me, then he will protect my soul from sinning, which includes sex outside of marriage."

"This may surprise you, but I like you. I'm looking for a soul mate, a valentine." After stabbing at his salad a few times, he stuffed his fork in his mouth.

"That's good because it means you'll be concerned about her soul, as well as her mind and body."

While he crunched on a mouthful of lettuce, she could tell he was thinking. Maybe about what she just said. Gabrielle was beginning to warm to Cameron. She appreciated his candor. She thought he would lose interest like some of the other men when she mentioned she didn't indulge in one-night stands. It unnerved her that one-nights were considered to be commonplace. Gabrielle was a card-carrying member of God's Virgin Club—and proud of it.

They finished the rest of their meal in silence. She would tease him about rewriting a romance book later. "What time is your flight?" she asked, as they wandered back to the gates.

"Six twenty. They should start boarding in a few minutes."

"So you're going to Baltimore. Flight 1273." Gabrielle could run down the daily flight schedule with her eyes closed.

"You know your stuff. I'm attending a two-day engineering conference there."

As she ambled her way around travelers, she didn't realize Cameron had stopped in his tracks. Glancing over her shoulder, Gabrielle wondered what was wrong.

He didn't move from his spot. Curious, she walked back to his towering figure. His piercing eyes captured hers right away.

"What's wrong?" she asked, concerned.

"I'm just thinking . . ." Taking her hand, he squeezed it. "When I return, I hope you will change your 'if' to a dinner date. I don't know what type of man you think I am, but Jamiesons are programmed never to fail a test—never."

Bringing her hand to his lips, he placed a soft kiss inside her palm. Then, as if everything was all right in the world, Cameron linked his fingers through hers and tugged her along with him to his gate.

Chapter Ten

*G*abrielle. Cameron couldn't figure her out. He doubted she was playing games with him, but she was surely testing him. It had been two weeks since they had returned from St. Louis. Not a day had gone by without him imagining her smile, laugh, or the brightness in her eyes when she seemed to be up to mischief.

Out of the corner of his eye, he had watched her snoop inside his briefcase and scan through that dumb paperback. It was an embarrassing find, but he didn't mind her knowing a secret. After all, he purchased the book to get more insight about why she read so intensely what she did.

Settling in his seat on the plane, Cameron stared out the window. She defined making love as sex. Whatever term Miss Dupree wanted to use didn't matter to him. The act itself was a two-way street.

Women slept with men to possess them. She didn't come right out and say it, but he suspected she had kept herself from a man. Was that supposed to scare him away or challenge him?

Whatever happened between them, so be it. He wasn't going after her for a conquest—okay, maybe initially, but now he was genuinely attracted to her.

Arriving in Baltimore at the conference, his mind continued to stray to Gabrielle. During the day-long seminars, Cameron couldn't recall half of what the speakers were saying, so he gave up on trying to concentrate. When the sessions ended, he would purchase the recordings, go back to his suite, and listen to them. That way he would know if he had questions for the speakers before the final day of the conference.

His first order of business was to make a call to Talise when he returned to his hotel room. Unfortunately, Cameron had to endure five minutes of conversing with Ace. After that, he questioned Talise for as long as Ace let him.

"What can you tell me about Gabrielle?"

"It depends. What would you like to know?"

"Anything: favorite color, flowers, more about her education, background . . ."

"Socioeconomic status?" Talise asked in monotone. Cameron couldn't tell if she was teasing or chastising him.

"I'll take that hit, but I'm beyond that. Gabrielle and I have called a truce about my clumsy introduction. What is she looking for?"

Talise took her time answering, "Be yourself. Show her the Cameron who befriended me when I was pregnant. She's a romantic. I'm not just talking about in the relationship department. Gabrielle is the type of person who sees hope in impossible situations.

"She taught me a Scripture about how man looks on the outside, but God looks on the inside. She strives to be an 'inside person.' The bottom line is she won't make a move without an okay from the Lord. The payoff being that she expects God to deliver on happy endings."

That's why she reads those fake romance novels, he thought.

"Gabrielle is very special to me. Like you, she was there for me when I needed her. She deserves the best, in my opinion. If you're not willing to give her that, then please leave her alone. My husband is a recovering sinner, I would hate for him to have a relapse and jump you."

"Right, I'm scared. I love family. I don't fight them."

"Good. Maybe you can learn to love Gabrielle because she's close like family to me."

They talked a few more minutes about Talise's favorite subject, the baby, before he reluctantly had to let her go.

The next day, a few hours after the conference came to a close, Cameron boarded the plane. Hoping Gabrielle was at work reminded him that he didn't have her number. But he planned to rectify that soon. Before the flight took off, another woman snagged the seat next to him. This time he did peep at her legs; her every movement was a seductive production.

Looking the other way, Cameron really wasn't in the mood for any pleasantries. Pulling out his iPhone, he fumbled in his jacket pocket for his miniature headphones. It was a time for concentration. He needed to identify his challenger—was it God, Gabrielle, or both.

He had nothing against God. His family worshiped Him and he respected the Lord, but Cameron didn't see a need to be overzealous. What separated him from his brothers and cousins was their passive thinking to wait on Jesus for everything. Even Gabrielle had said as much, but Cameron was proactive. He always had been.

God gave men the ability to make things happen for themselves. It wouldn't hurt to ask for His assistance with Gabrielle, however, but he planned to have an active role.

Before leaving Boston, he had boasted about never failing a test. But there was one that he barely passed in college. It was a lesson learned the hard way: alcohol and studying don't mix. Fortunately, he rebounded quickly. In school and life, Cameron valued a clear mind—at all times and at all costs. He could count on one hand the last time he even had a beer.

As the music soothed him, his eyes closed, setting the scene to conjure up images of Gabrielle. At times, he could recognize the fire in her clear brown eyes, which were a shade lighter than her flawless brown skin. She seemed ready to do battle. Other times, there was a softness that would make any man want to please her.

It seemed as if she yearned to believe in him, but withheld her trust. Time was running out. The countdown had begun for him to relocate permanently to St. Louis. He didn't believe in long-distance relationships, but to win her over, he would try for a little while.

When Cameron walked off the plane, he made a beeline toward the ticket counter where she was working when he had flown out. Getting in a short line, he approached a petite female ticket agent with an engaging smile.

"Hi, I'm looking for Gabrielle Dupree. Is she working today?"

The young lady shook her head. "She won't be back for a week and a half."

Cameron frowned. "Is she sick?"

"Oh no, sir. She's on vacation." The agent cordially dismissed him and motioned for the next person.

Vacation? Gabrielle never mentioned it to him. Her lack of trust to confide in him stung, although Cameron had no problem with earning it. Yet it still wounded his pride. He snatched his phone out of its case and tapped a name in his contacts.

Ace answered, "Hey, cuz—"

He didn't have time for any pleasantries. "I need Talise . . . please."

Ace snorted. "Well, hello to you too. My wife is busy. Can I help you with something?" Judging from the exaggerated calmness of his voice, Cameron was certain Ace was just trying to irritate him.

"Unless you can give me Gabrielle's phone number, no."

"As a matter of fact, I probably could, but it wouldn't matter."

His cousin was really beginning to irk him. "Why, Aaron?" Cameron asked, using his legal name.

"She's out of the country. Unless you have an international calling card, you'll have to wait for her to return from Greece."

Stopping dead in his tracks, he had just made it to the baggage claim area. "Greece!" Cameron yelled, then looked around and mouthed his apology to the other passengers, "Sorry."

Returning to his phone conversation, he asked, "What's she doing in Greece?"

"She took a vacation." Ace became quiet. "You know, if you step up your game, not only would you have Gabrielle's number, but you'd know her whereabouts too."

Throwing up his hands in frustration, Cameron didn't even say goodbye before he disconnected the call. Spotting his bag, he grabbed it and stalked out of the airport, fuming.

Trip or no trip, Gabrielle was running from him. She didn't know that he would chase her to the corners of the earth—because something inside of him kept saying don't let her get away.

Chapter Eleven

*A*board a Lufthansa jetliner, Gabrielle clicked her seat belt and prepared for her twelve-hour flight to Greece with a layover in Germany. Although she had downloaded plenty of books onto her eReader, she couldn't resist packing some new Christian romance paperback novels.

Gabrielle would never read another romance book without thinking of Cameron. It was endearing that he was reading alongside her instead of chatting up a storm with his fellow seatmate. Then too, it was how he had marked up the book with his opinions. If she gave it too much thought, she would laugh uncontrollably on the plane.

That would make a good conversation piece if she decided to go out to dinner with him. Cameron was so intense when it came to pursuing her. She was almost certain that after one date she would want more to follow.

One thing for certain, the man had been right. Instead of reading about it, she wanted to experience the intensity of love, minus the sex and lust, of course. She desired the pure love of a man for the woman he had chosen as his wife. Unsure if Cameron could be that man in her life, she dozed off dreaming about him.

Sweet thoughts lulled Gabrielle into a deep sleep until the first part of her trip ended. She landed in Munich, where she changed planes. On the second leg of her journey, she returned to the enchanting dreams that Cameron seemed to orchestrate.

In the wee hours of the morning, a flight attendant, who spoke with a proper English dialect, welcomed the passengers to Athens.

Fluent in Russian, Spanish, and broken Creole, Gabrielle enjoyed listening to other languages around the world in hopes of learning and some day mastering them. Back home, there was the intriguing Gullah language, which was fiercely preserved, so not to sever its identity with Africa. Undoubtedly, she was a language junkie. If left up to her own devices, instead of her parents' threat to cut off funding her education, she would have earned a double major in world languages and linguistic anthropology.

After retrieving her carry-on, Gabrielle focused on the present. She followed the instructions for those who were part of the tourist group. Her excitement was mounting, and she couldn't wait to begin their exploration.

At the baggage section, a chauffeur held a sign marked "Starks Sunset Tours." She joined a large group that was flocking around him. Minutes later, they boarded a bus for the six-hour ride to Thessalonica where their cruise would originate.

Gabrielle was all smiles as she greeted several other passengers. Making her way through the bus, she claimed a seat next to a woman who reminded her of Grandma BB from Talise's wedding. Unable to resist the temptation, she peered at the lady's footwear—tan Naturalizer sandals—and exhaled.

Turning around, she caught a few men ogling her, but she ignored them. Whenever Gabrielle was in a foreign country, it wasn't unusual for natives to mistake her nationality for Egyptian, Syrian, Somali, or some other. In a sense, they were correct. Since mankind began in

Africa, her heritage included a diverse ethnic makeup.

Using her international calling card, she phoned her parents to let them know she had landed safely. They would then get the word to her brothers, who would worry until she was back on American soil. Upon her return home, her three big brothers would resume their usual concerns about American criminals. After watching the movie *Taken*, starring Liam Neeson, who played a former spy, her brothers acted as if Jesus wasn't a Protector.

However, Gabrielle was aware that she had to be smart traveling alone, so as not to become a victim like the teenage daughter character. In the movie, the girl was abducted for slave trade after going to a foreign country without a chaperone.

But, not to worry, Gabrielle knew the Holy Ghost had her back. Relaxing, she admired the passing scenery. Her mind drifted. It had been a while since she stopped counting the number of times she had flown to Europe solo. She smiled, recalling the fabulous experience of remaining in college an extra semester. It was a clever way to complete her second minor as a cover to travel in the summer-abroad study program.

One advantage of being single was that she could up and go at a moment's notice. For instance, there was the time when her brother Philip, an evangelist, conducted a revival in Ethiopia. She had joined him for two days.

Soon her excitement began to wane as the time difference began to overtake her body. Gabrielle hadn't realized she had dozed off until the woman next to her nudged her.

"Wake up, sweetie. We're at our hotel."

A bit drowsy, Gabrielle followed the others off the bus. After she checked in, the bellhop secured her luggage. As soon as she reached her room, she took a shower and then laid down for a quick nap that turned into a night's sleep.

The next day, Gabrielle awoke refreshed, but starved. Dressing in light clothing for the warm weather, she met others in her party downstairs in the dining room. Within the hour, they boarded the bus for Philippi.

For the next week, each day was an adventure. There were plenty of stops and picture taking at sites where the apostle Paul lived, preached, and wrote letters to the church at Corinth. Observing sites such as where Paul and Silas were confined in prison, Gabrielle marveled as her imagination mentally transported her back to biblical times.

Fast-forwarding to the present, there she stood as a modern-day convert of the apostle's ministry. She hoped to embrace whatever spiritual understanding God would reveal to her. Gabrielle was always in awe of the early church and the adversities early Christians faced. She praised God that she hadn't lived during those times of persecution. She was thankful that God allowed her to be alive after the Comforter had come, as the Bible teaches in the books of Acts.

Jesus, thank You for my salvation, she prayed silently.

Her vacation sped by, which included a three-day cruise to the Greek islands. On the last day, Gabrielle silently said goodbye to the places she had personally witnessed from the New Testament.

During her 4,600 mile trip back to the States, a somewhat weary, but happy traveler opened her Bible and re-read the passages that spoke of the places she had visited. As the words blurred and her lids fluttered, the clarity of a handsome face with dark brown eyes, silky brows, a goatee, and a clean-shaven head reappeared for the first time since she had arrived in Greece.

It's time to get back to reality, she thought, pinching herself.

Bills, work, and decisions about job offers weren't the only things waiting for her in Boston. So was Cameron Jamieson.

Chapter Twelve

Gabrielle had been back in the States for a few days, and her body was still struggling with the time-zone change. The next day she would return to her nine-to-five job, which often seemed more like five in the morning to nine at night.

She had been praying for the Lord's confirmation about which path He wanted her to walk in her career and personal life. With no word from heaven as yet, she put those decisions off for a little while longer.

A few evenings later, while in the middle of trying her hand at duplicating an authentic Greek salad like the ones she devoured in Macedonia, the phone rang and interrupted her. It was Denise calling.

"Glad you made it back. I just got my postcard from Greece. Wow, I'm sure the pictures don't do it justice. I know you had a good time."

Gabrielle closed her eyes and smiled, just thinking about it. "I did. God's handiwork was breathtaking. I'm surprised you got it so fast. I wonder if my parents and brothers got theirs. Hold on." She paused to bless her food. "So what else is going on, you wedding crasher?" Gabrielle teased and slipped a fork full of romaine lettuce into her mouth.

"Girl, everything is moving so fast. My sisters and I would like for all of the siblings to meet. My knucklehead brothers say to leave well enough alone, but I've already set things in motion. I can't repeat the term one of my brothers called Ace and Kidd, since their mother was single when she had them. I'm ashamed to say it was cruel."

Cringing, Gabrielle didn't want to imagine. Clearly, her friend hadn't thought about the fallout from meeting her other siblings.

"I refuse to let them kill my joy. Anyway, my sisters and I have been finding information online for free. Besides that, Cameron's oldest brother, Parke, really has been a big help. I'm suggesting a big family reunion . . ."

The excitement in Denise's voice was building; Gabrielle couldn't help but believe God was going to work everything out.

"I spoke with another family member while you were jet-setting across the globe. It seems Cameron's having problems tracking *you* down."

No comment.

"Nothing to say? Why won't you give him a call? He's good-looking, well-educated, and employed—all prerequisites for husband material. The bonus is he's my cousin."

Gabrielle could hear the pride in her friend's voice. "Denise, I'm not saying I have no attraction to him. But the few times we've been together, I feel it's the battle of our wills. Why would I want a relationship with a man who I'll constantly clash with?"

"Okay, here's how this is going down. If you don't call him, I'll give him your phone number, home address, work number, parents' number . . ."

She knew her friend was serious. "Okay, okay. I'll call him."

"When?" Denise demanded.

"Ah, tomorrow . . . after work. It's late, almost nine thirty now."

"Girl, please. You're not a telephone solicitor. As of his recent birthday, Cameron is a thirty-two-year-old young man, not eighty. I'm sure he's up. I've never known you to be a procrastinator. I do owe him. He did act as my go-between with my half brothers."

What about me? Didn't she deserve some credit? Gabrielle was the one who mentioned the Jamieson wedding to Denise in the first place. Plus, in a way, she paid for the trip with her buddy airline voucher.

Humph. Something had to be wrong with her. In the past, she never wavered from her decision concerning a man.

"Stop it, Gabrielle. I know you. You're thinking of all the imaginary reasons not to go out with him. There are none. He's a nice guy."

Am I looking for permission to call him? How many of the heroines in her romance novels or movies always needed a nudge to go out on a date? Was she like one of those characters? One thing for sure, she didn't want to get sideswiped by Cameron's looks and charm.

"Well?"

Taking a deep breath, Gabrielle made the commitment. "Okay."

"Great. I'm going to hang up now so you can do that. Smooches. Talk to you later." Denise disconnected.

"Right." Gabrielle was in no rush. She finished eating and helped herself to seconds. Methodically, she tidied her kitchen. Still not ready, she folded her arms and strolled through her two-bedroom apartment.

Before she could make a move, the phone rang. It was Denise. "Did you call him yet?"

"No, I was enjoying my dinner . . ."

"Gabrielle, I am warning you—"

"All right. Let me do this before I excommunicate you."

"Good," Denise sounded as if she was about to disconnect. "Oh, I will call you back!"

"Goodbye!" Closing her eyes, Gabrielle whispered to Jesus, "Lord, You know my heart and my desire for a godly man. I know that Cameron isn't him."

"*Trust in Me with all your heart and lean not on your own understanding. In all your ways acknowledge Me, and I will make your paths*

93

straight," God spoke Proverbs 3:5–6.

"I trust You, Jesus. I don't trust me in this flesh," she mumbled, as she went into her bedroom. On her dresser, under a vase, lay the envelope filled with dried rose petals. She pushed them aside to get to the thin, heart-shaped sticky-note pad.

Flipping through the sheets, Cameron had scribbled his phone number on every page, leaving no room to write anything else. It was silly, cute, memorable, and . . . romantic.

Closing her eyes, Gabrielle counted to three and tapped in his numbers on her cell.

"Why should I be your valentine?" she asked when he answered on the second ring. It was like an instant shot of morning java.

"Gabrielle," he said with relief in his voice. "Denise is officially my favorite cousin. And why should Gabrielle Dupree be my valentine? Because I won't hurt her heart. I promise."

"You're putting a lot of work into assembling your team to sing your praises. In Talise's eyes, you can do no wrong. And now you've put my best friend up to doing your dirty work? Why? Why all the trouble, Cameron?"

"You have no idea how much I would enjoy answering all your questions until you drift into a peaceful slumber. But then you won't go out with me. How about dinner Friday night at Vlora Restaurant? It's practically in your backyard. I'm sure you'll enjoy their Greek dishes."

It took all the control within Gabrielle not to laugh at his dig at her recent whereabouts. For some reason, she enjoyed being a mystery to him.

"Right. I'll meet you at the restaurant about six thirty."

"This *is* a date. I prefer to pick you up," Cameron countered.

"I prefer to drive, in case the evening doesn't turn out amicable."

Cameron released a heavy sigh. "Give me a blind chance, Gabrielle, please. Whenever you're ready to leave, I'll take you home. If you don't trust me, you can always use your Mace. It won't be the first time you've attacked me."

Rolling her eyes, she groaned. "Have you ever heard of 'let it go'?"

Before he could respond, Gabrielle was already inviting God along. *Okay, Lord, I'm going to trust You and see what happens. Just don't leave me stranded, please God.*

Finally giving in, she told Cameron, "My address is . . ."

Chapter Thirteen

*F*inally, it was Friday. Cameron took extra care in his grooming for the evening. He didn't want Gabrielle to see any flaws in his looks, personality, or heartfelt intentions. He had even started to sport a beard like his middle brother.

With the goatee, admirers compared him to actor Laz Alonso. Cameron happened to be a huge fan of whatever character he played. Now with a beard like Malcolm's, people commented that he resembled a younger version of former NBA player-turned-actor, Rick Fox.

A half-hour later, after double-checking his cologne, deodorant, and popping a breath mint, Cameron walked out the door and slid behind the wheel of his black Audi, hopeful that Gabrielle would want to know what made him tick. He conceded that he possessed an extra dose of self-confidence but commended his parents on instilling that quality in him and his brothers. As a Black man, he was always expected to do better than Whites just to—in their minds—compete with them.

Stereotypes were real and had caused harm down through generations. It was an unfair burden for society to put on one particular ethnic group. If one Black man behaved badly, his actions couldn't possibly represent the whole race. How ridiculous.

Yet, it was the motivation that drove Cameron to be the best and succeed over adversity. As a newbie chairperson of the engineering department, and the first African-American at that, Cameron had to be on top of his game. And he aimed not to disappoint anyone—himself included.

What Gabrielle and others viewed as cocky was him stepping up to the plate and telling the world that he had arrived and would not be intimidated. What was wrong with that? Inevitably, that was the definition of a strong Black man.

Leaving his Winter Hill condo in the Somerville area near the MIT campus, he drove across the bridge over the Charles River. His mind was still counting his many virtues.

Gabrielle didn't live very far, in the Mission Hill neighborhood near downtown Boston. Unfortunately, Friday evening traffic was a nightmare.

Being late wasn't an option. He wouldn't give her any excuse to dismiss his presence. Successfully maneuvering through the streets, Cameron had seven minutes to spare when he pulled in front of her building and parked. As he got out, he scrutinized her neighborhood for safety concerns and nodded in approval.

Jogging up her stone steps, he pushed the intercom and waited.

"Right on time. I'll be right down," she said.

As soon as Gabrielle opened the door, Cameron held his breath. When he exhaled, it came out in a low whistle. "Wow and double wow!" he exclaimed.

A dress never looked so good on a woman. "You do have that can of Mace, right?" he teased openly, but secretly he struggled to keep his naughty thoughts at bay.

"If you even think about undressing me with your hypnotic eyes, I just might use it." He hoped she was only teasing him, especially after she was so apologetic after the wedding incident.

"I have three brothers. Believe me, I know how to defend myself."

"Noted." He withheld a smirk. They were in each other's presence less than five minutes and, already, she was drawing the line.

Escorting her to his car and helping her inside, Cameron snuck a peek at her shapely legs. How was he supposed to behave himself with so much temptation? He wasn't married. So he could look all he wanted as long as he didn't touch her, couldn't he?

When he got in and buckled up, Cameron adjusted the car temperature and headed toward Boylston Street in Copley Square. To impress Gabrielle, he chose Vlora Restaurant, which was actually about fifteen minutes from her apartment. The establishment was known for their authentic Greek food.

"Thank you for going out with me." He smiled, stealing a glimpse at her. She was a beautiful woman who didn't have to flaunt it. He bet she was a spoiled brat as a child and a heartbreaker as a teenager, especially with big brothers.

"I couldn't just have you showing up at my doorstep. Denise warned me that she would disclose my address." She scrunched her nose and laughed. "Do you always expect to get what you want?"

"Is this a test?" He was determined not to make their date a battle of wills all night. Either she didn't trust him or herself.

"Life is a test," she told him.

Cameron shrugged. "In all honesty, yes. I work hard and play just as hard. And I've earned everything that I have."

Surprisingly, Gabrielle sat quietly and didn't have a comeback. Despite the traffic, they got to Copley Square in no time. But finding a parking space was a task. He circled the block twice before stumbling across a spot someone had just vacated.

Grabbing it, he came around to help Gabrielle out. The two leisurely strolled to the entrance of Vlora. Cameron had to touch her, so he kept his hand on the small of her back. A gentleman opened the door and they walked inside to a woman behind a podium.

"Good evening," she greeted them.

"Reservation for Jamieson," Cameron said.

The woman nodded as a hostess appeared and led them to their table. With a quick survey of the area, Cameron was grateful for the privacy. Once they were seated, the hostess placed menus in front of them and advised that their waiter would be with them shortly.

As Gabrielle opened her menu, Cameron admired her long slender fingers that were minus a ring. The first time they met, she mentioned she was waiting on God to give her a companion. Really? Had God not sent what she wanted, perhaps in him? Or, had she rejected every man's intentions and planned to add him to her list? Before the night ended, he would have his answer.

A young man approached the table, introducing himself before he recited the night's specials. Cameron waited for Gabrielle.

It didn't seem to take her long to decide. "Hmmm. I will have Chicken Mediterranean kabobs and an orange salad."

Facing Cameron, the young man asked, "And you, sir?"

"I'll take the bone-in rib eye and a house side salad."

"And to drink, may I suggest a bottle of Riesling or Pinot?" the waiter asked.

"Gabrielle?" He wasn't much of a social drinker, but he did indulge from time to time. That is, despite the little fib he told the young woman on the plane who invited him for drinks.

"Iced tea for me."

Hiding his disappointment, Cameron dittoed Gabrielle's choice. After the waiter left, he asked, "Do you enjoy a glass of wine occasionally, or do you abstain?"

"I abstain."

"For religious reasons?" he pressed.

"Maybe." She shrugged and avoided eye contact. "Somewhat. I had to make some lifestyle choices, and my personal convictions hold me to them."

Really? Now he was getting somewhere about the personal life of

Miss Dupree. "Why do I sense there's a story behind your statement? Did something happen that you regret?"

Again, Gabrielle looked away. She seemed to struggle with whether she wanted to confide in him. He reached across the table and rested his hand on top of hers. She didn't pull back. "Please give me the benefit of the doubt. You can trust me."

Slowly she nodded. "I couldn't wait until I went away to college, so I could be free from rules. One night, Denise and I, along with three other girls, went out on the town. We were looking hot to pick up some guys."

Cameron wiggled his brow and his nostrils flared as his imagination painted the picture.

"We were drinking to be cool. One friend made a connection with a good-looking guy. They left the bar and moved to a corner booth." She paused and swallowed. "Anyway, the rest of us were distracted and almost missed the guy when he helped Shannon stand and took her to the door. We all rushed to her aid, but the guy started answering for her . . ."

Cameron knew how this story was going to end. "He gave her a date rape drug."

Gabrielle nodded. "Yes. I was so scared about what could have happened. I sobered up real quickly. When she woke up the next day, I guess you might say the incident literally scared the devil out of her. "

Thank God it didn't happen to Gabrielle or any of the other women for that matter. "I'm glad everything turned out all right." Cameron's heart pounded in fear of how things might have turned out.

"We made a pact that I would be the designated overseer of the group and the driver if anyone went out again. But later that night, when it really hit me about what could have happened, I prayed and cried. I recalled the stories in the Old Testament where the kings did right in the sight of the Lord, but their sons did evil. I didn't want to imitate that bad generation."

Gabrielle paused when the waiter approached their table and placed their iced teas in from of them.

"I knew drinking was just the beginning of the trouble that I had planned to get into, despite my saved upbringing. Eventually, I was able to witness to my friends. Besides Shannon, one other girlfriend repented, and together they surrendered their lives to Jesus. I describe it as they experienced their Nicodemus moment. Those girls gave God more than lip service. They followed His complete plan for salvation."

Lip service. He wondered what she meant by that, but he wasn't about to discuss religion over dinner. Cameron changed the subject. "Where in Greece did you go?"

"Who told you?"

"It seems like everybody, but you. I was disappointed—no, hurt— when I returned from my conference and you were gone." Cameron hoped he masked his vulnerability.

This time, Gabrielle rested her hand on top of his. With tenderness, she massaged it. "I'm sorry, I've been purposely ex-ing you out of my life." Suddenly, she covered her face.

Cameron panicked. He hoped she wasn't about to cry. "Why?"

"I'm ashamed to admit it, but you overwhelm me."

The night was about to go downhill as her eyes misted. Attempting to recapture the moment, he changed the subject and asked about her trip.

That's when Gabrielle's eyes lit up, as she took a deep breath. Smiling, she quickly became animated. "Ooh, there were so many places to see in a short period of time. Besides the biblical hot spots like the ruins of where Paul and Silas were imprisoned, monasteries in Athens, then Thessalonica, Rhodes, Athens, Greek islands . . ."

Listening intently, Cameron multitasked and soaked in her beauty while she rattled off the sites and monuments as if she was the tour guide. The only intermission occurred when the server placed their plates in front of them.

Reaching across the table, Cameron squeezed her hands, closed his eyes, and bowed his head. "Jesus, thank You for this incredible opportunity to break bread with Gabrielle. Bless our food and sanctify it from all impurities, in Jesus' Name. Amen."

She repeated Amen and then delicately stabbed her salad. Cameron cut into his steak and looked up to see her smiling at him.

"Although you are mesmerizing right now, what's so funny?"

"I'm not laughing, but smiling. I love to hear a man pray. It's comforting and almost romantic."

"That's your idea of romance?" he snickered.

"Why? Do you want to add a footnote like you did in that romance book you were reading?" She teased, giggling. With a dab of her mouth, she confessed, "I couldn't help but read it that day when I saw it sticking out of your briefcase.

Although Cameron was embarrassed at the time, he had gotten over it. "That was homework."

"Homework? Ha!" By this time, Gabrielle was laughing until a tear fell.

Cameron just watched her. He didn't care about being the butt of a joke. He'd rather see tears of joy, than misery.

"Umm-hmm. What kind of homework?" She stuffed more salad in her mouth and crunched, waiting to hear his explanation.

"Everything that I've done from the moment of your rescue to this dinner and all things in between is because I want to know more about you. Your hobbies, likes, dislikes . . ."

Gabrielle sobered and her eyes misted again. "That's sweet. Thank you, Cameron, for going through so much trouble."

He dabbed his mouth and leaned close. "If a man is attracted to a woman, he'll do everything in his power to win her heart. I am that man, Gabrielle," he whispered.

Sucking in her breath, she could only stare. When he sat back, Gabrielle reached for her glass of iced tea. Her hand was shaking. After taking a sip, she swallowed. "What makes you think that? You barely know me."

"A man knows. I'm not trying to make you uncomfortable, but my feelings have been pent up for weeks, and I'm running out of time to share them with you."

"I know."

When their waiter returned and asked if they needed anything else, Gabrielle shook her head.

"So tell me why you chose to visit Greece."

"I love the ruins of things that once were. There's so much history and culture, and I understand the Greek language has been spoken for at least 3,500 years."

"That's fascinating. I'm impressed." Cameron winked and witnessed her slight shiver. "What was your major at Howard?" he asked out of curiosity.

"BA in liberal arts. I double-minored in linguistic anthropology and world languages. While I lived in Dallas, I earned my MBA at the University of Texas."

Cameron dropped his fork. He blinked. She was accomplished in her own right. He had definitely misjudged her. Wow. That shut his mouth. He had to thank God for putting this incredible woman in his path.

"How many foreign languages do you speak?"

"Spanish, Russian, and broken Creole. I'm better at speaking Chinese than I am at reading it. Before I flew to Greece, I started to learn the language online," she said and placed a piece of chicken in her mouth.

"Why are you working as a ticket agent at the airlines?"

"I'm not. I was a trainee supervisor until about a year ago. Then I was promoted because of my MBA. But it seems like I'm doing the job of three people. That's why I've been job shopping."

"Really? Any offers yet?"

She shrugged. "A few."

"Have I earned a stripe for you to share that information with me, or will I forever be on the sidelines? I assure you any legal or personal background check would show you I'm trustworthy," he asked.

"We do have things in common, including the two women in your family whom I love. But Cameron, it's the mismatched things between us that scares me."

"We can make things fit, remember? Here's one more thing we have in common. You love ancient civilizations and ruins, and I enjoy learning about my ancestors."

Gabrielle was curious. "Speaking of ancestors, why weren't you skeptical of Denise's story?"

"I'm about family preservation. I've researched ten generations back. When I found the descendants of Orma, the information eventually led me to Samuel, Ace, Denise, and the other siblings. While attending MIT, it just made sense to track down Ace and his brother since they lived here.

"Ace and I bonded like brothers, so I temporarily put that first family on hold. Although I already knew about Denise and her siblings, it blew my mind when she actually came to her stepbrother's wedding. That was pure coincidence."

"That was God's plan to bring the family together. There are no accidents, coincidences, or mistakes. Jesus has a precise order to our lives, and I'm thankful someone is looking out for me," Gabrielle countered.

"What about our meeting? Chance or destined?"

She grinned. "I'm not backpedaling. It was destined. Maybe I was supposed to spray you with the pepper spray instead of that drunk."

Cameron laughed. "Got me." He paused to admire her. "You have the prettiest smile."

Blushing, she thanked him. "You mentioned ten generations. There were plenty of public records that had been preserved. But how is that even possible when we're talking about an individual who is essentially unknown to the masses, and in some cases unidentifiable in slavery?"

"It's not impossible. It takes some diligent detective work, but I encourage it. There are public documents in the dusty back rooms of courthouses. A person could also find obits and grave sites and marriage certificates. But the court records are the best. I'll never forget this one case in St. Louis, Missouri, about a freed man who was held in slavery. His name was Carey Ewton. He was born in 1790 as a slave to some man named Robertson in Petersburg, Virginia. When he was about eleven years old, he was sold to a Richard Cox to execute a will."

Although Gabrielle was wearing a frown, she listened without interruption.

"Anyway, Cox took him to Washington County, Kentucky, where he was bought and sold by several men over the next twenty-eight years of his life. That took him to several states. Eventually, William Ewton bought him and held him in bondage. When William died, Benjamin Wilder bought him at the estate sale. Carey Ewton argued to the judge that since he lived and worked in Illinois—a free state—that entitled him to his freedom. "

As tears pooled in Gabrielle's eyes, Cameron waited. "I don't have to continue," he said softly. "I get carried away with the details of a person enslaved," he stated, somewhat apologetically.

"I can't imagine one human being buying, selling, trading, abusing, and doing whatever to another human being. In the Bible, Hebrews or Israelites were enslaved and early Christians suffered persecution. That was long ago, but this Black man seems so close to home. Please go on. There's always a rainbow. Did the court ever grant his freedom?"

It was Cameron who hesitated. What more could impress him that night about her? The average woman cannot stomach any mention of slavery; they simply refuse to listen.

The thought of women being raped was accepting a part of

American history. Men also suffered physically with whippings on their bare skin. Adding insult to injury, they were dragged into jail. Unfortunately, there was no way for him to sugarcoat the past. With that understanding, he and his brothers had risen beyond that mentality by pursuing higher institutional education. Beyond that, they embraced an education not learned in school, but through historic documents.

Forcing a brief intermission, their waiter returned and asked if they needed anything. She declined and he followed suit. Then resuming his account, Cameron was happy to inform her that the former enslaved man did win his freedom.

While continuing to chat about various topics, they completed their meals. The server reappeared once more, handed them dessert menus, and waited.

"Whatever the lady wants," Cameron advised.

Gabrielle smiled and pointed at her menu. "I think I'll try the Albanian-style bread pudding with walnuts and pistachio crème anglaise."

"The Kompekai." The waiter beamed. "That's an excellent choice." He was about to leave when she asked for two forks. Cameron lifted his brow.

"It's time to share."

Chapter Fourteen

*I*t was time to put Cameron out of his misery. By sharing her dessert, Gabrielle was extending an olive branch from her heart. Maybe she had misjudged him. She was now convinced that he wasn't self-centered, but a sensitive man. That was priceless.

"I'll share anything with you," he whispered, reaching across the table. Cameron swept up her hands in his and brought them to his lips. Without taking his eye off hers, he brushed a soft kiss on them.

Whew. Gabrielle needed a fan. Maybe she should ask for a knife to slice the sensuality between them. Realistically, if she could keep him talking instead of touching, she'd be all right.

"Tell me more about the king and queen in your family tree?"

Cameron chuckled, as their pudding was set between them. She said a quick prayer then dug in first.

"Are you going to leave me any?" he teased.

"Every man for himself. You'd better jump in."

Soon it was the battle of the forks, and they fought until they were down to the last morsel. Cameron conceded, but when she was about to scoop it up, he took the fork from her hand. Coaxing her closer, he fed it to her.

Closing her eyes, Gabrielle savored the moment and the flavor. She liked him as a person and enjoyed how he treated her.

When she opened her eyes again, he teased, "Welcome back. I thought you went to sleep on me."

"Funny," she replied, as she dabbed her mouth and leaned back. "Okay, so tell me about your king and queen."

He grinned. She could sense that Cameron Jamieson was in his element when he talked about African-American history and his genealogy.

"Actually, it was King Seif and Princess Adaeze of the Diomande tribe. Paki was born in December 1770 in Côte d'Ivoire, on the Gold Coast of Africa. His name means 'a witness that this one will not die,' and it held true for him. He lived a long life, long enough to see slavery abolished in the United States.

"In the fall of 1790, slave traders attacked and savagely beat Paki and his warriors before kidnapping them. He was among hundreds of thousands who were hauled to the Gates of No Return castle.

"Some of the ships the captains used to transport their human cargo had biblical connections, like *Good Ship of Jesus*, under the command of Sir John Hawkins. Another one was named *Snow Elijah*."

Gabrielle considered herself a good Christian, but the thought of using biblical references for devilish purposes incensed her. "Those slave masters—"

"Ah." Cameron shook his head. "Many genealogists refer to them as slaveholders, not masters."

"You're right," she said with conviction. "There's only one Master—Jesus."

"*Snow Elijah* landed first in the Caribbean and dropped a payload of human cargo before heading to the Maryland coastline." Cameron whistled. "Now that state was known for harsh slave laws, especially for women.

"Automatically, my tenth great-grandfather was separated from his bodyguards. Because of his stature and strength, Paki was sold at the highest bid of $275 to a wealthy slave owner, Jethro Turner, in front of Sinner's Hotel."

"At least they got the hotel name right. Humph," Gabrielle huffed, with a touch of defiance.

They exchanged high-fives. "Paki fell in love with Elaine, the slaveholder's only daughter, and the two ran away together. She began a journal of their triumphs and trials. Quite miraculously, we have history because of her simple entries."

Interesting. While Cameron's distant grandmother preserved history in a journal, Gabrielle preserved the secrets of her heart in a handbook of romance.

"I commend your family. I know of my grandparents and great-grandparents on both sides. Beyond that, I never gave it a second thought."

"Enough about me. What other mysteries do you hold? Besides being friends with Talise and Denise, I know where you work. I know that you're an alumna of the prestigious Howard University and that you like to travel the world. I also know that you have three older brothers. One, by the way, who I don't think likes me for some reason."

Gabrielle laughed. "Don't take it personal."

"I didn't. That's why I called you. What's your middle name? Are your parents still alive? What do they do?" Cameron had endless questions.

"Gabrielle Francesca. My father is a doctor and my mother is a retired educator. We have Morehouse and Spelman in the house. I have a preaching brother, a judge, and a district manager of Kansas City area McDonald's restaurants as my siblings. We hail from Louisiana . . ."

"Louisiana?" Cameron shook. "That's a whole different definition of slavery . . . unlike the rest of the country, where one drop of Black blood means you're Black. In that state, a person with one-eighth Negro and seven-eighths White blood was considered an octoroon. A quarter

Negro and three-quarters White was a quadroon."

"You do know your history, and it appears my history too. I'm impressed."

"Finally." Cameron pumped his fist in the air.

"Just so you know, Mr. Jamieson, I've been impressed all night." She stuck out her tongue.

"Have you ever run the Boston marathon, or any marathon?"

"No." Gabrielle frowned. She was all for fitness and healthy eating most of the time, but she wasn't about to run in the streets with anybody for any reason. Period. "Why?"

"I was thinking, since our days are numbered, that we could do a dating marathon. You know, movies, dinners, concerts, or whatever you like."

"How about church?"

"I attend church, but I don't make a habit of mixing religion with dating."

What was it with men and church? Suddenly, Gabrielle was coming back to reality. If disappointment mirrored on her face, she hoped Cameron could read it in large, bold letters.

"Tell me about your salvation walk."

"First, I believe in the Lord Jesus Christ, I repent nightly at bedtime, I give back to the community, and I treat others as I would want to be treated," Cameron said matter-of-factly.

"That's not enough for me," she said, frustrated.

"I'm not a Bible scholar. However, I know enough to know we don't live under the law of the Old Testament. Jesus gave us grace in the New Testament. Therefore, there are no more laws. We judge ourselves; if we make a mistake, we repent and then go on about our business. It's a circle."

"Umm-hmm. Well, while you're repenting from a revolving cycle of sins in this world, you'd better hope Jesus doesn't return to rapture

His people. Because sin is sin and you might not get a chance to ask for forgiveness."

Taking a deep breath, Gabrielle gathered her purse and shawl. "Thanks for dinner. I'm ready to go home now, please."

Cameron squeezed his lips but didn't say a word. As he reached for his wallet, he summoned their waiter for the check. While they waited, he stared into her eyes. She recognized his confusion.

"I'm in the doghouse, aren't I?"

"Yep."

"If you believe I'm a sinner, then I challenge you to show me the error of my ways."

"Don't test me on this, Mr. Jamieson. I take my salvation seriously and it's either pass or fail. The Bible doesn't mention purgatory either."

Chapter Fifteen

*B*ack in her apartment, Gabrielle reflected on the highs and lows of the dinner. In one night, it was the most exhilarating, enchanting, and disappointing date she had ever experienced. Even with all his arrogance, she was attracted to Cameron. The flesh definitely couldn't be trusted.

He was beginning to become the most complex man she had ever met. In a way, she was relieved he was moving. Let his family handle him. Pride before destruction.

"Stand firm." Once again, God reminded her of Exodus 14:13.

God had given her that Scripture before. *Okay, Lord, what is my role in his life?* Without a response, Gabrielle grabbed her Bible. Before she opened it, she prayed, hoping the Lord would speak to her through His Word. About twenty minutes later, she had finished several passages without any further clues about what Jesus wanted her to do.

When it was time to prepare for bed, she got on her knees and talked to Jesus before getting under the covers.

However, there would be no rest for Gabrielle. After an hour of tossing and turning, she reached for her cell phone and sent Cameron a text: I'm sorry if I ruined our night.

Despite the lateness of the hour, he replied quickly. Sorry if I ruined your impression of me. Of all the women I've known and have yet to meet, I doubt any of them will have the effect on me that you do. Good night.

Smiling, she rolled over. For some unknown reason, Gabrielle was starting to like his hot-and-cold personality. Closing her eyes, she now believed she would sleep like a baby.

———～〜———

Early the next morning, Talise's phone call jolted her from a peaceful slumber. Gabrielle barely said hello when her friend started singing Cameron's praises, pulling her into the present.

"Cameron is complex. It seems like all these Jamieson men are. At least, that's what their wives tell me. Even Grandma BB chimed in. Too bad he's moving and you're still there."

Gabrielle remained silent on that subject. She wasn't about to hint that she might relocate to St. Louis too. Talise would probably be on the next plane out to help her pack, if she decided to accept such a job offer.

Listening to Talise chatting endlessly about her family, Gabrielle suddenly changed her mind and braced for the impact. "To bring you up to date on my job hunt, I've had several job offers and I'm currently entertaining two near you."

Talise squealed. "How close?"

"Hmmm. How close are you to . . . St. Louis?"

"Are you serious?" Talise screamed.

"Yes." Gabrielle could hear Ace in the background, asking if she was okay.

"I'm fine, babe," she answered softly.

"You sure? Is Gabrielle okay?" Ace sounded concerned.

"She's moving to St. Louis . . ."

"Talise, I didn't say that. I said I'm thinking about—" she tried to correct her friend.

"I just know you're going to say yes!"

Gabrielle wasn't so sure.

When she didn't confirm right away, Talise pressured her. "Girl, how can you pass it up? I know they're offering you good money, or you wouldn't even consider it. Plus, I'm here, your godbaby is here, Grandma BB is here, and she says you're her hero ever since your pepper spray attack. She loved it!"

"And Cameron will be there. God knows that man has me praying not to lust."

"As an official Jamieson wife and mother, that is hard to do. Good luck with that, girl."

"I'll pray on it. Now go spend time with your baby and your baby's daddy," Gabrielle teased and disconnected.

Gabrielle didn't move from her chair right away. She closed her eyes and bowed her head. "God, I know if I earnestly seek You, You will reveal Cameron's purpose in my life. I know my real job is to be a light that will lead him to Your complete salvation in the magnificent Name of Jesus. Amen."

Complete. It wasn't that Cameron didn't confess his belief in God. What bothered her was his complacency to stay at his current level with God instead of growing to overcome his temptations to curse or whatever else he did that offended God.

One thing her evangelistic brother taught her was never to discount a person's walk with Jesus but encourage them to seek more from God. "Lord, give Cameron a hunger and thirst that only You can fill."

Gabrielle spent her day off doing laundry, cleaning, and cooking meals for the following week. Later that evening, as she was about to begin her roundup calls—a term for which she dubbed her weekly calls to her brothers and parents—Cameron called.

"Hello?"

"What are you doing next weekend?"

Not a repeat of the previous night. That was for sure. He had tenacity. She would give him that. "I'm driving up to Hartford to see Denise."

"I was hoping we could spend my last weekend in Boston together." His deep voice revealed a tinge of disappointment. "How about some company? I'm willing to drive, and it will provide a perfect opportunity for me to meet the rest of my kinfolks."

What was it with these Jamiesons and their inclinations to invite themselves to places no one had extended an invite to?

"I know you're moving to St. Louis, Gabrielle. You're not going to get rid of me . . . yet."

That big mouth Talise. Although Gabrielle was swaying toward St. Louis, she hadn't committed and could change her mind at the midnight hour.

"It's not set in stone, yet."

"If this will help you make up your mind, I'll drive and let you talk about Jesus all the way."

Gabrielle smirked. Was he serious? Then the man must really like her.

"I'll be good company. I promise."

"Cameron, why all the trouble, really?"

"Because you're worth every moment of torture you're putting me through."

Lord, I am in way over my head with this one.

Chapter Sixteen

*I*f Gabrielle moved to St. Louis, the possibilities to woo her would be endless. Cameron thought he had struck out at dinner the other night, but when she texted him, his heart rebounded with more determination to work at smoothing out the rough edges.

The hour-and-a-half drive to Hartford was twofold. He would meet other Jamiesons and be with Gabrielle. Cameron planned to let her say anything she wanted to say about a burial in Jesus' Name or Holy Ghost fire. She could quote numerous Scriptures about Jesus. He would politely listen, but wouldn't comment. That's how a man stayed out of the doghouse.

Earlier, he had phoned his older brother and alerted Parke about his pending trip to Hartford to meet Ace and Kidd's half siblings. As the family's most aggressive genealogist, Cameron's former priority was to connect the dots to all the descendants from his tenth generation grandparents' five sons. Now his focus was on getting Gabrielle to see the true him that otherwise she might not see.

"If Kidd really had this Nicodemus conversion, it seems to me that he would forgive and forget about what Samuel did. After all, neither he, nor Ace, nor any of his half siblings played a part in their father's misconduct," Cameron told Parke, as he grappled with his own personal relationship with the Lord.

"God does require us to forgive others as He forgives us. Only He, according to Micah 7:19, can throw our sins in the sea of forgetfulness. In other words, He doesn't remember them anymore. Although He gives us the power to forgive, sometimes we hold on to things that we need to let go of. The Lord removed the raw anger, but Kidd's wound is still tender concerning his dad's abandonment." Parke then advised, "It takes time. It was a battle getting him to the altar. Like so many, he struggled before surrendering to Jesus for complete salvation."

Parke always detoured to Jesus as if Cameron didn't know Scripture. But, at the moment, he wasn't up to a sermon. He had simply made a courtesy call to let Parke know that he was about to meet more kinfolks. Cameron redirected the conversation. "Ace doesn't have any issues meeting them. But, as long as Kidd is the holdout, Ace probably won't budge."

"Stubborn Jamiesons," Parke said snidely.

Chuckling, Cameron shook his head. "Yeah, I've heard that's the rumor. We come from the same tree." They talked for a few more minutes before disconnecting. Honestly, Cameron couldn't relate to his cousin's pain. Oh, he understood about family drama, but Kidd had supposedly embraced God's complete plan of salvation, yet he was still battling issues. So how was Kidd's salvation walk any different from his?

Before he jumped into the shower, Cameron packed his laptop. It contained every file, photo, and miscellaneous document he had researched over the years.

While showering, Cameron reflected on the status of his family. His father, Parke V, and Charlotte Jamieson had been happily married for almost forty years. There were no other Parke Jamieson V rugrats running around to be discovered.

When he moved to Boston to attend MIT, he tracked Kidd and Ace down. At first, Kidd didn't trust his motives, nor did he want anything to do with Cameron. With his free spirit, Ace was the opposite. The two cousins connected instantly and were almost inseparable on the weekends until Cameron introduced Ace to Talise.

From a distance, he had watched the couple's relationship blossom then disintegrate over a misunderstanding. Basically, the breakup was Ace's doing when he couldn't come to terms with Talise's pregnancy. First Kidd, and then Ace, moved to St. Louis. When their mother, Sandra, packed up and followed them to be closer to her granddaughters, Cameron decided it was time to go back home too.

Little did he know that, once he made the decision, he would meet a woman who had the potential of wrapping him around her finger. Was it fate? And now, was it destiny that the same woman would be relocating to St. Louis? There were too many coincidences to ignore.

Gabrielle was waiting for God to send her a godly man. Cameron snickered as he splashed aftershave on his face and neck. Because of fate, God set him right in front of her.

Mentally, Cameron took inventory of his qualifications. He had read enough of his Bible to quote a good amount of Scripture. Next, he attended Sunday services whenever the mood hit him. He was just in church a few weeks ago for Ace's renewal ceremony, so there. He had justified himself. "What else do you want, baby?" he asked his reflection.

By the time he finished dressing, his mood had become somber. One week to the date, he'd load all his belongings into a U-Haul, severing ties with Beantown and all the things he enjoyed there. Parke and Malcolm would fly up the night before. Bright and early next Saturday morning, the brothers would begin the long drive to the Gateway City and away from Gabrielle Dupree.

"Make the best of your time left with her, Jamieson," he ordered himself, as he snatched up his keys and an envelope, then headed for the front door.

It was ten o'clock on a lovely Saturday morning. The springtime weather beckoned to shoppers, who were sprinkled everywhere along Cambridge Square. Using his hands-free phone, Cameron eagerly called Gabrielle.

"Good morning, lady. Have you had your cup of java? Do you want me to stop and grab anything for the ride?"

"That's sweet of you," she said, as he imagined her smile. "I prepared a snack for us. How close are you?"

"About twenty minutes away. Thanks for letting me tag along. I really am looking forward to meeting another side of the family."

"Thanks for driving. I'm a fly girl."

"That you are, Miss Dupree. You are fly at that. See you soon."

Twenty-five minutes later, he arrived at her Mission Hill apartment building. The Boston cabbies commandeering the road were to blame for his slight delay.

Gabrielle sat outside on the steps, watching for him. Her hair was tied back into a ponytail, but a breeze loosened a few strands. If he had been a professional photographer, he would have snapped away at her beauty.

Casually dressed, she was nothing less than gorgeous. As he got out and walked to her, the only thing on his mind was a good morning kiss—then he remembered her Mace. Plus, he wanted them to get through the day without causing her to pull away from him. Still, the closer he got, he couldn't resist. "You are beautiful," he said in awe. "I have a request, a kiss or a hug, which would you grant me?"

Tilting her head to look in his eyes, she said softly, "A kiss."

"Ah, yeah." Cameron puckered up and closed his eyes. The next thing he felt against his lips was Gabrielle's hands.

He obliged and she giggled. "I'll get you for that one," Cameron warned and laughed. "Ready?"

Nodding, she slipped on her sunglasses and handed him a large tote. It was stuffed with bottled waters, apples, and other wrapped items.

Cameron also eyed some books. "You aren't planning on reading while I'm driving, are you? As the copilot, you're supposed to make sure I'm alert and don't doze off."

"It's mid-morning. I doubt if you'll catnap," she said over her shoulder. He opened her door and waited for her to get settled.

"No way, with an attractive woman in my company." He winked and walked around to the driver's side.

Once Cameron was behind the wheel and had clicked his seat belt, he checked his rearview mirror and pulled away from the curb. Glancing over at Gabrielle, he saw that her eyes were closed and her head bowed.

He didn't interrupt her as he exited on I-90 westbound. When she mumbled an Amen, she opened her eyes and looked out the window.

"Did you just pray?"

"Yep."

"Do you always pray when you get in a car? I don't recall seeing you do that when I took you out to dinner." The woman knew how to kill the mood, but he agreed to let her have church. If she wasn't verbally talking about Jesus, she was acknowledging Him in some other way.

"Whenever I take a trip, regardless if it's in a car, on a boat, or in the air, I've made it a habit. I take nothing for granted, whether it's waking up in the morning or returning home in the evening. My life is in God's hand."

Cameron nodded and then reached for a knob on his console, selecting a jazz station.

Angling her body, Gabrielle squinted at his GPS monitor. "Denise is ecstatic that you're coming. Are you excited?"

"About?"

"About meeting your relatives, silly."

"Hmm. If you weren't with me—yes. Right now, all I can think about is you."

Gabrielle blushed and lowered her lashes. She was trapped in the car with him for the next hundred miles. As far as he was concerned, this road trip was mostly about convincing Gabrielle to take whichever job offer that would bring her to St. Louis. His main desire was for her to give them a real chance.

"Gabrielle, distance won't keep me from you—" he began, keeping his eyes on the road. Just then, her cell phone chimed.

Pulling her phone out of her purse, she laughed at the caller's ID. Leaning over to read his GPS, Cameron breathed a whiff of her perfume. *Sweet*, he thought.

"We're about to get on I-84." She paused. "We're less than an hour away. Yes, your cousin is driving." She faced Cameron and mouthed, *Denise*. He winked.

She ended the call and reached in the backseat for the tote bag. When poised to twist the cap off a bottle of water, her phone chimed again.

"You think Denise is excited?" he joked, as Gabrielle answered.

Turning toward her window, she mumbled into the phone.

"I'm not by myself . . ." He strained to eavesdrop.

Rage was building within him. So another man was vying for her attention. Cameron gripped the wheel. If he wasn't trying to pass a semi, he would swipe the phone from her ear and talk to his competition himself.

"Yes, I know you don't like Cameron . . . We're driving to see Denise . . ."

When the man roared back over the phone, Cameron identified the caller. He smirked as Gabrielle continued to cajole her brother and persuade him that her riding companion was harmless.

"I will, as soon as I get back. I'll tell him." She eyed him. "Love you too. Bye." Gabrielle ended the call with a deep sigh.

"Are you going to tell me what Drexel said?"

"Maybe, one day."

Forty-five minutes later, the GPS guided Cameron to Bloomfield, Connecticut, on the outskirts of Hartford. Cameron whistled as he made a right on Jerome Street. "It appears my family is doing quite well," he said proudly, nodding his head. He couldn't help but boast, considering not only that they were Black, they were members of his family.

Earlier in the week, he and Gabrielle had a short conversation— her choice of topic. And, of course, it became a battle of wills when he pointed out that having possessions proved that God had blessed a person.

The comment put Gabrielle on a Bible bandwagon. "Material things alone don't define a man's true worth. Think of it this way. It's fine for health professionals to promote a balanced diet with plenty of exercise. But that's not enough. God tells us through 3 John 1:2 to have a balanced diet of physical and spiritual prosperity.

"Yes, you give God thanks for the things He's allowed you to accumulate, but what about totally submitting to God's will? I can't separate the two. The man I commit my heart to has to be spiritually grounded. I won't compromise." She had scolded him before giving him an excuse to get off the phone.

Her resolve left Cameron considering his own successful means. When it comes to prosperity, Gabrielle preferred spirituality overall. Not only did she want him to thank God for the tangible things he possessed, she expected him to show God his appreciation by devoting his precious time. Well, he had that covered too. He put time into his foundation work, which contributed to several charities.

Besides, didn't Scripture say God causes His sun to rise on the evil and the good? And that He sends rain on the righteous and the unrighteous? Well, as far as he was concerned, an impressive two-story home with a two-car garage proved God could bless whomever He wants.

As soon as he parked behind the line of cars in the driveway, Denise opened the front door and raced out.

Denise took them by surprise when she passed Gabrielle and ran straight into Cameron's arms. He matched her enthusiasm and returned her hug, while Gabrielle pouted and stomped her heel on the ground.

"So it's going to be like that, huh?" Gabrielle positioned her fists on her hips.

"He's my cousin. You're just an old friend," Denise taunted, then released Cameron and gave her friend a tight hug. Looking toward the front door, he eyed a group of men, who reminded him of linebackers. He grunted. Jamieson men were built steady like a Ram truck.

The two friends linked arms and strolled up the pathway. Reaching into the backseat, Cameron retrieved his laptop. With long strides, he easily caught up with them and heard Gabrielle comment, "I see my boyfriend is here."

"Yes, he is. I drove, remember?" Cameron said. Strolling alongside them, they were both startled. "Sorry, there's an 'only one Jamieson per woman' rule. And I've got you, babe," he whispered.

She exchanged a glance with Denise. Almost in unison, they whispered, "Wow, wow moment."

Chapter Seventeen

Gabrielle tried to ignore Cameron, but she shivered anyway. Only when coming face-to-face with Denise's brothers did she recover. Denise had been right. The resemblance to Talise's husband was striking. They were definitely handsome—tall and buff, with rich, dark skin.

Denise scooted everybody into her house and made the introductions. She regretfully added that one brother couldn't rearrange his work schedule but looked forward to meeting them at another time.

Almost immediately, Cameron commanded an audience, receiving accolades for his research on the family tree. In spite of all the attention, his manner remained low-key.

Gabrielle didn't even try to keep the names and faces straight. She noted the twins had graying at their temples. Neither was married. Gabrielle guessed they had to be close to forty. As a matter of fact, out of seven siblings, Denise was the only one who was currently married.

"Hey, stranger." Denise's husband, Jacob, welcomed Gabrielle and they exchanged a hug and kiss.

"Lacey? You're here?" Gabrielle turned to Denise's older sister, smiling; she embraced her. Gabrielle got to know Lacey when she visited Denise a few times at Howard. Lacey had dated her childhood sweetheart, married, and then divorced him. Gabrielle never asked Denise for the details.

Denise instructed everyone to make themselves comfortable. While the family got acquainted with Cameron, Gabrielle strolled around the living room admiring her friend's latest decorating flair. She recalled the home was almost perfect when Denise purchased it three years earlier. Only the upstairs bathrooms needed an immediate makeover.

"So what do you do, Cameron?" asked Denise's youngest brother, Zaki, who seemed indifferent from the moment the door closed.

"Until this week, I was a consultant for two engineering firms and an instructor at MIT. At the end of the week, I'm heading back home to St. Louis. I'll be the first African-American chairperson at Washington University."

He glanced at Gabrielle. "I'm humbled by being the first and readily accept the huge responsibility placed on me."

His subdued admission earned a soft spot in her heart. Perhaps, one day his tenderness would blot out his irksomeness that had also settled there.

"I'm so glad Gabrielle invited me to come along so I could get a chance to meet more family members."

"How are we related again?" one of Denise's twin brothers inquired.

"We're all cousins by being descendants of brothers' children." Gabrielle heard Cameron say before she wandered into the kitchen where Denise was unwrapping trays of food.

"This is just like being at Talise's wedding. I'm surrounded by Jamiesons, *ggrhh*," Gabrielle joked and lifted the foil covering a platter of veggies and hot chicken wings. *Mmm. Junk food.* She shook her head, intending to indulge without a conscience before she and Cameron left later that evening.

"You could be a Jamieson," Denise suggested off-handedly.

"No kidding. I'm surrounded by enough of them."

"But only one of them has a jump start." Cameron's booming response surprised her, as he swaggered up next to her. As though he hadn't uttered a word, he spoke to Denise. "Cuz, your brother says you've already set up Skype time with your sister in Oklahoma City."

"Yeah, give me a sec. Queen wished she could be here too. Since her only sister passed away, she's eager to become part of a bigger family. She's already called twice."

Quickly changing subjects, Denise dried her hands on a cloth towel. "Everything's ready. I thought you might be hungry," she said with a warm smile.

"I'm always hungry." Cameron patted his six pack.

"Let's eat first. Then we can get started." Denise walked out of the kitchen with a tray containing a crystal pitcher filled with punch and some glasses.

Turning around, Gabrielle stared into Cameron's face. "You're like a panther, sneaking up on me like that. You were just talking seconds ago in there."

With no response from him but a shrug, she lowered her voice. "Everyone seems to be accepting of you. Is it always this way when you meet distant relatives?"

"It's a mixed bag. Some relatives want to be found. Others barely want to give a handshake." He nodded, matching her low tone. "I can tell the youngest brother is a bit reserved. I would hate to put him and Kidd in a room together. I thought Kidd was the poster child for the angry Black man, but I think that brother is a close second. If they got into it, I don't think Jesus could break them up."

"He holds the power of the world in His hand. He can break up two knuckleheads by simply breathing on them."

"It was a joke, Gabrielle. Relax." Reaching for her hands, he squeezed them. "I don't want to fight you word for word."

"That's just it. If I don't fight back, I'll succumb, and I don't expect to fall."

He must have recognized the frightened look in her eyes. "I assure you that I wouldn't do anything to hurt you—ever. I don't expect either one of us to fall. But as God is my witness, Gabrielle, you will not be a fallen angel—because I'll be there to catch you."

—— ∞ ——

The Connecticut Jamiesons had done well for themselves career-wise. One twin was an early morning sports analyst at ESPN, a station Gabrielle never watched. The other twin was a manager at United Healthcare, and the others were gainfully employed by United Technologies, a top-ranked regional employer.

As an alumnus from her and Gabrielle's alma mater, Howard University, Denise held her master's degree in social work. She had been employed at the state's department of veteran affairs for years. Her husband recently joined AT&T in a top management position a year before they purchased the house in an outlying neighborhood of Hartford.

After the refreshments were devoured, Denise's dining room was transformed into a war room of computers and old documents. Watching the Jamiesons get situated around the table, Gabrielle remained nearby in a recliner.

"Oh no, you're part of this, babe." Cameron added the endearment in front of the others and Gabrielle's heart fluttered.

God, I wish I didn't have to fight him so much and just let things happen. She sighed, as he physically pulled her from the chair and ushered her to one next to him at the table.

Gabrielle was about to scold him when the activity of everyone gathering around Denise's computer monitor interrupted her. They all watched as a young woman—Gabrielle guessed to be in her early twenties—appeared with a beaming smile.

After greeting the group, the first thing out of her mouth was, "Is my cousin there yet, sis?"

Denise grinned. "Yes, Queen. Cameron's here, along with my friend Gabrielle."

Others moved aside and Cameron positioned himself so he could be in front of the monitor. The young woman greeted him enthusiastically.

"You're as beautiful as your name," he said to Queen.

"Stop flirting. She's your cousin." Gabrielle nudged Cameron and everyone snickered.

"Don't be jealous just because you're not a Jamieson." He inhaled and slowly released his breath, adding, "Let me know if you ever change your mind about exploring that option."

Leaving Gabrielle mesmerized, he turned back to Queen.

Explore that? If they were on the same page in the same book, then there would be no hesitation about indulging in a relationship with Cameron. *Take baby steps*, her heart coaxed her. She smiled to herself.

"Depending on how far back your research took you, the information you uncovered may have revealed that we're descendants of royalty, King Seif and Princess Adaeze."

"Wow, I didn't know . . ." she replied in awe. "I've always said if I ever get married and have a daughter, I'd name her Princess."

"You'll be taking advantage of the royalty instilled in you." Cameron paused, as if he was flipping through a mental Rolodex. "Your eleventh great-grandfather, Orma, and his wife, Sashe, had two sons, Kingdom and Harrison. Then Candy and Paradise came along.

"Kingdom named his firstborn King. The next sixty years, or four generations, firstborn sons were named King II, III, and IV. I found King II on the Freedom Bureau marriage registry online."

One of the twins cut in, "I found some of that information too, but by the time I got to the third King, I said forget it. My head was spinning. Couldn't he find a more common name?"

As others around the table murmured their agreement, Cameron rested his arm on the back of Gabrielle's chair and toyed with her ponytail. In all her years of dating, she recalled one or two men who tried to play in her hair. She had objected then, but with Cameron, she didn't resist.

His gesture seemed natural and genuinely comforting, as the group looked for him to further explain the Jamieson lineage. "I agree it's frustrating, but it wasn't unusual for a name to be passed down from one generation to another. As researchers, sometimes that's our only clue. It gets crazy when you have brothers and sisters naming their children after their grandparents. That was common among Whites back then."

Gabrielle would never say this out loud, but Cameron's intellect really impressed her. Although she graduated summa cum laude, she didn't try to retain everything she learned in her studies or from her travels. Instead, she thrived on memorizing and studying Scriptures as a challenge to herself. Cameron's gift was definitely from God.

"Denise and I have tried to pick up where my deceased sister left off, but someone told us to follow the slaveholder," Queen explained.

Cameron nodded. "That's a good rule when you're tracking the enslaved woman because sometimes she's sold with her mother. But Paki and Elaine's children were born free. As far as I can see, only your eleventh great-grandfather gave up his freedom for Sashe. Mind you, for a free Black man to surrender his God-given rights at the mercy of a slaveholder, that was not a mindless decision. Can you imagine how much tongue biting he had to do so that he wouldn't be sold away?"

That's love. Gabrielle sighed. She couldn't imagine a greater love than for a man to give up his pride for the woman he loved.

"I so loved the world that I gave My one and only Son, that whoever believes in Him shall not perish but have eternal life," God reminded her of John 3:16, correcting her thinking.

Gabrielle swallowed and refocused. *Yes, Lord.* She closed her eyes. *Help me never to forget about Your ultimate sacrifice on the cross,* she silently prayed.

Opening her eyes, it was a shock to see Cameron staring at her. She frowned. "What?"

"Romantic?" Cameron asked, as the others watched.

"Ah, yeah," she stuttered with her mind still on the Lord's chastening of her thoughts.

"Well, our people must have had some crazy love to survive the death trap of slavery," Denise added. "We found a letter written by Robert Jamieson Jr., but we couldn't read it. My eyes and mind were strained from trying to decipher the alphabet."

Her brothers agreed.

"Do you have it now?" Cameron asked.

Nodding, Denise stood. "Let me get it."

While she was gone, one of the twins spoke up. "We tried our hand on this tree and found some Jamiesons we thought could have been related, but they were White."

"That doesn't mean they're not related to us. An enumerator would take the information, and it was up to what he or she saw that was recorded. If you were dark skinned, you were hands down deemed Black. If you were fair skinned, he marked Mulatto, to keep you in your place. However, if you were light enough and could pass as White, some did get by," Cameron explained.

"I, for one, am not mad at them." Lacey raised her hand in the air. "There wouldn't have been a need for affirmative action programs if hiring managers didn't self-appoint themselves 'enumerators' and noted one's skin color when making a determination about granting a position. Whenever coworkers inquire about my skin or hair, I shock them when I say I have ancestors who were White slaveholders or overseers."

Lacey smirked devilishly. "You should see their faces. But the kicker is when I inform them if I have White blood in me, they'd better check their tree because Black blood would surely pop up."

Denise returned with a copy of a handwritten letter and sat at the

130

table. Peering over her shoulder, Gabrielle squinted. "Goodness. You need a microscope."

"Got it," Cameron said and went to his computer bag. After a few minutes, he produced a magnifying glass.

"You come prepared," Queen said through Skype.

He grinned and scanned over the document. After a few minutes, Cameron slowly shook his head. "Unfortunately, I can't read this either. I'll have to send it to a friend of mine who studies paleography."

"May I see it?" Gabrielle slid the document closer to her.

Eying her suspiciously, Cameron handed the tool over to her. She accepted, ignoring his curious expression. It was obvious from the yellowing of the paper that the letter could be over a hundred years old.

Squinting, even with the magnifying glass, Gabrielle read the contents silently. She didn't realize others were waiting on her until Denise called her name.

"Huh? Oh, sorry. I can make this out." Gabrielle focused. "This is a letter from H.S. Jemison. It appears he's heading to an army camp in Florida and asking for one hundred and fifty dollars. He was in the army before and said it was rough without a boy or Negro," she said, giving an overall view before reading from the document: "'I need him and am not afraid of him running away from me. I know how to manage him. I can learn from the Negroes. Jarrett says he will never go back to the . . . anymore.'"

Gabrielle paused from reading and interjected. "I guess that's the name of the young boy." Then she went on, "'I'm afraid if he does, the Yanks will get him . . .'" She continued deciphering the rest of the letter.

Cameron was obviously impressed. "How can you read that?"

Denise answered for her. "I forgot my girl studied paleography at Howard. It was part of the linguistics program."

"What kind of graph?" one of the twins asked.

Meeting Cameron's stare was a mistake. Gabrielle tried to pull away. It took determination, but she broke his spell and faced everyone, who seemed amused at her and Cameron's interaction.

"It's called paleography," Cameron answered for her. "It's the study of ancient handwriting . . . and you never thought about researching your family tree? Amazing."

He didn't skip a beat, turning back to the monitor and Queen. "The letter is signed 1861. The location is Alabama and the spelling of the name is off, which isn't unusual."

Genealogy was a team effort, and Gabrielle didn't realize it until that moment. Although she deciphered the missive, Cameron gave his hypothesis.

Soon the discussion turned to other missing links in the family. Queen suggested a family reunion.

"Sounds like a plan," Cameron said absentmindedly. "They served as a gathering for ex-slaves throughout the South."

"We definitely need a Jamieson reunion. Everyone from our eleventh great- grandparents," Denise piped in.

"Paki and Elaine had five sons. Besides Parker, there were Aasim, Fabunni, Orma, and Sarda," Cameron advised. "Two lines are represented here, Parker and Orma."

"That means there are three missing links," a twin said.

"Actually, there are two," Queen said. "Fabunni's grandson 'passed' until his descendants assumed their race was White. We know where they are, but they're in politics and have gone to great lengths to separate themselves from their African heritage."

Cameron shrugged. "It happens all the time, but it doesn't change that drop of Black blood."

At that moment, Jesus dropped into Gabrielle's spirit the truth about His blood and how it will never lose its power or strength. Keeping that revelation to herself, she secretly thanked God for faithfully renewing her mind with His Word.

Chapter Eighteen

*C*ameron shook hands with the twins and their reserved younger brother, Zaki, who barely said two sentences to him during the entire visit. Denise and Lacey made up for his coolness with their warm hugs, as he and Gabrielle said their goodbyes.

"We all have to get together again soon," Cameron said sincerely.

"Count me out," Zaki said. "At least my father had remarried when my two other sisters were born. It's shameful that my father cheated on my mother with *their* mother." He refused to say Ace's and Kidd's names. "I want nothing to do with them. Good night." Getting in his car, he drove off.

One of the twins defended his brother's actions, "I was at the place mentally where Zaki is now, so I won't apologize for his attitude. It will take time."

Cameron was silent. He recalled that Parke had similar words about Kidd needing time. Then he thought about Kidd's mother. Did Sandra know about Samuel's marital status at the time of her affair? That was none of his business.

"I'll be praying for a change of heart," Gabrielle softly offered, coming to Cameron's aid. He didn't realize he had zoned out.

Once he and Gabrielle were in the car, she stretched. "I'm glad you came."

"Finally, I'm appreciated." He snorted. "On second thought, is it because I'm the designated driver?" he teased.

"Well, now that you've mentioned it." She gave him an enchanting smile before adding, "Actually, you're good company."

"You're the amazing one. So, on top of the rest of your impressive qualities, you can read ancient handwriting. Gabrielle Dupree, I have never met a woman like you." And he meant it. She was special, and for the first time in his life—Cameron Jamieson felt out of his league in a woman's presence.

"Thank you."

Pulling out of the parking space, Cameron turned up the music. In no time, Gabrielle drifted off to sleep. About thirty minutes into the drive, his phone played a tune, indicating it was Parke. He hurried to answer before Gabrielle woke up. He liked the feel of her trusting him with her life on the road. If only he could get her to trust him with her feelings. If she were to give up her deep reservations about him.

"Yeah," he answered lowly.

"How did it go?"

"Actually, it went well. Everyone was warm, except for the youngest brother who had resentment written all over his face. He followed that up with his verbal bitterness."

Parke didn't say anything right away. "Yeah, that's the risk we run in genealogy. Some don't want the family connection because of the past. I respect that. So where are you, and why can I barely hear you?"

Cameron stole a quick glance at Gabrielle, then back at the road. "It's an hour later on the East Coast, remember? Gabrielle dozed off and I don't want to wake her."

"Really?" Parke teased. "Does she live close to you?"

"Not far—in Mission Hill."

"Have you made up your mind about her?"

Cameron exhaled and lowered his voice even more. "She's the one, bro. She is definitely the one."

"A church girl, imagine that. You might as well give up like the rest of us. If you're falling in love with her, then you're going down, my man."

"Talk to you later." Cameron grinned and disconnected. He would put up with his two brothers soon enough when they arrived later in the week to help him drive back to St. Louis.

A church girl. How ironic that all his life he avoided mixing religion with other aspects of his life. Now, the woman who had stolen his heart wouldn't let him avoid the subject. If he wanted Gabrielle, then he would have to go toe-to-toe with her. He wasn't concerned about losing, which was very unlikely. No way would he accept that he could lose her over something so simple.

"Seek My kingdom first and My righteousness, and many things will be given to you as well," the Lord whispered *"Read My Word in Luke 12."*

Cameron wasn't a heathen, but he wouldn't consider himself a saint either. Still, he knew without a doubt that was the voice of God. Despite his own physical and mental strength, he shivered in God's presence.

Meditating on what God had said, he parked in front of Gabrielle's apartment. Before waking her, Cameron stole a few minutes to soak in her beauty inside and out. Only God knew what Gabrielle would decide about their relationship. Only God knew when Cameron would lay eyes on her again.

Releasing a frustrated grunt, he reluctantly nudged her awake. Gabrielle stirred and her thick lashes fluttered. She met his eyes with a dreamy smile. As a yawn escaped, she covered her mouth. "Sorry. I'm not good company."

"You don't have to say a word around me. Just knowing you're close satisfies me." Cameron got out and walked around to her side of the car. She stepped out in a drowsy state, like a defiant child wanting more sleep. He steadied her, while gathering her purse and tote bag.

With his arm wrapped around her, she slumped against him. He escorted her to the front door. "Okay, sleepyhead."

She blinked and he waited until he thought she was coherent.

"Gabrielle, I really want us to try. I'm game. You don't have to fly to St. Louis. I'll come to you."

Her dreamy eyes focused on him. "I'll pray on it, Cameron." Standing on tiptoes, she brushed a kiss on his lips and grabbed her stuff.

"What was that?" he asked, panting for more.

"A kiss, silly," she declared with a giggle. Then she turned to insert her key into the entrance door of her building.

Cameron steadied her hand. "Here's mine." Without any resistance, he cuddled her in his arms and kissed her until she pulled back.

"That's how I want you to remember our first kiss. Good night."

Inside her apartment, Gabrielle locked the door in a daze. She hadn't planned on kissing Cameron. The shock on his face was priceless. When he reciprocated, the passion he showered on her was fierce.

The moment had seemed right, not for sexual intimacy like some commercials promised for older couples, but for a sweet, brief brush across his lips. That had been a miscalculated move on her part because his response was totally possessive of her emotions. Cameron had said he would catch her if she fell. Those words were comforting, but she needed God to keep her from teetering on the line of temptation.

Walk upright before Me, God spoke powerfully.

"Yes, Lord, I hear You," Gabrielle responded out loud.

A big concern was in Cameron moving away. She knew he wouldn't lack female attention, especially once he recited his *résumé*, something that he loved to boast. It didn't matter. Long-distance relationships didn't work. It wouldn't matter even if she could fly free.

Dragging her body into the bathroom, she went through the

motions of preparing for bed. Donning a nightgown, she scrubbed her face free of makeup and applied moisturizer. It was a regimen that Talise, an accomplished hair stylist and beauty consultant, had drilled into her head. Finally, after she wrapped her hair and brushed her teeth, she was ready for a good night's sleep.

Gabrielle glanced at the clock before she slid to her knees to pray. Years ago, her brother Philip had challenged her to give Jesus a minimum of three minutes in prayer time. Now years later, she hadn't broken the habit.

Almost five minutes later, she ended and climbed into bed, snuggling beneath the covers. Gabrielle was asleep in minutes.

On Sunday morning, the phone jostled her awake before her alarm clock sounded. Leaping from under the covers, she reached for it to silence the nuisance.

"Hello."

"I wanted to make sure that the bad news guy brought you home safely," Drexel's commanding voice greeted her. "I advise my baby sister to stay away from trouble and what does she do? Rides shotgun with him out of town."

An hour-and-a-half drive was not what she considered going out of town. His over-the-top needless scowling just cost her forty-five more minutes of sleep.

"Good morning, big brother," she said sweetly to shame him.

He sighed. "Sorry. Good morning to you too. I just get bad vibes about him."

Frowning, she sat up in bed. Gabrielle respected her brothers' opinions and considered carefully their advice. In the end, it was God's counsel that she would heed. It just so happened that currently, she was struggling with that. "What kind of vibes?"

"Although I trust you, I sense he's a man on the prowl."

"Aren't all men? Anyway, you can regulate your heart rate. He's moving back to St. Louis before the week is over. End of story." Gabrielle advised, as she stepped out of bed and headed for the bathroom.

"Not until you decide which company's offer you'll accept."

"I'm close."

"As much as I love you and would enjoy us spending time together on some weekends, I suggest you take the position in San Diego."

"San Diego. Why? Aren't you the one who was selling me on St. Louis?"

"I can't help but feel that Cameron has been giving you a sales pitch too. You could get hurt with him living nearby. That guy has 'love them and leave them' written all over him. I've only jumped one boy over you and that was in high school. Those days are over."

"You do realize that Cameron and I have lived in the same city for two months without a brotherly chaperone? God has been my constant escort." Gabrielle paused, thinking about the passionate smooch she shared with Cameron just the evening before, a kiss that she initiated.

She felt God was keeping a close eye on her, trusting that she would not shame Him. That kiss could never happen again. Squinting at her morning reflection in the mirror, Gabrielle had to deliver the news she knew Drexel didn't want to hear.

"Thanks for being my alarm clock for church this morning. However, Cameron is committed to making this work between us, even long distance. He knows that to be with me, he has to step up his prayer life. So we'll see."

"Sis, you can't change a man who doesn't want to be changed," Drexel counseled, followed by a heavy sigh.

"I know you're the judge in the courtroom, but I have to trust God to judge Cameron's heart."

"Okay, you know I don't care for people who say, 'I told you so'. I hope I don't ever have to say that to my baby sister."

"Me too."

Chapter Nineteen

The Jamieson brothers arrived in Boston late Friday evening. Parke and Malcolm would help Cameron drive the twenty-plus hours back to St. Louis.

In the eleven years Cameron had lived in Beantown, he hadn't realized how much he missed home until Ace joined his brother, Kidd, and moved to St. Louis. When their mother, Sandra, who treated him like a son, packed up a few months ago, the void was even more tangible.

In a matter of months, Gabrielle had filled the emptiness. Now he was walking away from her and possibly his future. Not professionally, but emotionally. Cameron had to convince her to take the job in St. Louis. Every day and moment he had spent with Gabrielle, he had learned something new about her and himself.

"What's got you so quiet?" Parke asked from the front passenger seat while Malcolm sat in the back, texting his wife.

"I've just got a lot on my mind." Without offering any further comment, he detoured to go by Gabrielle's place for memory's sake.

Having memorized her phone number, he called Gabrielle every evening this week. Last night, she had informed him about her upcoming maddening day. His heart went out to her as she shared her concern about an extra long shift.

After they said their goodbyes, Gabrielle offered to pray for his trip. Avoiding a spiritual tug-of-war moment, he consented and silently prayed along until she became longwinded. That's when she lost him, and Cameron impatiently waited for an Amen.

"You know you just made the wrong turn to get on I-90 West," Parke advised.

"Did I?" Cameron's answered, annoyed at the intrusion of his thoughts.

"As a matter of fact, you did," Malcolm chimed in. "If you slow down long enough, you just might see her."

Peeking in the rearview mirror, Cameron waited for Malcolm to make eye contact. He didn't, so he concentrated on creeping past Gabrielle's building. She had texted him that morning: **Still thinking and praying for your traveling mercies. G.** Cameron had texted her back, but he hadn't heard from her. After weaving between cabbies, he pointed his Audi toward the interstate.

"Nothing to say?" Parke taunted him.

"I'm concentrating, if you don't mind."

"On driving or on Gabrielle?" Parke asked. "I just saw the sign that we were in Mission Hill. You know, your heart's not in this move. It's hard to walk or drive away from her, isn't it?"

"Man, as much as we love you," Malcolm chimed in, "it seems like you need to stay behind and work . . ."

Older brothers. He tuned them both out as they offered unsolicited advice on how to go about winning Gabrielle over. Of course, for them, that conquest would include a greater walk with God. When Cameron didn't engage them, they moved on to their favorite topic. Chatting about their children and what their wives were doing was priority number one.

All these years, Cameron had told himself that he was a good catch:

extremely handsome, with worldly possessions over which some men would salivate. Not to mention, the practically free higher education he derived from the numerous academic scholarships bestowed on him.

He had it going on, or so he thought, before Gabrielle Dupree breezed into his life. Cameron wanted the kind of permanent companionship that his brothers had too. But he refused to let a woman put spiritual demands on him to obtain that.

After a while, neither Parke nor Malcolm mentioned Gabrielle's name. But his mind hadn't set aside its memory of everything about her for one minute. That's when he had his own quiet talk with God.

Jesus, I got this. Amen.

———✺———

Holed up in her office, Gabrielle was ready to place her final call for the morning. Although she was still waiting on a word from the Lord concerning Cameron, Sunday's sermon had helped her reach a decision about her career. She hadn't shared her answer with anyone yet: family, friends, or Cameron.

"Why do we ask for God's direction and then ignore His instructions? Jesus will not steer you the wrong way," her pastor, Bishop Wilfred Ransom, had preached. "What are you afraid of? Did He not send a pillar of fire by night and a cloud by day to guide the Israelites in the wilderness? These are questions to which you already know the answer."

Gabrielle's attention immediately perked up when the pastor said, "And, just in case you're having some confusion about what God is telling you, Jesus will send a confirmation letter . . . be honest with yourself today. You can no longer hold back. Make your decision to say yes, Jesus, I'll take Your blessing . . ."

Pastor Ransom hit home repeatedly until he concluded with, "Stop listening to family and friends, if it doesn't line up with what God is telling you."

As others around her stood and praised God, Gabrielle remained seated and asked God for her confirmation letter about where should she go.

The Lord's answer was soft and swift, *For your happiness, go near home.*

That message pointed her in the direction of St. Louis and Nestle-Purina, which not only was a global company, but within close proximity to Chicago and her family. Her heart fluttered when she thought about Cameron. At this early stage, she couldn't allow him to factor into her future plans. Things might not work out between them because she was not budging on her spiritual demand that he walk closer with the Lord.

Now Gabrielle toyed with a pen as she waited for her regional manager to come on the line. A few hours earlier, she called the companies in San Diego and Tucson, thanking them for the job offers, but declining.

"Chandler Dawson," he greeted over the phone, interrupting any further musings.

She cleared her throat. "Hello, Mr. Dawson, I wanted to verbally give you a two-week resignation before I emailed you my formal letter."

"Oh, Ms. Dupree, I'm sorry to hear you want to leave our company, especially after the promotion we promised you," he said, making her feel a bit guilty. Although he had to accept blame that the promise had yet to materialize over the past year.

"I know, and I'm appreciative of the opportunities and the perks that came along with my position. But, I miss my family, and it's time for me to move closer to home," she explained.

"Well, that's understandable. Know, Ms. Dupree, that your dedication will be missed. The door will remain open if you feel you want to return within the next few years."

"Well, thank you, sir."

Once they disconnected, Gabrielle exhaled. She was fully aware that Chandler Dawson didn't give second chances and seldom granted management rehires. Lifting up her hands, she praised Jesus for the words to say and for His favor. Now, the only thing she needed was the strength to withstand Cameron's masculinity.

That evening, she called her parents and brothers. Everyone was elated, except Drexel. He called her stubborn. She left a voice message with Philip who was in Canada conducting a revival.

Looking around her apartment, Gabrielle couldn't believe she had accumulated so much stuff. One thing she didn't believe in was moving junk from one place to another. That determination motivated her to start compiling a to-do list. She would give away clothes that were too tight, her collection of Christian romance books, and various other nonessential items.

The next day, Philip called. "Evangelist! How is my dear brother?" Gabrielle was giddy with excitement over speaking with her favorite brother.

"Greetings to you, in the precious Name of Jesus, Sis. I received your message. It's good you're moving closer to everyone. I'm excited for you, but what's this mention about this man Cameron? Should I be concerned?"

"You should be praying," she replied seriously. "I'm scared of my emotions around him."

"Hmm. I know what type of man attracts you, so what is it about him that distracts you?"

"He recites Scriptures, but my spirit just doesn't connect with Cameron about his commitment. He admits to not going to church regularly—"

"Stop right there. You have a right to be concerned. You've turned away men in the past, so why is he so hard for you to handle?"

She was ashamed to admit to her brother—a man of God, at that—but she had fallen prey to the package instead of the contents. "The attraction is there and I can't turn it off."

Philip gave his manly take and then his spiritual advice. "You can't turn off your attraction and as long as he respects you, I would say it's safe to go out with him."

With a brief pause, he added, "Don't lose sight of who you are in Jesus. Remember the Bible asks the question, 'Do two walk together unless they have agreed on things?' Everyone isn't going to be on one accord with everything, but it's a must when it comes to salvation in Jesus."

She knew Amos 3:3 well. That Scripture has always been her golden text when it came to dating. Consequently, her interest in Cameron caused her some confusion. They didn't agree on their commitment to the Lord.

Her brother's sternness recaptured her attention. "Remember to set the Christian example. Always be prepared in season and out of season . . ."

Gabrielle smirked. Philip knew 2 Timothy 4:2 applied to preachers, but he was ever ready to impose the edict on all practicing believers as well.

"Okay, Sis, I need to go, but let me pray for you first."

Bowing her heading and closing her eyes, Gabrielle submitted to her brother's prayer.

"Dear Jesus, we come boldly to Your throne of grace where we may obtain mercy. My sister is falling in love . . ."

Gabrielle gasped and silently denied such a thing, but she dared not interrupt him in the presence of the Lord.

"She needs Your guidance to make it through this situation. Jesus, You are the God of revelation. Be with her in thought and conversation. We know You are able to keep her from stumbling, tripping, and falling, according to Jude 1:24. Lord, strengthen her heart to be a witness for You because her desire is to not fall . . ."

By the time Philip finished, Gabrielle sniffed as tears streamed down her face. Her brother's earnest prayers always seemed to wrap her in a warm cocoon where she felt safe and protected. If Philip wasn't her brother, she would marry him. In lieu of that option, she wanted a godly man like her brother. So far, from all appearances, Cameron wasn't the one.

"In Jesus' Name, Amen, Amen, and Amen," they said together.

"Thank you and I love you," she said.

"So when is the big move?"

"This is Boston, I'm sure I'll find someone to sublease my apartment within a few weeks. Meanwhile, I have to pack my stuff, blah, blah, blah . . ." she went on. Feeling somewhat giddy over the reality of it all, she was unable to hold back a chuckle.

"Then you should be in St. Louis in a month."

"About a week before that is when I have to check in as CEO over my division." Smiling at the thought of breaking the news to her friend, she added, "Talise will be ecstatic when I tell her."

"Excellent. Like the title song of an old movie, *Meet Me in St. Louis.* In a month, I'm doing a three-day tent revival there. Once you get there, I'll give you the details."

Gabrielle screamed her delight. If Philip would be that close to home, no doubt her parents and brothers would come to town. She'd try to get a place fast so they could all stay together. If not, it would be a hotel stay for the whole family. She was finally seeing how God's hand was tying the strings of her life together.

"And if Cameron does have serious intentions about you, bring him along," Philip concluded the conversation. "I'll meet him at the altar."

Chapter Twenty

Like the movie, Meet me in St. Louis, meet me. I took the job! G

Sitting up straight, Cameron grinned and his heart pounded wildly when he read Gabrielle's text. Right away, he attempted to call her but got her voice mail. Cameron replied with a text: Yes! Tell me what you need and when you need it and I'll make it happen. I can't wait to see your beautiful smile.

Cameron and his brothers were in the middle of the second day of their journey home. Parke was behind the wheel after their last stop to gas up.

"Boy, something has transformed your scowl to a smile," Parke commented, snooping for information.

"Umm-hmm. Gabrielle is moving to St. Louis."

Parke's eyes bucked. "You're kidding. She doesn't seem like the type of woman to run after a man, especially one as stubborn as you."

"Humph. She's not. Evidently, she accepted the job at Nestle. But I do plan to make the best of her relocation so that it's permanent."

"Now you're talking like a Jamieson," Parke said.

"I need to get home. Can you pick up your speed or let me get behind the wheel? I have things to do before she gets there."

"Is she boarding a plane right now?" Parke asked.

"I doubt it."

"Then there's no rush. There's a reason for a speed limit that you seem to ignore. How can you obey God's law when you ignore man's laws?"

Cameron grunted. "Give me a break, Parke. Some rules are meant to be broken."

"God's aren't, and He strictly enforces them at all times. If you're really serious about Gabrielle, you'd better get with the program. Quick," Parke advised him with finality and punched in the gospel station on Cameron's satellite radio.

It wasn't the first time during the trip that Cameron had tuned out his brothers. But, he did feel like God was giving him a second chance with Gabrielle. Closing his eyes, Cameron began to brainstorm how he was going to take advantage of the opportunity and win Gabrielle over—once and for all.

Crossing over the Mississippi River into Missouri, Cameron began his countdown for Gabrielle's arrival as soon as he saw the Gateway Arch. Although it was a popular St. Louis tourist attraction, it also served as a beacon to natives that they had made it home.

Without a second thought, he texted her and offered to fly back to Boston and help Gabrielle pack and drive. She thanked him but declined because Drexel had already committed.

Cameron cursed under his breath. He wondered how much trouble he was going to have with the judge. The next time he saw Gabrielle's brother, he planned to nip any misunderstandings in the bud.

Days later, the first week on campus, it seemed as if Cameron had endless meetings with the dean and provost. Next, he took a careful walk through the twenty-eight-hundred square foot house he practically hand-picked online from Boston. When he inquired about the age, he was impressed to learn it was built during World War II.

After his St. Louis family checked it out and thought it was a smart investment, Cameron made an offer that was ten-thousand dollars less than the four-hundred-thousand-dollar asking price. The seller accepted and now he was officially signing the contract, so he could move in immediately.

Although most of the family lived in historic neighborhoods in North County and St. Charles, he opted for city living. As a teenager growing up, Cameron was always amazed at the architecture of the enormous houses in the Central West End.

Plus, his commute to the campus by car was only minutes. Outdoor cafes littered street corners, reminding him of the East Coast. And he could appreciate Forest Park's scenery while jogging along one of its trails.

In Boston, he limited himself to the confines of a condo. But now, as the department chair of the school of engineering, Cameron planned to spare no expense. He wanted to look the part, knowing that he could surely deliver.

Although it was mid-June and he had the entire summer to review the curriculum, procedures, and accreditations for the upcoming semester, he didn't waste any time getting up to speed on his responsibilities. Refusing to be bogged down when Gabrielle came was of upmost importance.

The weeks dwindled down to days, and now Gabrielle was hours away. On Friday evening, Cameron was relaxing in Ace's lower level family room, watching a baseball game. Lauren was sitting contently in her father's lap.

Staring at the screen, he couldn't concentrate. All he saw was Gabrielle's shapely face and the lips that teased him the night he took her home.

"Tomorrow's the day, huh?" Ace asked.

"Yes, eighteen long hours away. Sixteen, if I was driving," Cameron answered, annoyed by his cousin's interruption.

"I know you avoid talking about Jesus. But, cuz, take it from me. You can't say you love the Lord and your actions are contrary. If you want her, you've got to make some changes."

"I believe like Gabrielle and you all believe. None of us are perfect. I repent, I'm forgiven, and I move on."

"Parke taught me that striving for perfection begins in the heart and that dictates our actions."

Cameron cringed. *Parke again.* He was sure his brother was trying to make him look bad because he wasn't a regular churchgoer.

"Ace, I know the Scriptures better than you. At the moment, church is closed, so please stop with the sermon." Cameron didn't feel like constantly rehashing this same conversation with his family. Not even for Gabrielle did he plan to go to a prayer altar and relinquish more of his free will.

"Suit yourself. You can run, but no man can hide from God. Believe me, I know." Ace then turned his attention toward his beautiful little daughter. She had a ready smile for anybody willing to play with her. When Talise came down the stairs, Ace immediately ogled his wife. Lauren reached for her mother.

"Gabrielle will be here tomorrow," Talise gushed, as she took the baby from her husband.

Cameron nodded. "And I plan to win her over by any means necessary."

"Uh-oh." Talise moaned. "My girl better look out because you Jamiesons are unstoppable when your minds are locked on a target."

"Yep," Ace agreed. "There was no way I was willing to let you get away, and I needed God's help on it."

Except for the religious reference, Cameron confirmed her words with a wide grin. Moments later, the couple went upstairs and walked their guest to the front door.

Before saying goodbye, he made one last declaration. "Make no doubt about it, Gabrielle is a marked woman."

Chapter Twenty-One

*D*rexel was about to beat a dead horse until it came alive again, as far as Gabrielle was concerned. Cameron's name had come up countless times during the one-thousand-mile trip to St. Louis. Every time she received a text from Cameron, Drexel would pick up where he left off after the last text. It was an endless cycle.

"At first, I was all for your relocation, but since Cameron has manipulated his presence into your life, I have mixed feelings about this move. Yes, I want you close to me, but as far away from that Jamieson guy as possible."

Gabrielle listened quietly.

"Why are you subjecting yourself to a man who, obviously to the naked eye, has carnal intentions toward you?" Drexel asked from behind the wheel of the U-Haul with her Chevy Malibu hitched to it.

This was day two on the road. Cameron had offered to return to Boston and help her drive back. Two things for sure, the conversation would be better and Drexel would be livid. Good thing they were only four hours away from the city she would now call home for as long as she decided to stay. Or, perhaps, until Drexel forced her to consider moving again.

In the end, it would be God's will. Any other woman would have told her sibling to back off and mind his own business. Gabrielle glanced out the window as she gathered her thoughts. She couldn't dismiss Drexel's concern. He would always be her voice of reason until she heard God's voice.

Common sense told her to cease all communication with Cameron, but Jesus' presence reminded her that He wouldn't let her fall. Honestly, she liked having someone to talk to throughout the day or sometimes at night. When Cameron called constantly, it let her know how often he thought about her. And she liked that.

"I somehow feel that I've met my match with him, Drex. He's never tried to seduce me, and that has definitely garnered my respect." *Forget about the kiss. Don't think about the kiss,* she kept telling herself.

"He could be biding his time. That's what charmers do, Sis."

"Have you forgotten that I've been approached by men of different ages, nationalities, and religions? Regardless of their status, I've handled myself accordingly. I think you and God would be pleased." She paused and crossed her arms, after turning the tables on him. "Besides, it's not like any of those female attorneys, court clerks, or other judges haven't tried to seduce you. How many times have you been forced not to undress them with your eyes and mind?"

Drexel bobbed his head. "That happens all the time, but you know I'm a praying man. Not only do I not want to tarnish my professional reputation, but that goes for my spiritual garment all the more. For me, sin is not an option. It's not easy, and I do call on the power of the Holy Ghost to look away."

Her brother's words weren't judgmental, but filled with empathy. "The only thing I ask is that you pray for me. I know this is a trial, but I don't have to run away from my feelings to win."

He grunted and accelerated his speed. Moments later, he mumbled, "If you don't have the power to walk away, resist the devil, and he will flee from you."

"James 4:7," Gabrielle identified immediately. "That entire passage keeps me rooted. It reminded me to consult with God and ask Him to reveal my purpose in this situation. Several times, God has told me to stand firm and see His salvation. The Holy Ghost keeps reminding me to walk upright before Him. That message came again recently."

Drexel was thoughtful and didn't comment right away. "Who am I to go against the Wonderful Counselor? If Jesus has helped me throughout my thirty-seven years, then He can help you too, Sis."

Satisfied with his response, Gabrielle yawned and closed her eyes. Sometime later, she didn't even realize that her brother had stopped and gassed up until he was climbing back into her car and clicking his seat belt.

Through blurred vision, she frowned at him. He laughed. "It happens every time. A road trip knocks you out. You know you're not much company when you're snoring, right?"

"I do not snore!" Sulking, Gabrielle scooted down in her seat. At least, she hoped she hadn't in Cameron's car.

"And close your mouth too," he added, entering back onto the highway.

Punching Drexel in his arm, Gabrielle could feel his muscle tense. "Don't hurt your hand," he teased.

"Right. I'll call Talise to let her know we're close." She tapped her friend's number and waited for an answer. "Hi. We're about forty-five minutes away."

"Good. I've been praying for safe travel. I'm so excited, I could cry. You were such a blessing to me in Boston, and now I can return the favor."

"You owe me nothing, girl. I'm a card-carrying godmother of a beautiful little girl. And I've got a new job," Gabrielle said proudly. "I would say I'm blessed and expecting more blessings to come my way. That is, as long as I pray the devil out of the way," she added, unable to hold back a big smile.

"That sounds like a Scripture in there somewhere."

"It is. I'll share it with you later. But first, is the plan still for Drex and me to meet you at your house, eat something, and then you'll show me to my new place?"

"Yes. I still don't see what the rush is. You could have stayed with us."

"Ha! And be scorched by the sizzle between you and Ace? Nah." She laughed as Talise joined her.

Theirs wasn't the ideal love story Gabrielle would have created, with Talise getting pregnant outside of marriage. But Ace and Talise's happy ending would make Cinderella weep tears of joy. The couple had repented of the lifestyle they once lived. God washed them clean and filled them with power to live right.

Gabrielle turned to her brother. "Talise has prepared a light snack for us, so we're going there and then heading to the apartment."

He squinted at the GPS and nodded. Gabrielle resumed their conversation until Lauren began to cry in the background.

"See you in a few." The two friends disconnected.

Continuing westbound on I-70, they spotted the Arch, crossing the bridge over the mighty Mississippi River into downtown. Minutes later, Drexel pointed out the area where he and Gabrielle had eaten at Crown Candy when she was there for the renewal ceremony.

"Well, at least when I come to visit, I know where I can get a good meal," he joked, knowing Gabrielle loved to cook when she had company. Gabrielle familiarized herself with the sights until they pulled up in front of Talise's home.

With Lauren in her arms, Talise stepped outside to greet them. She was all smiles. Once Drexel parked and helped Gabrielle from the car, she hurried to her friend's outstretched arms. In a loose group hug, Gabrielle squeezed the baby and Talise.

"I'm so glad you brought Gabrielle. Otherwise, I would have worried about her," Talise said to Drexel before ushering them into the house.

"I'm still worried about her." He smiled at Talise and gave Gabrielle a pointed stare.

She ignored him as she kicked off her shoes in the foyer—a habit she had developed whenever she spotted light-colored carpet—and then made a beeline for the restroom. After freshening up, Gabrielle walked into the dining room to discover Talise's light snack was actually enough food for a hearty meal.

"Drexel, please do the honors of saying the blessing," Talise asked, as Lauren became impatient to eat.

"Heavenly Father, in the Name of Jesus, we thank You for this meal and fellowship. Thank You for Your grace and the blood that You shed on the cross for us. Please sanctify our food and help us to be a blessing to those who have not." He paused. "Jesus, rebuke the adversary and the wolf in sheep's clothing and the devil . . ."

Gabrielle nudged him.

Opening his eyes, he feigned innocence. "I'm just covering all the bases, in Jesus' Name. Amen."

Talise eyed Drexel then smirked at Gabrielle who was rolling her eyes.

"Brothers," she griped.

"I wish I had one."

"You can have him." Gabrielle tilted her head toward Drexel, who was already stacking his plate with pasta salad and beef smokies.

In a hurry to get to her apartment, Gabrielle didn't want to linger after they ate. She was pleased when Ace arrived. He had come home early from work. After kissing his wife, he shook Drexel's hand and hugged Gabrielle. Taking their baby, Ace assumed his fatherly duties while Talise grabbed the car keys to show Gabrielle her new place.

Alone in the car with Drexel, this time Gabrielle lit into him about embarrassing her in front of Talise. "I'm offended that you have no confidence in my salvation around Cameron. Why don't you just lay down your Dupree law the next time you see him."

155

"Not a problem. When I see him, I'll be sure to make that my first order of business."

Although Drexel's persona was meant to intimidate, Cameron didn't come across as a man who feared too much, maybe even God. Gabrielle shivered at his ignorance. She feared going to hell. That was her incentive to walk right before the Lord. Plus, she loved Jesus. If Cameron didn't get with the program soon, then he would be excluded from hers.

Chapter Twenty-Two

*C*ameron's heart pounded wildly in anticipation. Gabrielle was within hugging and kissing distance. One day was a long time to be away from a woman who had blindsided him in less than sixty seconds. Waiting a month seemed unbearable, but knowing she was relocating made it worthwhile.

Arriving on campus earlier than usual that morning, Cameron immediately prioritized tasks, so he could leave to meet Gabrielle. Of all days, he could barely make it out of his office. Duty called as he got caught up reviewing current policies and making suggestions about implementing new procedures at the university. Adding to his delay, since he was the new kid on the block, everyone wanted to introduce themselves after an alumni luncheon.

Although he was up for the challenge at work, with Gabrielle, it was questionable. Relying on Talise to keep him informed, he wanted to arrange a surprise meeting at her new apartment. Not long ago, Talise called and informed him that Gabrielle and her brother were parking outside her house.

Cameron sprang into action. By the time he made it to a flower shop, Talise phoned that they were heading to the apartment. She also cautioned him that Drexel seemed to be on the warpath. That tidbit didn't faze Cameron.

Quickly, he paid for the bouquet and sped off toward Gabrielle's apartment. Fifteen minutes or so later, he cruised through the wrought-iron, unmanned security gates at Willow Estates community complex. To his surprise and relief, he had beaten them.

Turning off the ignition, Cameron touched the control to lower his window. The warm mid-June breeze was quite welcome before the summer heat roared in. He glanced around the grounds and nodded. His cousins had chosen a picturesque location for Gabrielle. The now flourishing complex didn't exist when he went away to college more than a decade ago.

As a matter of fact, it was the site of a deteriorated school near the airport. A crew had razed Berkeley High School and replaced it with an exclusive collection of townhouses, two-bedroom bungalows, and luxury apartment buildings. The landscaping alone was immaculate.

With Ace's mother living nearby in one of the bungalows, Gabrielle would know at least one neighbor. Cameron glanced at his watch. There was still no sign of her car and U-Haul truck. Leaning back on the headrest, he closed his eyes and tried to relax. He and Gabrielle had taken baby steps toward a relationship through phone calls and texts while apart. Together again, the possibilities were endless.

The sound of a truck motor alerted Cameron to open his eyes. He looked around and spotted Gabrielle's car latched onto the U-Haul truck trailing Talise's new SUV. Stepping out of his Audi, he slipped on his sunglasses and leaned against the hood of his car. Gabrielle was now on his turf, and he was about to negotiate the rules of engagement.

———— ꕥ ————

Cameron. The last text Gabrielle received from him stated he was busy at the university but couldn't wait to see her. Her heart fluttered the moment she laid eyes on him. At the same time, Drexel mumbled, "What's he doing here?"

He's here because I'm here and we missed each other, she thought but dared not mention the truth.

Before Drexel came to a complete stop, Cameron pushed off the hood of his car and began his swagger toward them.

She had to give it to him. He wore the persona of a brainy professor with a GQ edge in his khakis and dark polo shirt; his build was an object of appreciation. Cameron was still eye-stopping handsome. In his hand was a bunch of flowers that popped with bright colors. She recalled his first flowers the day at the airport.

Once he realized she wasn't driving, Cameron walked around to the passenger side, cutting off Drexel from opening her door.

Gabrielle exhaled as she came face-to-face with Cameron in dark shades. Neither uttered a word. She wondered which of the expressions he was reading across her face: longing, happiness, or uncertainty.

Accepting his flowers, Gabrielle forgot about Drexel, Talise, and the world. "Thank you," she responded, wishing he would remove his dark glasses so she could stare into his eyes.

In a split second, he unbuckled her seat belt and lifted her out of the seat. When Cameron engulfed her in his arms, she clung to him. "God knows I've missed you," he whispered, as Gabrielle inhaled his cologne and was content cherishing the feel of his strength. She could have lingered in his arms longer if it wasn't for Drexel.

"I guess you didn't hear a word I said." Drexel cleared his throat and turned to Cameron. "As you can see, it's far too early for Gabrielle to entertain guests. My sister's just moving in," Drexel smarted off. He squinted at Cameron. "And it doesn't appear you came dressed to help."

Removing his hand from the spot on her back, Gabrielle could feel Cameron tense. She recognized the testosterone standoff and began to pray. These were two professionals, surely they were not about to embarrass her in a brawl.

Taking off his glasses, Cameron dismissed Drexel. "Don't let my appearance fool you. I am fully capable of lifting, moving, and dusting. Bring it on." With that sharp rebuke, he reached for Gabrielle's hand and squeezed it. If it was an intended gesture to irk her brother, he had succeeded.

"I wanted to be here to welcome you to St. Louis. I came straight from the university, but I'm here to work," he explained himself to Gabrielle.

Before she could reply, her brother cut in, "Jamieson, this is my only sister. She's not a toy for you to play with. I know what you want, but—"

"Good," Cameron stepped closer, "as long as we have an understanding that I want your sister with the sincerest intentions."

Cameron's boldness caused Drexel's nostrils to flare and his hands to ball into fists. Gabrielle could tell her brother was using all the restraint God gave him.

Dignified, mild-mannered, highly educated, loving, and walking with Jesus, Drexel didn't let people get under his skin. Somehow, Cameron had succeeded, and this was only the second time the two met.

Not good. She didn't want to add friction to her life. But right now, she was standing beside a major source. Gabrielle desperately wanted the Duprees' stamp of approval on Cameron if they were going to spend a lot of time together. There was no doubt about it; he was going to have to come around soon.

A honking car and yelling ended the stalemate.

"Fight, fight!" Grandma BB shouted from the window of a dark Hummer that pulled up next to Talise.

Gabrielle cringed. "What is she doing here?"

"That seems to be the number one question of the hour," Drexel said snidely.

Gabrielle hoped she wasn't bringing "ghetto" to this idyllic neighborhood. First, two men were poised to throw a warning punch. Now this crazy woman pulled up, hanging out of a vehicle, encouraging a fight. Were there any more surprises waiting to happen? she wondered.

"At ease, men," Grandma BB commanded, as a bear-sized man assisted her out of the SUV. "Before the boxing match begins, let's get your girlfriend moved in and then I'll referee the fight."

Grandma BB made her way to Gabrielle and embraced her. "Let the good times roll."

Decked out in her Stacy Adams shoes, Grandma BB didn't look dressed to lift a box. Talise quickly came to her friend's rescue. Looping her arm through Gabrielle's, she steered her away from the drama.

"Grandma BB hasn't stopped singing your praises about your Mace incident at my nuptials. She has replayed the scene numerous times to the Jamieson wives. You've become her hero, you know."

"Okay." Shrugging pensively, Gabrielle still didn't understand.

"She's here to convince you to team up with her for covert activities in her neighborhood, in case you get bored." Repeating the elderly woman's words, Talise tried to explain. With a clueless expression, she finally threw up her hands. "Hey, don't ask me. I'm just celebrating my six-month wedding anniversary."

God, if this is Your will, I'm definitely not getting off to a good start. Everybody seems to be crazy. Somewhat perplexed, Gabrielle wondered again if this was a good career move.

"Since none of our husbands were available to give you a hand, Grandma BB enlisted help from some of her personal assistants," Talise further explained.

She stepped closer. "Before you do, don't ask. I can't imagine what work they do for her. Girl, wait until you see the muscles on those men. Whew. I had to close my eyes and thank Jesus for the good man I have."

Gabrielle laughed. "You've got a praying man. That's worth money, looks, or health. You are truly blessed."

Suddenly, the devil taunted her. *Look at you, you've been faithful to*

God longer than your friend, and what has He given you? A man who you'll have to compromise to have . . .

Before Satan could continue his lies, Gabrielle called on the Name of Jesus and rebuked the seeds of doubt. She may not get a mate that she so much desired, whether Cameron surrendered to Jesus or not. But she was determined to get God's reward for righteous living—a crown of life, according to James 1:12.

It seemed as if God sent a distraction when Grandma BB came to her side. Glancing over her shoulder, neither Cameron nor Drexel had budged. Instead of a physical exchange, they were having a heated debate.

As a judge, Drexel believed in solving worldly matters in the courtroom and spiritual struggles in the prayer room. Nevertheless, he would return a swing if necessary when it came to defending his sister. She had witnessed it while growing up.

"It's a matter of time before you go down, chile." Grandma BB shook her head, as her three workers/bodyguards/boy toys waited near the Hummer for her instructions. She winked at Gabrielle. "Just don't go down without a fight. But right now, we need to separate them two."

Swallowing hard, Gabrielle could only stare in bewilderment.

Jesus, what have I've gotten myself into?

Chapter Twenty-Three

*L*ook, Drexel," Cameron tried to reason with Gabrielle's brother, "we're both men who could have our pick of women. I've made my choice—Gabrielle. There's something about your sister that makes me crazy without her. For that reason, to keep my sanity, I need her in my life."

"She deserves better than you," he snapped.

"Better?" Cameron laughed. "I'm the descendant of an African king. I have a bank account that might surprise you—"

"Surprise me."

Cameron ignored the bait. "I am a newly appointed chairperson of the engineering—"

"Listen, Jamieson," Drexel cut him off again and folded his arms. "Public records are just that, public. If I want to know anything about you, I can obtain your background information through legal means. However, my concern is your intentions. Since you're bent on giving me your résumé, I would be interested in hearing what you do for the Lord."

Recognizing the trick question, Cameron didn't back down. "I donate time and money to various organizations." He began to list his philanthropic deeds.

Drexel sneered. "You're too smart for your own good. You can always tell a saint of God because he has a ready testimony of what God saved him from." He glanced over his shoulder and so did Cameron. Gabrielle gave them both a worried look. Drexel faced him again. "If you don't have one yet, keep living. Sure enough, by the time my sister finishes with you, you're going to be praying for deliverance."

What was that supposed to mean? The man was crazy. Gabrielle had tried and failed to run him away. Jamiesons had staying power. Cameron could only shake his head at her brother's absurdity. He and Gabrielle were getting along just fine. And as long as they kept Christ out of their personal conversations, they would have perfect harmony in their relationship.

—⁂—

The following week, things were already not going as Cameron planned. Somehow, instead of exploring the new hot spots in St. Louis with Gabrielle, he got stuck babysitting the men in his family.

Grandma BB had just upped him by orchestrating a women's-only housewarming party for Gabrielle. He became suspicious when Gabrielle told him no men were allowed besides those who were paid to wear aprons and serve the ladies. Grandma BB was legendary for being the life of the party, or, better put, bringing mayhem to a shindig. So what was she up to?

His family, who met the sassy senior while he was away in college, said Grandma BB was harmless. However, rumors involving her reached him all the way in Boston. If a person didn't know that she shot Parke's father-in-law, served jail time, and escaped from a nursing facility—along with other outlandish tales—they would think she was just a sweet old lady. What havoc was she looking to reap in his life with Gabrielle?

"It's great to have you living back home, Cam," Parke said, interrupting his musings.

"I know. The more Jamiesons, the merrier. I was long overdue returning, especially after the Boston bad boys left town," Cameron joked. He was referring to Ace and Kidd before the Lord saved them. He stretched out his legs on an ottoman. "It's hard to separate us. And we're what generation of cousins?"

"Twelfth," Parke confirmed.

"That doesn't matter, we have each other's back," Ace chimed in, bumping fists with Cameron. "Through thick and thin . . . and through Drexel and Drexel." He snickered.

"Don't go there," Cameron warned. He had nothing to prove to Gabrielle's brother, only to her. "Anyway, we might not have ever connected if it wasn't for the genealogy quest in our blood. That's why it's important to connect with other members on the Jamieson tree." He spied Kidd's reaction.

Kidd scoffed. "It's a good thing you and Ace connected, because I had already written you off as crazy. But now, in hindsight, I see the dots that God connected to lead me to the beautiful wife I have. With that said, I believe in leaving well enough alone."

Ace's older brother wanted Cameron to butt out of any discussion around bonding with recently discovered half siblings. At first, Cameron had agreed to honor Kidd's wishes, but he couldn't let it go and eventually changed his mind. After meeting Denise at Ace and Talise's reception, Kidd's request now seemed unreasonable. *This is about family,* he reasoned to himself.

His cousin may not be a Bible scholar, but Kidd always had one Scripture handy. Whenever Cameron attempted to reopen the discussion, he would quote chapter and verse. " *I have learned to be content whatever the circumstances,* Philippians 4:11", Kidd would inevitability say.

"I'm content. I'm saved in Jesus and happy to be a husband and father. Let it alone, cuz," he said repeatedly.

165

For now, Cameron would respond inwardly.

Tonight, he turned his attention to the other Jamieson men in the sunroom. They were feasting on hot wings, soda, and pizza. Engaged in a friendly family rivalry, they watched an unusual baseball matchup between the National League St. Louis Cardinals and the American League Boston Red Sox.

During the commercial break after the Sox took the lead by scoring one point, Cameron broached the subject again. Denise was depending on him to convince Kidd that regardless of the sins of Samuel Jamieson, they were all brothers and sisters and should meet each other.

"What do you all think about a Jamieson family reunion, get-together, or what not?" Cameron took another shot, shrugged, and crossed one leg over his knee. Casually, he exchanged a quick glance with Parke. His brothers had already agreed to help sway Kidd's mind.

"Don't we already have one at Jamieson family game nights? Speaking of which, it's at your house next," Kidd said with a grin. "I cleaned up for hours after y'all left."

Not to be sidetracked, Cameron pressed, "Well, I thought we should expand it a bit." He wondered if Kidd suspected a setup.

Kidd had a hard edge. Not much fazed him unless it came to his brother, mother, wife, or daughter. Ace was the free spirit in the family. Although he was willing to meet Denise, Ace wouldn't go against his brother if Kidd wasn't on board for a large-scale meeting.

"You'll have to admit that without my zeal, you wouldn't have met your wife. Can you imagine what else you're missing by not knowing other family members in the Jamieson bloodline . . . such as your half siblings in Oklahoma City and Hartford? They are all eager to meet you. Denise took a chance coming to Ace's ceremony, not knowing how she would be received." Once Cameron opened up the floodgate, he wasn't about to back down.

The one tidbit he omitted was that Denise's youngest brother was just as adamant as Kidd about not meeting his half siblings. Zaki was a carbon copy of Ace in looks and mannerism, but he was all Kidd in attitude. The man's raw emotions stood out when Cameron and Gabrielle visited Denise.

Throw the two brothers in a dark alley, and it would have been a pit bull fight. Cameron agreed with his brothers, with that type of mindset, a person like Kidd needed Jesus. When his cousin couldn't control his emotions and temper, church was the necessary alternative to change his lifestyle. On the other hand, he himself didn't need to be caught up in the religious whoopla; his life wasn't in disarray. At least, that was Cameron's assessment of how he and Kidd differed.

He looked at Parke to back him up, and his big brother stepped up to the plate. "Kidd, man, we're all part of Paki and Elaine. No one has a big happy family—without skeletons in their closets. Over the years, we've taken chances when we've contacted folks," Parke explained. "More than once, we've been hung up on or told we had the wrong Jamieson when all the information pointed to them. All we want to do is reach out, even if it's just a hello and goodbye."

"You're the lone holdout in the group, Kevin 'Kidd' Jamieson," Cameron asserted. "Is it going to be a hello or goodbye?"

"They know about us. We found out about them, isn't that enough?" Kidd argued back, throwing up his arms in frustration. "When I say I'm content with my life right now, I am." Then, just as Cameron expected, Kidd quoted Philippians 4:11. Afterward, he added, "I've lived with drama all my life thanks to my absentee father. I don't want to meet any more victims of his mass destruction."

"That's understandable, but we've got to have each other's back. I remember when I was barely a teenager. Our grandfather, Parke IV, had a favorite saying, 'Be kind to one another because you never know whose hand is going to give you that last piece of bread.' You never know when you may need something or somebody," Cameron advised.

Parke nodded in agreement. "Yeah, that was so long ago." With a quick shift, he then addressed Kidd directly, "Speaking of having each other's back, remember when you first came here and I was about to put you out of my house?"

Kidd lifted a brow. "You're telling that story wrong, cuz, because I was about to leave."

"Whichever version doesn't defend your manhood. Anyway, even though you and I were in the middle of an argument, I still needed you when Grandma BB had her stroke. Just because we're grown men doesn't mean we're self-sufficient and don't need our families," Parke said.

"This isn't time for a parable." Cameron regained the conversation. "Denise wants to plan a family reunion with as many of the descendants of the five brothers as she can find. It appears your two older brothers—"

Kidd scowled.

"Face it. You're not in Kansas anymore. That was Samuel's first family. They're all older than you, except two, and then two other siblings died."

At the mention of death, his defiant expression softened. "How?"

Everyone in the room knew the story, except Kidd. Cameron swallowed and explained, "There were two sisters in Oklahoma. One died of complications from lupus. She was three years younger than Ace. That left the younger sister alone. She needs you, Kidd. The oldest son was killed in a car accident. He was behind the wheel driving drunk."

It wasn't meant to be a guilt trip statement; the others gave Kidd a moment to digest the information.

When the tied baseball game became lively again, all eyes focused on the screen, except for Cameron's. He squinted at Kidd, trying to read his thoughts. Not liking to be the bearer of bad news, he tried to lighten the mood.

"Hey, I just knew I was the lead genealogist in the family, but it appears I have some competition. I guess I became so engrossed in other areas of my life that I lost my edge. Denise and the others have found descendants of one brother, Fabunni, on the Ohio census, beginning as early as 1830. I don't know how I missed them. They were listed as White. I guess they could pass because they were never classified as freed Blacks, mulatto, or Black on any of the census data."

"Hmm." Parke tilted his head. "From what Elaine described in her journal, all her children had colored skin from dark to very fair. I guess Fabunni was fair enough and passed as White. The lie kept going until the descendants no longer knew it was a lie."

"Why does it have to be a lie?" Ace countered. "People should classify themselves however they want, Latino, Asian-American, whatever. When I wore my hair in a long ponytail, many people thought I was Cuban. Go figure."

"That classification thing is so annoying." Parke shook his head. "It reminds me of when I was talking about salvation to a group of men. One guy said he was Jewish, as if that was going to end the discussion. I told him I was a Gentile, and that ended the discussion." He grinned. "Later on, he came back and told me that I had blown him away with my answer. He totally expected me to say Baptist, Pentecostal, or some other denomination. In reality, Jesus is coming back for a church wearing His name only."

"We're digressing," Cameron charged, after Parke slipped his testimony into a conversation that had nothing to do with religion. "Back to what the pretty boy of the family was talking about." Cameron laughed and balled up a napkin, then aimed it at Ace.

"Let me clarify my statement. During slavery, all it took for Whites to keep Blacks enslaved was the one drop of Black blood. That's how they had you pegged. The same mentality is still used today where a person has to choose. Evidently, Fabunni's descendants are comfortable in their skin."

"And that's why folks need to leave well enough alone," Kidd stated.

Cameron noted his cousin's defiant attitude had returned, but he ignored him.

"Do you know if anyone tried to contact them?"

"No. One of Denise's twin brothers said he didn't want to interfere with their lifestyle."

Lifting his bottled water in a salute, Kidd nodded. "Smart man."

Cameron smirked. "It appears they've become very affluent. Lily white, if you will, and very secretive."

"Really?" Kidd sat straighter. Then, right before Cameron and the others' eyes, Kidd did a transformation. "Well, I guess it's time to shake some things up. I never did like snobs."

The roar of claps mingled with those from the TV set. The Red Sox won and so did another generation of Jamiesons. The family reunion was officially under way.

Chapter Twenty-Four

*S*taring into Cameron's seductive eyes, Gabrielle never thought it would be like this. It was their first official St. Louis date, taking in the sights of the city. They had just left the art museum in Forest Park. Throughout the afternoon, she had enjoyed Cameron's whispers tickling her ear. When he held her hand, she had a feeling of blissful contentment. *Is this what falling in love is like?* she wondered.

Gabrielle could no longer deny its existence; their sensual tension could light a match. *God, I did not sign up for this type of temptation,* she silently prayed.

Now they were enjoying the Brio's outdoor café at Plaza Frontenac. Anticipating another intimate moment, it was time for her to set boundaries.

"Cameron, I can't kiss you anymore." Instinctively, she braced herself for his rebellion.

His expression never changed, as he reached across the table for her fingers. "That's an extreme rule. I have no complaints about our first kiss—none. As a matter of fact, my heart has been set on getting one all day. It couldn't be bad breath because I don't miss a dental appointment."

That last remark made her giggle before she blushed. "You know that's not it."

"Okay, beautiful. Tell me what it is."

"I lost myself in that kiss. I can't handle the passion."

He nodded.

"I'm not sleeping with you either."

He bobbed his head and took a deep breath. "Anything else?"

"If you still want to go out with me, I'm sure more will be forthcoming." She withdrew her hands and folded them, waiting for him to say goodbye. Surely, there were women who would probably kiss him without asking. Gabrielle wanted so much for him to fight the devil to keep her.

"Let me tell you why I want you. Your beauty arrested me the moment I saw you. Your intellect mesmerized me, but your humbleness has shamed me. Since I've never met the other Duprees, and I'm assuming Judge Drexel represents them all, his protectiveness is what I would expect from someone with strong family ties."

Gabrielle teared. She was about to cry over his heartfelt words. It was the right answer.

"If you want to torture me, then I won't touch you."

"Now, you've gone too far." Gabrielle pouted. "I like your touches. Even a newborn thrives when she's cuddled and touched."

Cameron took a deep breath. "Well, Miss Dupree, you want your cake and eat it too."

"I know." Gabrielle bowed her head. No doubt, she was sending mixed signals.

"I will give you whatever flavor cake you want. If holding hands," he paused and laid his hands on the table with his palms up, "and hugging is permitted, then I will refrain from everything else to be with you. You're making it hard on a man, but you're my soul mate and I know it."

Sniffing, Gabrielle looked away. No romance book had come close to what he just said. "If you truly believe I am your soul mate, then guard my soul, Cameron." She rested her hands in his.

After a squeeze, he lifted his right hand and saluted her. "Reporting for duty, ma'am."

Gabrielle laughed at his antics, but Cameron didn't crack at smile. "You'll soon see I'm serious."

"Thank you," she whispered with a shiver. *God, this feels right. Please, let it be right. I will proceed below the speed limit with caution.*

Winking, Cameron opened the menu. "Okay, let's eat. You're zapping all my strength to walk this fine line."

———— ‰ ————

Although he never crossed the line, Cameron found other ways to express his magnetism. He treated her like a lady, he smothered her with attention, and he flirted shamelessly when they went out.

So, what could be her complaint? He never budged when it came to fully embracing God—and that was her constant source of frustration.

Cameron avoided any mention of Jesus beyond a few sentences. Clearly, he didn't want to engage in any church dialogue. That was a bummer.

To Gabrielle's disappointment and her brother's expectation, the object of her affection had yet to make an appearance at the church services she attended with Talise and her family. Instead, he always had a noteworthy reason.

"Let's get together later, babe. My frat brothers and I are taking a group of boys to see a Cardinals' game," he had offered for the first absence.

Every Sunday after that, he blamed a conflict in schedules—from golfing with colleagues, to tutoring those who were underachievers in school, and on and on. That was all good, but what did Scripture say? Only what you do for Christ will last. Where was Jesus on his schedule?

What sacrifice did Cameron make on behalf of Jesus?

The more her feelings deepened for him, the more she felt like a failure as a disciple for Christ. Clearly, Cameron seemed comfortable with his level of salvation and not interested in growing spiritually.

Yes, he could prove he had read the Bible from cover to cover. With a keenly sharp mind for memorization, he could quote Scriptures almost as well as Elder Johnny James, a renowned evangelist who didn't need a Bible when he preached. (Without a doubt, God had tremendously blessed that minister's mind.)

She also recognized that it was the Lord who gifted Cameron with knowledge and possessions. Yet Gabrielle wanted to hear about the faith he professed in God. He never acknowledged that it was God who blessed his life extraordinarily. There was no way Gabrielle could discount that omission. God had to be a priority in her mate's life.

One morning before work, Gabrielle lingered in prayer a little longer than usual. With many questions on her heart, she remained on her knees talking to God. "If he is gradually surrendering to You, Jesus, why isn't my spirit bearing witness? God, I've waited so long for a mate. I've turned men away because I couldn't see Your presence in their lives but foolishness lurking in their spirits. That was easy to do. In Cameron Jamieson, I see goodness, but I see pride too. And pride separates him from You."

When she ran out of steam, Gabrielle said Amen and then opened her Bible. Her heart was troubled. She felt like God was taking a backseat while her feelings for Cameron were accelerating.

Unable to focus on the words on the page, she sighed. With her concentration distracted, Gabrielle closed her Bible. It was time to get dressed for work. Standing, she glimpsed the worn journal she called a "handbook of romance" for so many years. She had pulled it from a packed box the day she found a rose under her windshield wiper.

The roses started to appear the day after their first official St. Louis date. For weeks, Cameron had driven to her apartment complex three times a week. There was never a message on the card, only his signature. No man had ever gone out of his way for her like that before. In comparison, her previous suitors' gestures seemed to be at their convenience.

On those days, Cameron's thoughtful touch always caused her to arrive at her office with a smile. Gabrielle would text him: thank you, setting up their day of text exchanges. Cameron always sent the sweetest thoughts: Give me your heart, you already have mine or I can't stop thinking about you or Your smile is ingrained into my mind.

Giving him enough of her thoughts for the moment, Gabrielle headed to the bathroom for a shower. Hours later at work, she stared out of her spacious office window. What was wrong with her? She was a woman highly favored of God. Yet her mind was completely distracted as she restlessly awaited the weekend. It was a day away and Cameron had already confirmed they would attend a concert Saturday night.

What Gabrielle really wanted was to take a weekend getaway alone. Although leaving the airlines was a smart move, she missed the perks of jumping on a plane to visit her parents in Chicago, or friends in Washington, DC, or Denise, or wherever her brother was evangelizing in the states.

"Help me to focus, Jesus, so I don't make You ashamed on my job by not giving my best," she mumbled, recalling Colossians 3:23: *"Whatever you do, work at it with all your heart, as working for the Lord, not for human masters."*

As CEO of international sales with offices in six countries, the majority of Gabrielle's staff was overseas. However, the personnel she oversaw in St. Louis were essential to the company's growth.

Gabrielle couldn't wait to take to the skies again. She looked forward to meeting her worldwide teams, especially those in the Philippines and Turkey. Whenever that happened, it would be her first trip since she and Cameron started dating. She had to admit that they were doing a good job of refraining from kissing. She was still blown away that he consented. Gabrielle smiled. She would miss him like crazy when travel time rolled around.

Work. It was hard for her to keep her mind off Cameron and do just that. With renewed determination, she delved into answering company emails. In the process, her phone vibrated with a text. Thinking it was probably Cameron, she grabbed it quickly. A huge grin came over her face as she read the message from her brother Philip. He asked her to call him whenever she could talk.

Getting up, Gabrielle closed the door to her office and tapped his number. Contentment washed over her as Philip's authoritarian voice answered.

After a few preliminaries, he said, "I was in prayer the other day and God placed you on my heart to really pray for you. Anything going on?"

Gabrielle closed her eyes and waved her hand in the air. "Thank You, Jesus," she mouthed. And she had thought God wasn't listening to her plea. "I'm just kind of second-guessing some things in my life."

"Such as," Philip prompted her, as if he didn't have a demanding schedule.

Sighing, Gabrielle didn't want to hear herself say out loud what she had been silently praying to God. "I have everything going for me, yet I'm empty inside."

Philip didn't respond right away. Whenever he was quiet, she sensed he was consulting the Lord on what to say.

"Does this have anything to do with the man you were seeing before you left Boston and now both of you live in St. Louis?"

"Yes. Cameron. He's got so much going for him, but it's the few things he's lacking that trouble me. If you've spoken with Drexel, I'm sure he gave you a list of things he doesn't like about him."

Philip chuckled. "You're our baby sister. We're not supposed to like any man who has eyes for you."

Gabrielle chuckled. "My feelings are strong for Cameron. He's a go-getter in his education, family, society—"

"But a slacker with Jesus," Philip suggested.

She nodded as though he could see her response. "I'm starting to ask myself if I should walk away or get on board the 'bring any man to church' campaign in order to get a husband. I want to be married, Philip, but God help me not to become so desperate where I close my eyes to keep from seeing red flags."

"It's okay to have a desire to be married. Is Cameron your desire?"

Gabrielle struggled with a truthful answer. "I'm crazy about Cameron." She exhaled. "In his current state, if he were to ask me to marry him and I said yes, then I'd feel like I'm settling. I need some signs that he's on fire for Jesus."

"Don't settle. You're a child of the King where blessings abound. You're not on spiritual welfare where you have to take a handout from the devil."

—⟋⟍—

On Saturday evening, Cameron stretched his arm across the back of Gabrielle's chair. They were seated in the auditorium of the Blanche M. Touhill Performing Arts Center. Either Gabrielle was enthralled by Herbie Hancock or she was unaffected by Cameron's presence. Because when he tried to inch her closer to him, she barely moved.

During intermission, they strolled into the lobby for refreshments. When he reached for her hand, Gabrielle stiffened before she relaxed. Once they accepted cups of ginger ale from the bartender, Cameron guided her to a secluded corner.

"What's wrong, baby? I thought you would enjoy this concert." Concentrating on her facial expressions, what he saw and heard had to be in sync. She was beautiful that night in her sleeveless gold dress and duster. Unfortunately, sadness or confusion seemed to fill her eyes.

"I just have a lot on my mind."

Cameron didn't like the sound of that. "The jazz concert was my way of relaxing you after a long work week. I'm a good listener." He gently brushed the back of his hand against her soft cheek.

The lights flickered, indicating the second half of the program was minutes away from beginning. Gabrielle was about to follow the crowd across the lobby without answering, but Cameron restrained her with his hand around her small wrist.

"Gabrielle? I wish you would talk to me."

"Would you want to hear it, even if I was badmouthing you?"

Cameron held his breath. This was serious, his woman wasn't smiling. "What did I do now?"

"Can we talk after the show?" she asked and resumed walking.

No, you have a problem with me. I want to hear it now, he wanted to demand, but he wasn't one to make a scene. Instead of sitting on the edge of his seat, enjoying the acoustics, he would be bracing for a tongue-lashing. "Sure," he answered.

When the concert ended, Gabrielle declined his offer to grab a bite to eat. "Can you take me home? We can talk on the way."

Cameron did just that, but once they were in his car, she wasn't forthcoming, so he had to prompt her.

"I'm ready for you to chew me out, although I have no idea what I did."

Turning away, Gabrielle glanced out the window. "It's what you won't do, Cameron. Every time I try and initiate a conversation with Jesus in the sentence, you shut down. Why is that a taboo subject with you?"

Gritting his teeth, he refused to snap his frustration at her. "I see no need to inject God into our discussions."

"Why? It's part of who I am," she said.

"Believe me, I'm a saint compared to what I used to be before I met you. And I was a good guy even then. For you, sweetheart, I have stopped cursing. I withhold from undressing you with my mind, and

I've refrained from kissing you. I'm definitely in sainthood if I'm not making love to you, which you call sex. What more do you want from me?"

His woman was pushing him and, as a man, he could only tolerate so much. It was time for her to give a little.

"I guess I want nothing from you, Mr. Jamieson, absolutely nothing," Gabrielle said with finality in her voice.

No other words were uttered. When Cameron walked her to the door of her apartment building, he couldn't stand it any longer. "I need a hug and I sure hope you're not about to deny me one."

When she collapsed into his arms, Cameron kissed the top of her head. "We'll work it out." He was about to add, *I promise,* but when it came to religion, Cameron couldn't hold to that promise.

Chapter Twenty-Five

*W*hy am I still chasing this woman?" he asked Ace. Standing on Cameron's back deck, they were preparing to barbecue for the upcoming Fourth of July celebration.

A designated family member always started grilling the meat a day before because it was such a chore to complete in one day. This year, his parents nominated Cameron, and Ace volunteered to help.

"This is the most frustrating relationship I have ever suffered through," Cameron continued to vent.

"Gabrielle isn't holding you hostage. Walk," Ace advised.

But that wasn't the answer Cameron wanted to hear, even if it did make 100 percent good sense. "My heart won't let her go," he admitted softly.

Cameron went on to share that Gabrielle started pulling away from him for no good reason. Ace listened to the whole story about their disagreements, interjecting his opinion. However, Cameron was careful to point out their spats were nothing serious. They hadn't even raised their voices at each other.

By the end of the conversation, he was regretful that he had confided in his cousin. Ace's comments had been no help. With disappointment in his voice, he told Ace, "Man, your brainstorming skills are sorely lacking."

"Then give the woman what she wants." Feeling the sting from Cameron's comment, Ace seemed thoughtful before his next statement. "Take it from a man who's done everything the wrong way: women, partying, jail time, and the way I went about winning my wife's forgiveness and love. Trust me. I've learned the hard way that you're never going to get what you want until you give God what He wants."

"And what does Jesus want?" Cameron flipped a couple of burgers.

"Your complete surrender."

"Listen to my preacher cousin. I never thought I would hear you telling me anything about Jesus."

"I never thought I would say the three forbidden words 'I love you' to any woman." Ace paused, as his face took on a somber expression. "I almost lost my happiness because of my warped thinking. At the time, I didn't know that Gabrielle was pulling for me and Talise when there was no 'us.' But, in hindsight, I see how God was connecting all the dots. You might as well surrender, man, if you have your heart set on her."

"Listen, man, I'm free from guilt. I have no regrets in my life. God gave me a certain number of talents, and I produce, so I'm not out of His will."

"Just because you think you're okay doesn't mean you're in His perfect will." Ace gave him a skeptical expression. "Gabrielle is high class and high spiritual maintenance. I would hate to see a Jamieson lose all his common sense in favor of book sense. Even though God gave you a double portion of that, you could flunk, man."

"Are you suggesting that I need to punch in a time clock at church?" Cameron chuckled at the obscurity of the thought. "I'm not anti-God. I'm pro-Jesus. If I'm not in church, most of the time I'm off somewhere doing a good deed."

"Cam, this is more than about you showing up every now and then at services. By the way, it's been a while, mind you. God gave Gabrielle a double portion of something too, and she's seeing right through you."

Lately Gabrielle made no secret of her disappointment with his legitimate reasons for missing church. She was a very desirable woman; one look at her could almost make him forget his name. Nobody was perfect. At the end of the day, couples have to compromise and overlook certain things about each other.

Huffing, Cameron turned and stepped back inside the kitchen to get more ribs for the grill. Somehow he knew Gabrielle was his equal, but church shouldn't be a prerequisite for a relationship.

Her brother Drexel had basically said that it was when they squared off at her apartment complex. In absence of the courtroom, Judge Drexel Dupree was attempting to put him on trial. Nevertheless, he would lose this case. Cameron wanted Gabrielle based on honest intentions. He didn't need church for that, and he wouldn't bow to any woman's demands regarding religion. That was still nonnegotiable.

Later that evening, after all the meat had been smoked and Ace had gone home, Cameron was alone with his thoughts. He was absolutely clueless how to handle the divide between him and Gabrielle. His mind told him to cut his loss and walk away; yet he resolved to stay and fight. The question was: Who was his enemy?

With his television on mute, he closed his eyes so that he could continue to mull over his dilemma in silence. Just then, his phone rang. When he answered, Gabrielle's sweet voice greeted him.

"I miss talking to you throughout the day," he told her.

"I miss you too, Cameron, but it's getting busier at work as I settle in."

Cameron was still adjusting in his position too. But he always made time for her, even if it was a quick text. On the other hand, he didn't believe in playing tit-for-tat. "You're not calling to cancel coming to my house for the holiday, are you?"

"No." The line was silent. "I just needed some distance to think clearly."

"I see."

Gabrielle cleared her throat. "My family will be in town next weekend to hear my brother preach. Remember I told you about Philip, who is an evangelist. He'll be conducting a tent meeting. Since he's in the States and close by, we're turning it into a family affair."

"Did you get it?"

"What?" He definitely confused her.

"Did the distance help you think clearly about us?"

When she didn't answer right away, Cameron assumed he had made her uncomfortable. So he switched the subject back to the barbecue at his house. "You'll get a chance to see all the Jamiesons since the renewal ceremony. We'll watch fireworks, play games, and get fat and full. There'll be plenty of food."

"I can smell the barbecue all the way in North County. Talise told me earlier that Ace was going to your place. Wasn't it a game night that changed Ace and Talise's relationship?"

"Somehow it got Talise speaking to him again." Cameron chuckled. He wasn't there but even back in Boston, he heard about how Ace was acting like a sick puppy.

Then she flipped the script on him. "I'd like to invite you to the tent meeting. It will be held in Forest Park on Friday through Sunday. Talise said you don't live far from there."

Cameron was conjuring up plenty of excuses, but his mind failed and his lips sabotaged him. "Sure."

"My brother preaches until the Holy Ghost descends in the midst of the people. God has truly anointed him to touch everyone under the sound of his voice."

Lifting a brow, Cameron withheld his smirk. Was that a challenge? Let her brother give his best shot to stir up anything in his spirit. When he did attend church with his family, they called him a spectator instead of a participator. Their summarization was accurate, and Cameron didn't see anything changing because of Gabrielle's brother.

—∽—

The next evening, Gabrielle drove through the gated Willow Estates complex after work and parked. While getting out of her car, Veronica Dupree's ringtone played on her iPhone. For an instant, her heaviness dissipated and turned into a smile. She had texted her mother earlier for a dessert recipe to take to Cameron's house.

"Hold on, Mom," she answered, as she inserted her key into her designated box to retrieve her mail. Next, she jogged up two flights of stairs to her apartment. "How's everything at home?" She tried to sound upbeat, knowing her heart was heavy with her growing feelings toward Cameron and how to tame them.

"I should ask you how things are in St. Louis. We missed each other's call this past weekend, so I thought I would check in with you before your dad and I go to a function tonight."

"I'm fine . . ." *And lonely.* But Gabrielle kept that to herself, as she opened the door to her apartment.

"What's wrong, sweetie? You sound down."

"Cameron Jamieson. I think we've reached our crossroads. We're not budging on our convictions. I've asked for distance to think and pray. He's given me that and I'm miserable," Gabrielle admitted.

Before heading to the kitchen, she kicked off her shoes. Immediately, she started warming up leftover steak and a baked potato. "But I'm all right. I know you don't have time to talk."

"There's always time for girl talk. Your father will wait because he only has one daughter."

"A voice inside of me says I would be a fool to let him get away, but I feel my spirit warning me not to compromise. With two warring factions in my head, I've been evaluating whether I'm judging him too harshly—"

184

"Never compromise when it comes to a man or salvation—never."

"Or I'll have regrets?"

"Regrets are part of life, but God rewards us if we diligently seek Him."

"Hebrews 11:6," Gabrielle whispered. She reached for lettuce and cranberry bits to make a salad. Her eyes misted. She dared not sniff or it would upset her mother, who would upset her father, then her brother would be mad. Before the night was over, they would be at her doorstep.

"Everyone wants companionship. It's natural. Remember, God made Eve for Adam, and He created animals in pairs. Pray without the fear of being disappointed. Then God will open your eyes and allow you to see what He wants you to see."

"But I am afraid of being disappointed."

True to her word, Veronica spoke with her daughter until Gabrielle felt her melancholy mood pass. She also gave her the recipe for a cool dessert. Seconds after they said goodbye, Cameron sent a text: We just took a recess, and all I can think of is you.

Smiling, Gabrielle instantly perked up. *God, there is no way this man could disappoint me. Is there?*

Chapter Twenty-Six

*C*all her old-fashioned, paranoid, or just plain saved and trying to stay that way. To Gabrielle, it was something about entering a man's house. With Cameron, she didn't trust the chemistry between them.

Even if they were surrounded by his family and friends for the holiday, Cameron would be the only one she would see. Was this the way love felt—uncontrollable? Oh no, was she really in love? Then she was in trouble.

Maybe she was getting ahead of herself. Personally, she considered her home a private domain and anyone who stepped foot inside had to be special.

Gabrielle pushed that anxiety to the back of her mind as she gathered the graham crackers, cream cheese, and sherbet for the strawberry lemon mousse tarts her mother had suggested. She prepared the dish in no time and cleaned up the mess.

Checking the clock, Gabrielle jumped in the shower. Unaccustomed to the St. Louis humidity, she dressed comfortably in a flowing sleeveless sundress, topping her look in heeled sandals.

With her dessert tucked away in a protective plastic container, she gave herself one last perusal and was ready to leave. Once in her car, she programmed Cameron's address and drove off.

Exiting off I-170 to Forest Park Parkway, she waited at a stoplight and noted the history museum that guarded the entrance to Forest Park. When she relocated to St. Louis, it didn't take long to learn it was one of the largest urban parks in the country—even bigger than New York's Central Park—and a major tourist destination.

In less than a week, Total Surrender Temple Church would set up a tent somewhere in that massive park and become the hot spot for a summer revival. Philip would preach and set St. Louis on fire with the Holy Ghost.

Once she passed Barnes-Jewish Hospital, Gabrielle turned left onto Euclid until she saw McPherson Avenue and made a right. The homes were magnificent in architecture.

A few cars crowded in the cul-de-sac around Cameron's abode. As she crept closer, an orange construction cone was planted on one side of his driveway, prohibiting anyone from parking in the spot.

She squeezed into a parking space a few houses away, unbuckled her seat belt, and then reached for her dessert. When she turned around, Cameron appeared out of nowhere and tapped on her window, startling her. Gabrielle unlocked the door and he opened it.

"Hey, it's about time you got here." He was all smiles as he bent and brushed a kiss against her cheek. Her heart fluttered. They had negotiated a kiss on the cheek as acceptable.

"Give me your keys," he said, as if he was a valet.

"Why?"

Guiding her outside, he shut the door and stepped closer until she could sniff his cologne. "Because," he said, pointing, "that space is reserved for you—always."

God, I want a man just like this, but one who loves the Lord so much that he's scared to soil his spiritual garment. With her silent petition finished, she appraised Cameron's outer appearance. He was to be admired in a sleeveless red T-shirt, blue Khaki shorts, and white sneakers. Cameron's sculptured muscles resembled a stone Adonis.

"Why?" she repeated.

Cameron stopped and stared into her eyes. "You have a standing reservation at my house. We need to have a serious talk tonight with or without my family nearby. You're killing me with this distance, baby."

Gabrielle exhaled and finally handed over her keys.

Allowing him to move her car, she stared at the two- and three-story monasteries on his block. As they neared the front door of his home, his little nephews raced out onto the porch with water guns aimed at each other. Gabrielle stepped back, so she wouldn't get caught in the crossfire.

When two of them pumped their guns, Gabrielle braced for a splash. Instead, bubbles floated into the air. She laughed and they giggled. Cameron hiked up the steps and slipped his arm around her waist. Welcoming his comfort, she leaned into him and hugged him back.

God, please keep me from falling.

He rubbed a kiss in her hair and whispered, "Lady, you are one beautiful woman." Before he could say more, one of the miniature Jamiesons distracted them. "I said you can play with them outside in the backyard, not on my front porch. Go on, you two," Cameron ordered.

Pouting, they did as they were told and marched down the steps and around the side of the house. As Cameron steered her through the door, Gabrielle recognized one boisterous voice. Evidently, Grandma BB was in her element and providing entertainment.

The woman paused in mid-sentence to greet her. Others followed suit and offered hugs while Cameron stayed by her side.

Remembering her dessert, she shoved the container in his hand. "This should go into the refrigerator as soon as possible. I think the children will enjoy it."

Cameron snickered. "I didn't even notice it. Sorry." Instead of doing her bidding, he passed the buck and placed it in his niece's hands. "Here, do whatever she says," he instructed Parke's only daughter.

Without an argument, Kami, who was always respectful, did as Gabrielle told her. Talise had raved about the child's scholastic achievements. Gabrielle had teased that brains and looks run in the family. That's when Talise had confided that Kami was adopted. Scrutinizing the child's features again, it was hard for her to believe the girl wasn't born a Jamieson.

Glancing around Cameron's house was like watching a reenactment of a United Nations meeting. There were guests from nationalities she recognized and others who Gabrielle wouldn't dare guess. That was another thing they had in common; she and Cameron enjoyed diversity in fellowship.

The chatter continued among the women, and she turned her attention to the interior layout. It was an older home that boasted rich character in its architecture. With a hint of elegance here and there, basically, the décor reflected his personality—contemporary, and that of an intellect who was accustomed to entertaining. The dark hardwood floors glistened and hinted that a fresh coat of polish had been recently applied.

His choice of stylish mahogany furniture appeared staged for a showcase rather than practical use. Yet she didn't sense he had any reservations when it came to his guests having a good time.

People were everywhere. Guests mingled in the living room and dining room and some even congregated in the kitchen. Gabrielle chided herself for worrying about being alone with him.

"So glad you finally made it, girl." Talise squeezed her shoulders. "Cameron was really working my nerves. You could have ridden with us."

Shaking her head, Gabrielle smiled. "Nope. When I'm ready to leave, I can get in my car and go without disturbing you and your family."

"Uh-uh. I've got your keys, remember?" Cameron snuck up behind her again.

She whirled around and scrunched her nose. "Uh-huh. I've got Mace, remember?" she teased, smiling.

"Ouch. I still have flashbacks about that horrible experience." He displayed a non-convincing, frightening expression and reached for the back of his neck. Gabrielle shoved him playfully, as she began to relax.

"I would have protected you from any harm," he whispered. As if he was reading her expression, he added, "And after our very first kiss, I knew I had to protect you against me even before you brought it up. But my plan didn't include a permanent sabbatical from your lips."

"Change the subject," she warned in a whisper, because his words were starting to subdue her and that was just as bad as an actual kiss. Despite the crowd, as she had predicted, they were sucked into a private moment. That is, until Grandma BB nudged her way between them.

Suddenly dismissing Cameron, Grandma BB introduced Gabrielle to another handsome man. It was mind-boggling. "Where do you find these escorts?" she asked the older woman.

"Craigslist," Grandma BB answered with a shrug that indicated Gabrielle should have known. "A seasoned woman like me needs one or two bodyguards from time to time."

"Don't get any ideas," Cameron spoke up after suddenly reappearing. "You won't need them for bodyguards or boy toys like Grandma BB."

Just then Talise stole her away before she could respond and ushered her into the kitchen. The Jamieson wives, Cheney, Hallison, and Eva, were manning the pans of food scattered across the countertops. The massive kitchen was another magnificent room with beautifully wood-carved French doors leading to a stone-covered patio. Gabrielle looked out and noticed a volleyball net set up in a yard that seemed as big as the house. There was a crowd milling about, and it appeared as though a game was about to begin.

Questions began to form in her mind. Gabrielle came from money. Only an affluent person could afford this type of property, which was usually in the hands of well-to-do Black folks with old money passed down through generations of doctors or other professionals. Her father was the second generation in the medical field. She knew Cameron was doing well, but he had to have paid a pretty penny for this place. In spite of his financial ability, this just seemed like a lot of square footage for one man.

Clearing her throat, Gabrielle blinked. She came to have a good time, not calculate a home appraisal. "I didn't realize there would be so many people. I definitely didn't bring enough dessert."

Talise waved her hand. "Girl, please. I've learned quickly that Jamieson wives cook, regardless whose house is having a party. There's always plenty of food."

Cameron's house seemed to be a living sponge of delicacies, as visitors either dropped off a dish or carried away a plate. Although he was busy entertaining, when she glanced his way, he always had his eyes trained on her. He winked.

As soon as the sun set, guests poured out of his house and gathered to watch the fireworks. Since Cameron's home was situated between downtown and Forest Park, there were nonstop explosions of bright colors lighting up the sky.

With her goddaughter cradled in her arms, Gabrielle sat on a porch step and watched Lauren sleep.

A few minutes later, Cameron snuggled beside her and exhaled. "Whew. Being a host is like a second job." He glanced at the baby. "She's getting so big, and she's a flirt too. Just like you."

"Me?" Gabrielle faced him.

Staring into his eyes, she watched the reflection of red sparkles that rained from afar. Gabrielle didn't notice the bottle of beer in Cameron's hand until he took a swig. It was a reminder of their different convictions.

He must have read the disappointment in her expression because he dropped the bottle in the nearest trash bin. Too late. Gabrielle had already been awakened from a spiritual slumber.

"I thought you didn't drink, or at least you don't when we go out to dinner."

"I don't drink hard liquor anymore. That's what I told you."

She never wanted to be a woman who ignored the warning signs. The red sparkles had just turned into a red flag.

"I messed up, didn't I?"

"Cameron, this is your house, and I'm one of your guests. If you were involved in illegal activity, I would have left right after I got here. You're not drinking and driving, so, technically, no laws have been broken."

He seared her with an intense stare. "What aren't you saying?"

"It's a Bible quote from 1 Corinthians 10:23."

"I know the gist of that book. What does that verse say?"

"Always be prepared to give an answer to everyone who asks you to give the reason for the hope that you have in Me. But do this with gentleness and respect." God spoke 1 Peter 3:15.

Softening her heart, Gabrielle said in her most nonthreatening manner, *"'I have the right to do anything,' you say—but not everything is beneficial. 'I have the right to do anything'—but not everything is constructive.* That's what 1 Corinthians 10:23 says." She thanked God for speaking to her Spirit beforehand because she was ready to snap and write him off—yet again.

"Where Christ is, there is liberty. No harm done," Cameron said, checkmating her.

For misquoting 2 Corinthian 3:17, Gabrielle wanted to slap his kissable lips with the pocket Bible she carried in her purse. Instead, she gave him a disapproving look.

Looking away, Cameron huffed. He seemed frustrated, but definitely no more than she was. "Gabrielle, for the months we've been together, I've walked a fine line not to offend you. That was a slip-up.

Occasionally, I drink a bottle of beer with my barbecue. But I don't have any habits I can't break."

I can name a few: pride, stubbornness . . . but Gabrielle held her tongue.

"Babe, I'm a one-hundred-percent man, who has given up so much to be with you. Eventually, you're going to have to make me a priority in your life like I've made you in mine. If you keep taking from me, one day I'll have nothing left to give you. And I'm not going to let that happen."

Cameron's words hit its target—her vulnerable heart. As the sparks in the air frizzled, so did their chemistry for the remainder of the night.

Chapter Twenty-Seven

W hy does love have to be so complicated?" Gabrielle mumbled, as she drove away. Then it suddenly dawned on her that she had said the word *love* twice in one day. Shaking her head, Gabrielle checked traffic before she exited onto Forest Parkway.

"Jesus, please keep me from getting caught up in the hype. I want to be loved, I want to give love, and I want to be a wife and mother. But Lord, whenever I think Cameron and I are in sync, You show me otherwise."

On the drive home, she poured out her heart to the Lord. After pulling in front of her apartment, she couldn't recall getting off the interstate, stopping at lights, or making turns. *Whew*, she thought. Jesus had definitely been her pilot.

A few minutes later as she turned the key to her apartment, her cell phone vibrated with a text. Know this. I am praying. More than I ever have, before I lose my mind. Kiss on the cheek. C

The message caused a bittersweet smile to appear with his reference to a kiss on the cheek. Her thoughts were jumbled with too many responses, so she simply texted back: Okay.

The following week, the Duprees arrived at Lambert Airport. While waiting in a line of traffic to get her parents, Gabrielle was reminiscent about her many years in the airline industry. The perks of family flying free and free employee parking were now gone.

However, in her heart there was no regret over the decision for a career move, even with her emotional state in turmoil. As CEO, when she stepped into the offices of Nestle, Gabrielle would always perform at the top of her game.

Her new position was definitely less stressful at times when someone called in sick. There was no need to wear three hats and play catch-up on the demands of the business. Her division focused on providing excellent customer service after every sale.

Within minutes of securing a parking spot in the garage, Gabrielle swiftly walked through the airport's double doors. It wasn't long before she spotted her mother and father, with a piece of luggage by their side.

Instead of hurrying to meet them, she held back and observed their mannerisms. Dr. Bernard Dupree was handsome, distinguished, and highly confident. Her father didn't need to wear a suit to command attention. He walked with authority in every step.

Her sixty-one-year-old mother was the epitome of beauty. Veronica sparked envy among many younger women because of her healthy skin and glowing hair. The gray streaks didn't age her, but added sophistication to her persona.

Watching her father's arm protectively wrapped around her mother's waist, Gabrielle sighed. Their forty years together held a tremendous amount of bliss. At thirty, she still had hope that such an honor would eventually come her way. It was well understood that her parents were remarkably of one accord about things. With the same mindset, they had no debates about God, on how to rear children, or how they would cherish each other for the rest of their lives. For them, faithfulness was a given.

Maybe those were the expectations that she and her brothers were holding out for—that one person who could connect with them like a puzzle. Was she trying to alter Cameron to make him fit in her puzzle?

Once her parents saw her, they quickened their steps. Gabrielle met them halfway. Their hugs were strangling, but felt good.

"How's my baby?" her father asked, as he stepped back and gave her a critical once-over.

"I'm well, Daddy," she replied before diverting his attention away from her. "And you look good, Mom. Tina Turner has nothing on you. You go, girl." Her mother blushed while her father beamed proudly.

Gabrielle's bonding with her mother was so easygoing that, at times, Veronica would step out of her motherly role and act like a silly girlfriend. Gabrielle missed those times when she could fly home at the last minute for a shopping trip on the Magnificent Mile. However, Veronica set boundaries too, and Gabrielle knew when not to cross the line.

"That's what a good marriage will do for you," Bernard smarted off, as he scanned the overhead signs for the exit. "A man had better know that, including Cameron, if he intends to bend his knee for a proposal." His familiar scowl meant that was his final word.

"*Shhh*, Bernie. Our daughter's waiting for the right one." Veronica's eyes sparkled at Gabrielle. "Will we meet Cameron while we're here?"

"We'd better," her father demanded.

They exited the terminal and strolled to Gabrielle's car. Once her father situated the large bag in her trunk, the conversation turned to her brothers.

She checked her watch. "Drexel said he was leaving directly after presiding over his last case. He should already be on the road and here soon." Since her middle brother lived in Kansas City, he was only three hours away and expected to arrive sometime that evening. "Dashan had a series of meetings this morning. He'll be here later on," she reported.

Although her apartment was spacious, Gabrielle doubted anyone would complain about comfort the next couple of days. It mattered that they were together. Her parents, as well as her brothers, could easily afford suite accommodations at a swanky St. Louis hotel.

Next, her mind went to Philip. He was the only exception. Whenever a church sponsored him for a revival, the invitation included travel and hotel accommodations. But not this time. Gabrielle asked everyone to stay at her new apartment, and they all obliged.

Strapped in their seat belts, she pulled out of the garage and into traffic. "Of course, our evangelist will get in late."

"My boy," Bernard said proudly. "I'm really honored that God has blessed him with the knowledge of His Word and the anointing to preach it." He grinned. "I'm proud of all my children, but I wish you all would marry. Not that I need it, but I'll be eligible for Social Security in three years. I'm not getting any younger, and I'd like to see another generation."

"Relationships aren't what they used to be when we dated, honey."

"A spouse should be special—man or woman," her father said from the backseat.

"Got it, Dad."

They chuckled and then bounced around other subjects for the rest of the ride. A short time later, Gabrielle arrived at Willow Estate complex. Her mother gushed about the property, which resembled a lush golf course with classy apartment buildings, bungalows, and townhouses.

Once inside the apartment, they took a brief tour. Gabrielle had spent all week shopping for knickknacks and accents. The second bedroom was furnished with a full-size bed set and a sofa sleeper smaller than the one she purchased for her living room. Her parents would take the master bedroom.

It wasn't long before Mr. Dupree changed his clothes and stretched out in the recliner. Grinning satisfactorily at his wife and daughter, Bernard reached for the remote.

Veronica shook her head as she trailed Gabrielle to the kitchen. Taking on her motherly role, she began scanning the shelves in the cabinets. "Did you remember to pick up some sea salt and red wine vinegar for the green beans?" she queried.

Happy to be sharing the moment, Gabrielle grinned. "Can't sauté the green beans without them, Mom." She reached for the spices as her mother opened the refrigerator door to gather the vegetables. "You know I could have picked up a meal from a deli or restaurant," Gabrielle fussed. She always felt bad when her mother came to visit and worked. Yet the two enjoyed being in the kitchen together.

Adorned with aprons tied around their waists, they worked side by side, seasoning skinless chicken breasts and other entrees. It wasn't long before her father had dozed off. Gabrielle took the opportunity to engage her mother in a hushed conversation about Cameron.

"I love him, Mom." She sighed. "I know this is going to sound crazy." Gabrielle couldn't believe she'd dare utter it, so she took her time to phrase her words. "Mom, I've been as faithful as I know how in walking with Jesus. In fact, I think I've been a textbook saint. But, after being around the happily-ever-after Jamieson wives, I'm wondering if I'll miss out by continuing to hold my ground on points that aren't important to God."

Lifting a brow, her mother resumed flouring some biscuits and didn't respond right away. Finally, she cleared her throat. "So you want to compromise?"

"I want to be loved and to love. I want children. Can a man who professes his salvation be enough to take him at his word? I feel like I'm starting to run out of options," Gabrielle whined.

Veronica rinsed her hands and dried them. Giving her daughter a hug, she replied, "Don't give up. God has the right man for you. Don't grieve God by dismissing what you know, even if your blessing is delayed."

Gabrielle refrained from voicing to her mother that she was tired of living alone, eating alone, traveling alone, and even going to bed alone. Cameron's looks, touches, and sweet words seemed to magnify the emptiness in her life. She wanted the companionship of a good saved and sanctified husband.

"If Cameron isn't the one, then we need to pray that God move faster. Between you and me, I'm becoming emotionally overwhelmed."

Trust Me, Jesus spoke.

God, help me, she silently pleaded.

"Is Cameron pressuring you?" Veronica asked, concerned.

Gabrielle smiled. "Actually, he's been very accommodating, but the carnal desires do rise up. He's a good catch, and he's cocky enough to know it."

Her mother responded, "I'm trying to read between the lines, and I'm not quite sure what you're trying to tell me by not telling me. My advice is to live your life free from the guilt of sin. Have no regrets about your steadfastness with God."

As Veronica slid the pan of biscuits into the oven, she hummed a familiar gospel tune. Gabrielle enjoyed the melody, as they worked together to clean up the mess.

Before Veronica took off her apron and walked out of the kitchen, she whispered, "Work with the Holy Ghost on this. Don't take the lead. God sees Cameron's heart, and He knows your desires. Just like Hannah prayed for a son, He knows you're praying for a husband."

Nodding, Gabrielle accepted her mother's advice with tears in her eyes. She wanted to go somewhere and hide; she felt like crying to relieve some of her pain. This whole love emotion had her heart aching.

While dinner baked, she sat quietly reflecting on her mother's counsel. Veronica had been married longer than she had been single. Her mother tied the knot at age twenty. Gabrielle just recently hit thirty.

Her phone vibrated, indicating someone had sent a text. Picking it up off the counter, Gabrielle tapped the screen: I wanted you to know

I'm thinking about you. Don't give up on us. Cam.

Typing back: Give me one reason, she pressed Send.

Because I love you, Cameron immediately texted back.

Those four words seemed to warm her heart. She thought about responding with her own declaration, but chose to withhold it. *Nah*, she said to herself while slipping the phone into her purse. That way she'd be sure not to forget it in the morning.

Being an old-fashioned girl, she would have preferred Cameron tell her face-to-face that he loved her. She had scribbled the anticipation of that "wow" moment in her handbook of romance a long time ago. More than the feeling of Cameron's comforting arms, God knew she needed to hear those comforting words.

In a reflective moment, Gabrielle closed her eyes and pondered Cameron's text. As her mood began to lighten, she took a deep breath. After a minute or two, she headed to the front bedroom. The additional bed linen she had purchased during a shopping spree with Talise was stored there.

Stepping out of the closet, Gabrielle paused, hearing familiar voices outside in the parking lot. She flung open the French doors and leaned over the rail, grinning from ear to ear. Drexel and her middle brother, Dashan, had somehow arrived at the same time. "Get up here, you two, so I can get my hugs," Gabrielle yelled, waving furiously as if they couldn't see her.

Buzzing them inside the building, she waited impatiently while they raced up the stairs. Dashan was first to lift her off the floor with a gripping hug. Drexel stood by until it was his turn.

Bernard had stirred from the recliner and was standing in the background. As the siblings drew closer to their parents, the brothers followed the ritual of shaking hands with their father and kissing their mother. Before the greetings ended, they smothered Veronica and Gabrielle with strong hugs.

Being surrounded by her family, everything seemed right in her world. For the first time in days, Gabrielle felt content. For a brief moment, she wondered how soon it would be before one of them expanded the fold. That thought caused a frown to appear on her face. Clearly, Gabrielle had been giving too much attention to marriage lately.

None of them seemed to be in a race to the finish line. Tall, with pecan-colored skin, Dashan opted for the bald look. Although she had to admit it looked good on him, Cameron wore the look better. Drexel preferred weekly barbershop visits and sported a well-manicured mustache. Still, there was no mistaking they were brothers.

Showing them to her guest bedroom, the two brothers good-naturedly joked about who would get the bed. Dashan concluded the dispute with, "You're the old man, bro. So you'd better take the mattress. It'll help your posture."

Drexel shot him a friendly warning look.

Once everyone was settled, Veronica announced dinner was ready. After washing up, they gathered around the bistro-height kitchen table ensemble.

With heads bowed, Bernard said the grace. "Oh, great and mighty God, we worship You for Your blessings on us today. Thank You for the spiritual health of this family. God, we praise You for allowing us safe travels. Protect Philip as he makes his way to join us. Please sanctify our food and help us to remember those who go without that we may be a blessing to them."

After the family ended the prayer with a chorus of "In Jesus' Name, Amen," the dishes and utensils began to clang. The mood was light and festive. First, Dashan complimented Gabrielle on her choice of living location and décor. His next statement was one that she could have lived without.

"Tell me about Cameron," Dashan asked before taking a bite of his biscuit.

Gabrielle knew that name would be mentioned sooner or later.

"When I first met him, I didn't get a good feeling about him," Drexel offered before she could say anything. "I don't care for his cockiness, as if he's God's gift to women. My spirit just doesn't bear witness with his as a practicing Christian. If I could get Gabrielle to come to Springfield one weekend, I would introduce her to some bona-fide, good Christian men."

Their father chewed his food slowly. He didn't comment, but she knew her father's mind was processing everything spoken. On the other hand, her mother seemed unfazed by Drexel's assessment. She was the next to speak up. "Son, you may preside over important cases every day. But outside the courtroom, we have to rely on God to reveal a person's motives. Gabrielle is steadfast in her salvation. She'll be diligent, watchful, and prayerful." She winked at her daughter.

"Thank you, Momma."

"Noted, but while Gabrielle is praying, you'd better believe I'm watching," Drexel said with finality.

"Now you have me curious about this Cameron Jamieson. Our brother has painted this picture of a monster. Hopefully, while we're here we can meet him and judge for ourselves. The pun is definitely intended. Court adjourned." Dashan grinned at his brother, then stood and headed to the stove for seconds.

Thanks to Drexel, Cameron was going to be a hard sell to her family. But Cameron's love for her was a source of encouragement. It gave her hope that he would admit to his shortcomings and completely surrender to God.

Once the dessert was eaten and the kitchen cleaned, the family reminisced about past vacations and even the old neighborhood. Everyone was trying their best to stay awake for Philip's late arrival.

The church's armor bearer would drop Philip off at Gabrielle's place.

As they waited, the day's travel began to take its toll. One by one, the family members nodded until the door buzzer startled them.

Scrambling to the intercom, Gabrielle verified her visitor and then flung open the door. Visibly exhausted, Philip dragged himself up the two flights of stairs. Once he cleared the threshold, everyone vied for his attention.

"Hungry?" Veronica asked but didn't wait for his answer. She immediately headed to the kitchen to warm up a plate.

A few minutes later, they gathered around the table for a second time. Between bites of food, Philip shared testimonies about God's amazing works during his recent revival services.

Finally, he wiped his mouth and pushed back from the table. Everyone took that as a signal to retire. Veronica made sure the kitchen was tidy before she joined her husband. Unfortunately, Gabrielle should have already been in bed. Without accruing any vacation days as yet, she had to work in the morning. Her family could rest or enjoy a day of sightseeing.

Gathering toiletries from her bedroom, Gabrielle headed for the guest bathroom. While she played with the water temperature, the thought of her family sleeping under one roof caused a feeling of security to sweep over her. Although she admired the Jamiesons for their closeness, her own family was just as close in their own way. No complaints.

By the time she finished and dressed in her pajamas, the apartment was completely quiet. Philip was already under the covers, knocked out on the sleeper in the living room. Smiling, she kissed her brother's forehead before claiming the other sofa.

After thanking God for His many blessings, she made herself comfortable and closed her eyes. Suddenly remembering her cell phone needed to be charged, Gabrielle reached for her purse laying on the end table. Instantly, she noticed an unread text. It was from Cameron hours ago.

Did your family make it in safely?

Yes, she typed and hit Send before going into the kitchen to retrieve her charger. Plugging in her phone, she saw that Cameron had already responded. It was about twelve-thirty. She was sure he would have been asleep.

I can't wait to meet them.

Gabrielle shook her head and responded. They're more eager to meet you. If you thought Drexel was a force to be reckoned with, be prepared. Warning: I'm the only daughter.

Cameron texted back again: Caution: I'm a man in love, waiting for a certain woman to return my affection. I'm fearless when it comes to you.

Rolling her eyes, Gabrielle blushed at the same time. Of all the men in the world, why did she have to be attracted to a man who seemed lacking in the one area she deemed most important? Why couldn't he channel that determination for Christ?

You are planning on coming to the tent meeting tomorrow evening about seven? Right? She texted back, holding her breath.

Yes. The Jamiesons will be there. My mother is preparing a spread at my house afterward. I'll see you then. Love, Cam.

Forget Battle of the Bands, it may turn out to be a battle of the families, she thought.

This ought to be interesting.

Chapter Twenty-Eight

Strolling through the door of his house, Cameron sniffed the aroma seeping from his state-of-the art kitchen. With a spare key, his mother had let herself in. She was preparing a repast for the Duprees after the tent service that night. He kissed her cheek and began to peep inside the pans.

"I like her," Charlotte Jamieson said, as if they had been in the middle of a conversation.

"I love her. You'll love her too, Mom." Cameron waited for his mother to say something. "You don't seem surprised. What tipped you off?"

"You know there are no secrets in this family. Your brothers told me that love is in the air. I noticed at the barbecue that whenever you were around Gabrielle, you had this certain softness. I could sense that there are sparks between the two of you, but she seems hesitant. Cameron, I don't have to tell you this, so I'll just remind you. Women need to be made sure of a man's intentions. Don't give her a reason to doubt your affections." Charlotte sighed. She was wearing a faraway expression that turned into a frown. "Don't mess this up, Cam. For some reason, my sons have an uncanny skill of initially running a good woman away. Thank God He gave the girls a change of heart."

"Relationships are about give and take." Cameron shook his head. "That woman challenges me on everything."

Charlotte's brown eyes twinkled with amusement. "Good for her!"

"Funny you'd say that. Gabrielle makes it seem as if the package I'm offering isn't good enough."

"Sometimes, it's not what's on the outside that a woman wants. It's what's on the inside that counts," his mother said.

"Right, she's had a glimpse of that part of me too." He glanced at his watch. "Thanks for doing this, Mom. I'd better shower and change."

"Son, I'll tell you like I've told your brothers. You may think you're all that, but usually what a good woman wants from a good man is the least he's willing to give."

Cameron lifted his brow. "I know you're speaking in some kind of female code, but I don't have time to crack it right now. I have to go and shower before it's time to go back into the hot St. Louis humidity." Then, reminded of the night's event, he threw up his arms. "The things a man endures for a woman. What's with this tent thing? Doesn't that church have a building to hold their services?"

"Stop being so puffed up. That's not who we are," Charlotte scolded. She snickered until it turned into a fit of giggles. "I guess since you won't come to church, Jesus is bringing the church to you. It serves you right that Gabrielle's brother is a preacher. You can't run from God now."

"Who says I'm running? I just prefer the comfort of a cushioned seat in an air-conditioned building," he said.

"And you barely come then. You didn't complain when it was just as hot and your house swelled with guests for the holiday barbecue," she reminded him. "God is user-friendly . . ."

To escape her harping on his lack of commitment to attend church services, Cameron headed upstairs. What was wrong with his family?

He did attend church. Then again, after taking a pause in his thinking, he had to admit it had been a while.

Cameron took his time showering and getting dressed. Later, when he returned to the kitchen, his mother was nowhere in sight. *She must have gone back home to get ready for the big night.* He chuckled at his own sarcastic thought.

Cameron didn't know which irritated him more, the St. Louis summer humidity or the fact that he had to impress Gabrielle's family by sitting through tonight's service. Listening to a man scream Scriptures for several hours wasn't exactly his idea of a fun evening. Begrudgingly, he got behind the wheel of his Audi. Ten minutes later, he was curbside in the park.

The gigantic, white vinyl, makeshift tent could not be missed. Stepping out of his car, Cameron stared. The time was a quarter to seven, and it didn't look like the preacher had much of a crowd.

He had just activated his car alarm and was about to cross the street when more family members' cars drove up to the curb and parked. Cameron smirked at the possibility that they had synchronized the time of their arrival.

Upon entering the tent, it didn't take much effort to spot Gabrielle and her family. Of course, they claimed seats near the front. Muscular built men seated on either side seemed to swallow up Gabrielle and her mother.

His family was eager for introductions, but Cameron held them off. He didn't want to overwhelm the Duprees and thought it best that he get in on their good graces first.

"You'll meet them afterward at the house," he told them. Making his trek down the grass aisle to the front, the only prayer Cameron wanted answered was an unrealistic one. He hoped that the service wouldn't last more than thirty minutes—and that was pushing it.

The older gentleman occupying the end seat had to be Gabrielle's father. Cameron kicked up his charm a few notches.

"Excuse me, sir. I'm Cameron Jamieson."

"Bernard Dupree." Her father stood and gripped his hand in a hearty shake.

Cameron returned his strength and maintained eye contact so Bernard would know he wasn't easily intimidated. "Nice to meet you, Dr. Dupree."

"This is my beautiful wife, Veronica," he boasted, as he motioned toward her.

She was a mature version of his lovely Gabrielle. "Mrs. Dupree," Cameron greeted. Her parents made a striking older couple. Both were casually dressed in cool, but stylish attire. Their polished mannerisms hinted they had class.

Cameron was in awe of Gabrielle's resemblance to her mother. If the myth proved true about how to tell what a woman would look like in her older years, by observing Gabrielle's mother, then he was in for a real treat. That is, if he and Gabrielle could move past their differences. She had yet to profess her love for him.

"Dashan." The man sitting next to Gabrielle said, as he rose to his feet and shook hands.

Reluctantly, Drexel—the judge who had judged him without knowing him—stood. But no handshake was forthcoming. The most Cameron got from him was a nod.

Gabrielle popped up from her seat with a smile that brightened her face and made him forget they weren't alone. He whispered in her ear, "You look so pretty." Then, without hesitating, he added, "I do love you."

She sucked in her breath at his face-to-face declaration. "Stop flirting with me in front of my family," she mumbled, then shooed Drexel to scoot down a chair.

"I hope you came with your praise shoes on, young man. My son is a gifted man of God," Bernard boasted, leaning across his wife and Dashan.

"I came interested in his style of delivering the message," Cameron said. Looking around, he caught his own brothers staring at him. Besides the Jamiesons and the Duprees, there were a few curious bystanders outside the tent who dared not come inside.

"I do hope more people show up."

"God has an appointed time for everyone to hear His message. They'll come," Mrs. Dupree said confidently.

As the musicians walked onto the stage and took their places, Cameron reached for Gabrielle's hand. "You really do look pretty and cool in this heat."

"Thank you. Compliments swell one's head, so I'll leave it at I'm glad you came," she replied.

"Did I pass my first inspection?"

Gabrielle shrugged just as a piercing sound echoed through the tent.

A woman fumbled with the microphone on stage. "Praise the Lord, everybody! Praise the Lord!" She clapped, as she attempted to stir up the handful in the audience to follow her lead.

Cameron heard shouts of "Hallelujah" from behind him. He didn't have to turn around to know the praises came from his clan. His family could always have church without being in one. It was no surprise that, at the mention of a tent meeting, they didn't even wait for an invite.

"We are truly in for a treat this weekend. God is good and we were able to snag world-renowned, Holy Ghost–filled preacher, Evangelist Philip Dupree. Let's pray that God will use him mightily to minister to the people of St. Louis."

She glanced down at a small piece of paper. "There are water bottles in the back and the ushers have plenty of fans to keep you cool. So relax and praise the Lord with us!"

As band members stood and blew their horns, the drummer set his rhythm. The same woman who greeted the audience got behind the keyboards. Within seconds, the crew had initiated a gospel music jam fest.

Gabrielle and her family were immediately on their feet. In sync, they swayed to the beat. Instinctively, his conscience told him to join them and follow suit, but Cameron reasoned he was his own man.

He was a leader, not a follower. Looking around for an usher, he requested a fan. After nodding his thanks, Cameron relaxed, crossed an ankle over his knee, and kept beat by moving his shoe.

The crowd began to grow until there was standing room only around the packed tent. It was hot, it was humid, and it was a Friday night. Yet these people made an effort to be there. Cameron figured it had to be the music that drew them.

As soon as the concert seemed to be in full throttle, a tall man who resembled Gabrielle walked up the few steps to the stage, carrying a worn Bible. In front of a folding chair, seemingly reserved for him, he turned his back to the crowd, knelt, and prayed.

Gabrielle tapped his thigh. "That's Philip."

"I could tell." But he had already lost her attention to the excitement over seeing her brother.

After taking his seat, Philip glanced in the direction of his family and smiled. It was the same smile Gabrielle had graced Cameron with many times. The evangelist made eye contact with him and they exchanged nods.

Several minutes later, after he was formally introduced, Philip stepped up to the microphone to a hardy and enthusiastic applause. Closing his eyes, he stretched his arms high in the air and instructed the crowd to shout praises toward heaven. Then, without further preliminaries, he dove into his sermon.

"Most of you are a bit uncomfortable because of the weather, so this won't take long. We're all about comfort. Heat in the winter, cool air in the summer, a luxury car, a spacious home . . ."

Cameron liked Philip already. Philip was speaking his language. Perking up, he folded his arms and focused.

"Our wants appear only to be a remote click away. What more could a man ask for?" He paused and looked around the audience.

"How about a three-car garage and a beautiful wife? And if she isn't enough, then add a few babes on the side. After all, everybody's doing it. Am I right?"

Various responses rippled through the crowd. Some snickered, including Cameron, but Philip's expression didn't change. Although Cameron never cheated when he was in a committed relationship, Philip's stone expression made him uncomfortable.

"I have yet to meet a man or family named 'Everybody' who I want to emulate." Philip continued running down a laundry list of the woes that come as a result of a sky-is-the-limit lifestyle. "Keep over-indulging, and you'll soon spin out of control. A portion of Luke 16:15 says, *'What people value is highly detestable in God's sight'.* Friends, money cannot buy you a reservation in the kingdom."

Lifting up his Bible, Philip shouted, "Jesus is the senior reservationist and the only one who can save you from yourself. In Him, we live and move and have our being. The Bible tells us in 1 Timothy 6:17, *'Command those who are rich in this present world not to be arrogant nor to put their hope in wealth, which is so uncertain, but to put their hope in God, who richly provides us with everything for our enjoyment.'"*

His dramatic preaching style charged the crowd. Chancing a glance around, Cameron was amazed that the audience had swollen, which made the air even thicker. The looks on their faces made many people appear hungry, like they were feasting on every word out of his mouth.

"If you want riches, power, and wisdom—look to Jesus. God put mansions inside of a house, not the other way around. Read the Scripture for yourself. In John 14:2, the King James Version says, *'In My Father's house are many mansions.'* That should blow your mind because I still can't fathom it." Philip paused to wipe his face with a handkerchief resting on the podium. The harder he preached, the more he sweated. Finally, he turned to the musicians. When he nodded, they began to play softly.

"This is the part of the service where God doesn't care what you look like, what you have or don't have. He's looking at a soul that needs nourishment. Won't you come today and let Jesus save you? Repent from where you are standing and come to the altar . . ."

Many rushed to the front almost in a stampede manner. Cameron couldn't believe the throng of people who flocked down the aisle. There seemed to be no end in sight. Some were in tears with anguish and sweat dripping from their faces. Philip patiently listened, then one by one, he laid hands on each person's head and prayed for them. He treated everyone as if they were the only person in line.

Cameron didn't see his folks until the crowd finally thinned. He excused himself from Gabrielle and headed toward them. Ace met him halfway.

"That brother can preach, can't he?" His cousin seemed impressed.

"He definitely fired up the troops."

"But did the Word light your fire?" Ace gave him a curious look.

"Everything was common sense." Cameron responded with a shrug. "Frankly, I was amazed that others found his preaching so mind-boggling. I know that everything I have, God gave me the ability to get it, and I thank Him every day. I don't live beyond my means."

Ace nodded. "True, bro, but your pride has pushed you to the brim. Step off your high horse and repent like the rest of us."

Before returning to his wife and child, Ace gave Cameron a mock salute. "That is all."

Chapter Twenty-Nine

*I*t was almost ten o'clock when Cameron's house came alive for the repast. The Jamiesons never missed a meal or a reason to get together as a family. Refreshed and energized, they barged through the front door. Despite the hour, the children looked ready to get into something.

When Cameron was a child, his father, Parke V, declared every Friday night to be game time as a way to strengthen the family bond. Plus, the weekly exercise served as an opportunity to ingrain their African-American heritage into his three boys. It was during that time when the Jamieson sons were recharged and reinforced to be the confident Black men their dad reared them to be.

As the three brothers grew older and became involved in school-based activities, the weekly family game night turned into a monthly event. Now, with expanding and extended families involved, it was a struggle to keep that tradition. Still, everybody was expected to show up for family game night every other month.

Cameron's house was abuzz as the Jamieson wives stormed in and took over the kitchen. Cheney and Hallison warmed the food that

Charlotte had prepared. Talise and Eva set the table with plates, napkins, and utensils.

What a contrast to the Duprees, who rang the bell and waited to be invited inside. Gabrielle's family would soon learn that they would only be treated as guests once. After that, they would simply be considered family. A round of introductions was made before Charlotte announced everyone could wash up and eat.

Unsure of how to address Gabrielle's brother Philip, Cameron decided he couldn't go wrong with the formal route. After all, in academia, he was addressed as Dr. Jamieson. Otherwise, he was comfortable with being called Cameron.

"Evangelist Dupree, do you mind blessing our meal?" he asked politely.

It was an honor usually reserved for Cameron's father, who understood and graciously acquiesced. Surprisingly, the blessing was short and to the point, not a sermonette. For that, Cameron was grateful. In unison, they all echoed, "In the Name of Jesus. Amen."

Although there wasn't a shortage of seats, the children preferred eating on the staircase, with the older children babysitting the younger ones.

Every time Cameron tried to coax Gabrielle to the side, one of the Jamieson wives grabbed her. The conversation bouncing off the walls consisted of a potpourri of subjects. When Cameron was finally about to pull Gabrielle from the clutches of the women, Philip stirred from his corner seat and headed toward the table for seconds.

"Thank you for the refreshments," he cordially said in a deep tone. "Do you have a few minutes for us to talk?"

"As long as it's not another sermon, sure," Cameron joked, as he led them to a nook off the kitchen. Initiating their talk, he addressed Philip, "You really work up a sweat out there without trying. Your message was so simplistic, yet the people responded as if their lightbulbs had just clicked on."

Philip nodded. "For some, it did. Jesus is deeply profound, yet the Bible says He saves us through the foolishness of preaching." He chuckled. "Who can figure out the mind of God?"

"If people read their Bibles, God will open their understanding," Cameron argued good-naturedly.

"Then perhaps you're familiar with Romans 10:12–15: *'For there is no difference between Jew and Gentile—the same Lord is Lord of all and richly blesses all who call on him, for, "Everyone who calls on the name of the Lord will be saved." How, then, can they call on the one they have not believed in? And how can they believe in the one of whom they have not heard? And how can they hear without someone preaching to them? And how can anyone preach unless they are sent? As it is written: "How beautiful are the feet of those who bring good news!"'"*

Cameron quietly considered Philip's explanation. Although he had a rebuttal lined up, Philip changed the subject.

"How long have you known my sister?" he asked casually, as though he were Gabrielle's father. Cameron guessed the two of them were about the same age.

Smiling, Cameron recalled the moment he laid eyes on Gabrielle. "We met at my cousin and Talise's renewal of vows ceremony in the spring."

"My sister is exceptional; she's not to be toyed with. I'm not saying you would harm her intentionally, but you need to know that she has a special place in my heart and God's. I love her and will protect her no matter how far away I am. However, make no mistake about this also. My sister is very capable of taking care of herself."

"Don't I know it," Cameron mumbled, recalling the Mace incident. Cameron wasn't offended by the older brother's protective stance.

Reaching inside his shirt front pocket, Philip pulled out his business card and handed it to Cameron. "I'm on call 24/7 for the Lord. In case you need clarification on anything we've discussed—about the Scriptures or my sister." He grinned with the same contagious smile as Gabrielle.

Cameron had the gist about the sixty-six books in the Bible. He already knew the major Scriptures, so there was nothing new Philip could bring to the table that his cousins hadn't previously attempted. Out of politeness, he accepted the card but doubted he would ever use it.

—⁓—

Gabrielle felt his presence before she heard Cameron's voice saying, "Excuse me, ladies. I believe you have someone who belongs to me."

Without protest, the women relinquished her, as if Cameron was the Big Bad Wolf. Stretching out his hand, Gabrielle accepted it without hesitation. She had wanted a moment alone with him. The two stepped outside onto the patio.

She shivered. Once again, he had succeeded in making her feel like they were the only ones in a room full of people—family, at that.

"Cold?" he asked.

"No."

In spite of her response, he put his arms around her. "I've got you, babe. And I've been waiting to hear something from you."

Before she confessed her feelings, Gabrielle had something else on her mind. She gazed into his eyes. "I belong to you, really? I belong to Jesus. He purchased my freedom with His blood."

"Why do our conversations always have to revert to biblical thoughts?"

"Because I'm programmed like that. But, with you in love with me . . ." When Gabrielle's eyes misted, she hesitated to continue and bowed her head.

Cameron captured her chin and lifted her face to meet his stare. His touch and expression were so tender. "But what, babe?"

"You were right about giving me so freely of yourself. But when it comes to any discussion of Jesus, you continue to cut me off. More than once, I wondered what you were thinking when Philip preached." She paused again. "So . . . what were you thinking this evening?"

"Things have changed between us." He lowered his voice, considering that the commotion around them meant someone might overhear. "You know that."

When she nodded, his smile was breathtaking. Tapping his temple, Cameron explained, "Inside of me is a man nobody knows. I barely recognize that part of me myself, but I know that I want to share him with you."

"What happens when I get inside but can't find my way out of your maze?" she whispered, still waiting for him to answer her question.

Reaching down for her hands, Cameron squeezed them. "Gabrielle Dupree, I have this feeling you're on a search-and-rescue mission. The crazy thing about it is you're my only way out."

"But will I get lost in the process?"

"We can find our way together," he said, gazing into her eyes.

Once she blinked, Gabrielle persisted for an answer. "What did you think of the sermon Philip preached?"

"He's the best I've heard yet, and the message was stirring." Cameron must have read the expression on her face because he lowered his voice again. "I will always tell you the truth and that is the truth. So am I in or out of the doghouse?"

Unable to hold back her feelings any longer, she laughed and gave him a tight squeeze. Seizing the opportunity, he trapped her in a long embrace. Finally, he rested his chin on the top of her head.

When they separated, Gabrielle walked ahead of him. Back inside the house, they headed for the living room where there was a bevy of activity. She noticed Philip dozing in a large chair, despite the boisterous conversations.

"We'd better go before Philip asks for a pillow and blanket," she whispered.

"Okay. I guess I need to put my folks out anyway."

They engaged in a longer embrace before Gabrielle announced it was time to leave. Cameron made good on his threat and cleared his house of all Jamiesons too.

A few hours later, Gabrielle lay awake stretched out on her sofa. Replaying Cameron's words in her mind, she conjured up Scriptures for and against Cameron. Then she chided herself, knowing what she was getting into after the first, second, and third date with him. Then too, at every step of the way, Gabrielle had second-guessed God when He reminded her that He could keep her from falling. She had to trust the Lord.

Philip's light snoring caused her to chuckle. After they had returned to her apartment, Gabrielle hoped to get Philip's take on Cameron, but he looked wiped out.

Another time, she thought. Rolling over, she closed her eyes.

Suddenly, a soft whisper was uttered from Philip's lips. "Who knows the mind of God? It's up to us to trust Him."

His words caused her to smile. He must have read her mind. "Thank you, brother," she whispered back.

"It's evangelist to you."

Chuckling, Gabrielle snuggled under the covers and drifted off to sleep.

On Saturday afternoon, Cameron returned to the tent revival without any prompting. Her heart warmed at the sight of him. Once again, he forced her family to move down and make room for him. Talise and Eva also returned.

Settling into the seat next to her, Cameron winked. She smiled and relaxed into him, as he stretched his arm over the back of her chair. For some reason, she was in a touchy-feely mood after their talk the previous night. Her wayward thoughts dissipated as Philip's electrifying sermon from Psalm 94:11—*"The Lord knows all human plans; he knows that they are futile"*—stirred her spirit.

Glancing at Cameron, who seemed more relaxed too, disappointment began to resurface. Not one "Amen" spilled from his mouth, nor did he offer one clap. But she had to stop judging him on what she saw or didn't see. God knew all things. The crowd was larger than the night before. It truly was a revival in the neighborhood.

The weekend sped by. On Sunday afternoon, the church that sponsored Philip's trip provided a celebration dinner for him. Then it was time for Gabrielle's family to leave. She bid Dashan and Drexel goodbye and they drove back to their respective homes. Now, at the airport, she and her parents had a few more minutes for goodbyes before they went through the checkpoint.

"Of all my children, I never worried about you making a bad choice in a mate. Maybe because you were always so choosy. Cameron has a great family. They're all fire and water baptized. He's connected to them, but I saw a slight disconnect when we spoke about God. What's his story?" her father asked.

"That's a six-hundred-page novel. There's so much about Cameron that's right, but a few things are making me proceed with caution."

"Honey, your mind might be confused, but your heart has left you way behind," Veronica told her daughter, as they hugged. "So now you're in the middle of the test. Study God's Word, so you'll pass. Failing is not an option."

Chapter Thirty

I am *so* jealous!" Denise practically shouted into the phone. After Gabrielle gave her a recap of the weekend happenings, she was beside herself. "You're spending more time with the Jamiesons than I am."

Gabrielle laughed, twisting the strand of pearls around her neck. She imagined her friend's fake pout.

Sitting in her office, waiting for an important call, she responded, "Well, don't be jealous. Philip was in town, and it was all about the souls."

Hoping to calm Denise down a bit, she explained everything. "I invited Talise, and the rest of the family decided to come along too. Then Talise and her sister-in-law, Eva, came back the next day. I have to tell you, when I saw Cameron walk in, I could barely believe my eyes. Since I've lived here, he's never made that much effort to come to a service with me."

"Hmm, so was his presence the proof you need to stop fighting your feelings? There are only so many men in the world. If you keep turning them down, you're going to run out of candidates. In my opinion, Cameron is the most qualified to give you your heart's desires."

"Sounds like nepotism to me," Gabrielle teased, relishing in how Cameron felt about her, but still withholding those words he wanted to hear.

"Listen, I'm not as spiritually connected as you . . ." Denise always began serious conversations this way. She was referring to Gabrielle having an edge over her with a preacher in the family. "But I believe in my heart that my cousin is a good guy," she stated emphatically.

Giggling, Gabrielle had to put an end to her friend's pleading. "Your cousin told me that he loves me."

"What?" Denise whooped and screamed in Gabrielle's ear. "You had me go through all that when evidently things seem to be under control."

"I wouldn't go that far and say everything's under control. However, it does change the dynamic of our relationship. But even for those three little words, I won't let my heart compromise. I want a godly man."

"Girl, please. Cameron is as saintly as you'll get. We all have a few vices."

Listening to Denise made Gabrielle recall one of her pet peeves: making excuses for bad behavior and wrong choices. Maybe that's why she was emotionally tortured when it came to Cameron.

"Some vices can't be overlooked. For example, what if I become sick after I'm married? There will be nothing more romantic and comforting than to hear my husband pray for me." She sighed. "That is making love."

"Yeah, well, we definitely have to get you hitched soon—if you think laying hands on the sick is making love."

"Love is more than sex, Denise. If I've submitted to my husband, then he'd better have a hotline to God and know how to handle me with tenderness."

"Girl, you really are a dreamer."

"I'm a romantic. In hindsight, maybe I should have never gone to din—"

"No, honey, I don't think Cameron would have let you walk away. I—and your friend Talise—had his back. So you were cornered, sister. He loves you and you might as well 'fess up your feelings. Everything will work out," Denise said.

Since Cameron and Denise have discovered they were cousins, Gabrielle was frustrated that it was harder to engage in an impartial conversation about the man. Still, she had concerns and planned on venting them, even if Denise did view her issues with Cameron as trivial.

"I'm forcing myself to pay closer attention to detail. Don't you think it's odd that everyone in his family—brothers, cousins, and parents—are passionate Christians, yet he acts as if he's numb to hearing God's Word preached?"

"Did you not say Cameron came both evenings?" Denise pressed on.

"Yes, and he sat through the whole time without mumbling an Amen or—"

"Hold up. You don't even sound like my friend. Remember the woman who is known for giving people the benefit of the doubt? Yet somehow doubt is running the show when it comes to you and Cameron. Stop looking for things to be wrong," Denise admonished her.

That statement about giving people the benefit of the doubt knocked the wind out of Gabrielle's argument, shutting her mouth. She had no further comeback. The line was silent.

Denise sensed that she'd probably given Gabrielle enough tongue-lashing. "In the end, you know, I'm always on your side," she uttered in a softened tone.

Clearing her throat, Denise then changed the subject. "Now what I was really calling for, before you distracted me, was to give you news about a Jamieson family reunion. My family and I have really been digging into old records online, the censuses, and the Jamieson message boards." Excitedly, she proclaimed, "And, I've found the perfect place!"

"Where?" Gabrielle asked, trying to shake off the hurt feelings. What Denise had said about her character was true. Up until she met Cameron, she did give people the benefit of the doubt. She had always searched for the best in others.

"It's our namesake, called the Jemison-Van de Graaff Mansion in Tuscaloosa, Alabama. Sis has been reading up on it. We're wondering if we may be distantly related to the original owner," Denise said with triumph.

Recovered from her brief pity-party moment, Gabrielle sat straighter. "Wow. You have been working. Do you really think that the name Jemison could be connected to your Jamieson name?"

"Well, it's not unusual to have different spellings for one name. I found Jamieson without the 'e' and Jemison with an 'e' instead of an 'a.' Now, get this." Denise picked up speed. "From what Cameron shared with me, Elaine, our great-forgot-her-number-grandmother, was the slaveholder's daughter. Paki—with the same-forgotten-number-grandfather—wasn't enslaved for long. I guess Elaine made sure of that. When they escaped her father's plantation, it was a Robert Jamieson who helped them along the way."

"Okay . . ." Gabrielle stuttered, totally confused. However, the last thing she wanted to do was downplay her friend's commitment to the project.

"Well, the nice Robert Jamieson is somehow related to this dude in Alabama who happened to be one of the largest slaveholders in the state. The mansion even has remains of slave quarters on the property."

Gabrielle shivered at the sufferings of people based on their skin color. It was one thing to study the atrocities of civilizations occurring thousands of years ago. But slave mentality still existed almost one hundred and fifty years after the Emancipation Proclamation and less than fifty years after the Civil Rights Movement. When Gabrielle thought about such disturbing times so close to home, she prayed for Jesus to return soon.

Denise finished talking and waited for her to respond.

Gabrielle exhaled. "Wow. Look at you, Detective Denise."

"I want you to come too."

She choked. "Me? I'm not family. I just know too many of you all."

"Don't go there. Who knows, you could be a Jamieson if you stop playing hard to get."

"I'll pretend I didn't hear that last part." She was not about to return to that topic. "When are you planning this big event?" Gabrielle held her breath. Maybe it would be while she was out of the country on business or something.

"Labor Day weekend."

"Like Labor Day two months from now? Why so soon?"

"We have a brother and sister who are already gone. Why wait and possibly lose another loved one? It won't be anything fancy. Plus, I'm a little curious to see if the White side of the Jamiesons will show up."

"I don't know. I'll think about it."

"Umm-hmm. That sounds too close to a no to me."

Gabrielle hurried off the phone before Denise could further pressure her to commit. A few minutes later, Cameron sent a text: **Missing you and still loving you. Cam.**

Fortunately, she didn't have time to think about it. At the last minute, Gabrielle had been added to a conference call, which lasted more than two hours. Where her morning had been a lull, her afternoon was a storm of activity with rumors of a new product launch.

She couldn't wait until the day was over, and it showed when she left thirty minutes earlier than normal. Having skipped over lunch, the only thing on her mind was food. Gabrielle was prepared to go home, throw together some spaghetti, and eat alone. Cameron had a prior commitment to some charity event or something.

She had to give him credit. No one could ever say Cameron Jamieson didn't give back to the community in the form of time and money. Everyone benefited, except the Lord.

Turning into the complex, she noticed Cameron's Audi. First, a frown appeared and then a smile. Why was he sitting outside on a bench near the front door? What a total surprise. She grinned.

Out of the corner of her eye, Gabrielle watched him as she parked. With a swagger he had copyrighted, Cameron was there to open the car door. "Why aren't you at home getting ready for your meeting or whatever?"

He didn't answer until he had helped her out. "Besides being tired and still missing and loving you, I was summoned to your place by a certain relative. She instructed me to use whatever means necessary to persuade you to come to the Jamieson family reunion. All in all, those were good enough reasons for me to bow out of my meeting."

Even in heels, she didn't match his height, but she met his stare. His good looks covered his weariness and his eyes didn't hide the excitement of seeing her.

"So I'm here to see my woman," he whispered.

Exhaling, she shook her head to break his pull. "Umph, umph, umph. That Denise." Gabrielle scrunched her nose and announced, "She could have saved you the trip. I had already figured if she could crash a wedding, I could crash a family reunion."

"Then my mission is complete. I wanted to see you, and I didn't care about the reason." Cameron unexpectedly grabbed her around her waist and lifted her off her feet. She screamed and playfully punched him in his chest. "Put me down."

He did. "Hungry? I can take you out."

"You didn't go to a meeting that I know was important to you. I can see how tired you are, so you don't have to take me out." Gabrielle swallowed. Could she handle being with him alone? They had been together for months and knew where each other stood. It would be a

225

test for both of them, that's for sure. "I guess that means you're invited to dinner. We're having spaghetti. I hope you know how to cook."

Cameron laughed. "My woman invites me to dinner and makes me cook my own meal too."

"You know it!" She said aloud, while silently, she prayed. *Jesus, please help me. I know I'm a big girl, but I still need my Daddy—You—to keep me pure.*

————ɱ————

Cameron studied Gabrielle's expression. He suspected she was deciding whether she could trust him with the two of them alone in the apartment or maybe herself.

No other woman ever hesitated to extend an invitation, but he didn't love any of them. For some reason, he had something to prove to Gabrielle. And he knew material things wouldn't cut it.

Cameron didn't want to pressure her; he wanted her to believe in him. He loved Gabrielle and wanted to hear those words from her lips.

After they entered her apartment, the first thing he noticed was how she had transformed empty rooms into a tasteful living space. Looking around, he complimented, "This is nice."

Resting her purse and computer bag on the table, she glanced over her shoulder. "Thanks. I forgot you haven't seen it since the day I moved in."

"Yeah." Stuffing his hands in his pockets, Cameron didn't remind her that she hadn't invited him.

"Come on in the kitchen and wash your hands."

He obeyed. Grabbing an apron from its hook, Gabrielle laughed as she held it up for him.

"What's so funny, me wearing a pink apron or me letting you do this?" he asked when Gabrielle stood behind him and tied it around his waist. Seizing the opportunity, he trapped her hands and brought them to his lips for a kiss.

"It's a toss-up," she said, prying their hands apart and backing away.

After changing, she returned to the kitchen and busied herelf bringing a pot of water to boil and then pouring pasta into it.

Left to his own creation, Cameron seasoned the ground sirloin and Italian sausage while she stood beside him, dicing onions and garlic. He caught her smiling again.

"You're very beautiful when you smile. I wish you were looking at me."

"I'm just happy." Gabrielle's eyes sparkled. Forty minutes earlier, she was just as gorgeous when she stepped out of the car in a designer suit and was now in an oversized T-shirt and Capri pants.

"Would I be conceited to hope that I have something to do with it?"

"God knows you make me happy," Gabrielle said with a sigh. "I just don't know how this is going to play out between us. There's a Scripture—"

He groaned but held his breath. The Bible was the last thing he wanted to talk about with his woman.

"No, wait. In Ecclesiastes 4, there's a reason why two are better than one: *If either of them falls down, one can help the other up. But pity anyone who falls and has no one to help him up.*' Just think how wonderful things could have been if Adam would have had Eve's back." She paused with a shrug. "Unfortunately, they fell together."

"How do you do that? Unbelievable. How can you take a simple statement and connect it with a Scripture?" he asked. Talk about sexual tension. Gabrielle gave him plenty of that, in addition to his own source of spiritual frustration.

Her eyes pleaded for his understanding. "God was in my life long before you. Now that you're in it, I don't want the Lord to leave." She stopped dicing and dried her hands. "As a saint of God, He expects us to walk in the natural and spiritual way. He wants us to be aware of the warfare going on in the spiritual realm for our souls. And right now, with us alone, knowing you love me . . ." Gabrielle shook her head and admitted. "I'm weak."

He couldn't take her philosophical argument any longer. Cameron cut her off with a slow, drugging kiss that seemed to set off an alarm. When they jumped apart, they realized it was the smoke alarm. The meat for the spaghetti sauce was burning.

They sprang into action. Gabrielle grabbed an oven mitt, reached for the skillet, and turned off the stove. The smoke began to billow and drift throughout the apartment. Cameron quickly opened the window over the kitchen sink and then hurried to open more windows in the living room. Just then, Gabrielle yelled.

He raced back to her side. "You okay?"

"I'm fine, but I spilled sauce on my shirt. I'll have to change."

He nodded and went back into the living room. While she walked down the hall into her bedroom, Cameron reached over a lamp table to open another window. He accidently bumped against it and a notebook fell to the floor. Placing it back on the table, he noticed his name scribbled several times. Curious—or maybe downright nosey—he peeped closely at it.

"I'll be right out," Gabrielle yelled from behind a closed door.

"Take your time," he shouted back. Flipping through some pages, Cameron realized it was a diary or journal of sorts. He smiled at the entry where she wrote the date, time, and location where she was when he texted that he loved her. *Romantic!* She had added to that entry.

Cameron shook his head. His woman had no idea how romantic things could be if she would only trust him. Grabbing a nearby pen, he scribbled in her diary, *I need to know if you love me. Tell me or text me. Cam.*

When he heard Gabrielle fumble with the doorknob, he put the notebook back in place and rushed to the kitchen. As she entered the room wearing another Boston University college T-shirt, he was trying to look busy doing nothing.

"There goes the masterpiece dinner," he joked, attempting to mask his suspicious behavior. "Why don't I help you clean up this mess, then we can go out and grab a bite. After all, it's my kiss that was a scorcher." He grinned and wiggled his brow.

"You are so cocky," Gabrielle said with a laugh. "I can't be mad at you about the kiss because I enjoyed it too. But God set off that smoke alarm."

God again. Cameron held his tongue.

Gabrielle didn't wait for a response and kept talking. "Actually, I'd rather stay in. I enjoy cooking when I have someone to eat with me. I was smiling earlier because I thought about when my mom was here. She helped me break in my kitchen, and we cooked up a storm."

After filling the sink with soapy water, she soaked two dish towels. She then squeezed one and threw it at him without warning. "Wipe off the stove," she ordered, adding a quick, "please." Her smile was priceless.

Cameron caught the towel, thanks to his sharp reflexes. "Yes, dear." He winked and did as he was told.

Suddenly, a somber mood seemed to come over her. "I also enjoy the process of preparing and tasting and tweaking meals. It's always exciting when you have someone to share the experience. Otherwise, it's a chore."

Opening the refrigerator, Gabrielle pulled out a bag of lettuce to make a salad. Grabbing a bowl, she rinsed off the romaine lettuce and then sprinkled cheddar cheese, dried cranberries, miniature mandarin oranges, and pecans over it.

He restored the stove back to its pre-disaster state and turned around. Taking the moment to observe her, Cameron admired how she fussed over the placement of the garnishments. She was so cute. In the back of his mind, he wondered when she planned to tell him what she had written about her feelings toward him.

Scrunching her nose when she caught him staring, Gabrielle slid a plate in front of him. "Here, eat this as an appetizer and I'll warm up some leftovers."

Bowing his head, Cameron silently said grace and stabbed at his salad. "Tell me more about your cooking escapades."

"Meals were always a big deal at our house. Dinnertime became a community moment because we all stayed at the table until everyone was finished. It's quirky, but it's a Dupree thing." She shrugged and punched in a time for defrost on her microwave.

"Anyway, I cooked at home alongside my mom and then in college with Denise. Even now, when I want to try a new recipe, I'll call my mother. Mom will walk me through it as if she were in my kitchen, telling me when to taste it." With a smile, she added. "That's how you got dessert on the Fourth of July."

When he finished his salad, he rinsed the bowl and forced Gabrielle to have a seat. He took over warming up what appeared to be meatloaf and collard greens. Without saying so, Cameron enjoyed the experience of them preparing, cooking, and enjoying a meal together. It was a sensual experience, a term he would have never associated with food alone.

After they had eaten, once again he assisted her in cleaning up the kitchen. From there, they moved to the living room where she showed him galleys of childhood pictures. Then came a bittersweet addition to the evening. With Gabrielle cuddled up next to him, Cameron "endured" a romantic comedy. The only problem was, the film couldn't hold his attention and he didn't see anything funny.

Although he enjoyed the intimate moment they were sharing, Gabrielle was oblivious to the fact that the window to her soul lay open within an arm's reach. Finally, bored from lack of concentration, Cameron gave up his struggle, picked up the remote, and clicked off the movie.

She frowned. "What did you do that for? It was just getting to the good part."

Cameron thought she was about to hyperventilate she was so mad, but he felt like a ticking time bomb too. He needed to hear three words from her. Standing, Cameron went to the table in the corner and picked up her notebook. The horror that raced across her face turned into fury.

"What are you doing with this?" She rushed over and snatched it out of his hand.

"I read it." Cameron blinked, anticipating his cockiness was going to earn him a whack upside his head, maybe more than once.

Instead, her eyes misted as she hugged the notebook to her chest. "You had no right. These are my private thoughts . . . in my possession . . . in my private domain."

"Well, my private thoughts are now in your possession too." Pointing at the book, Cameron's face showed his level of frustration.

Glancing down, Gabrielle quickly flipped through the notebook and scanned the pages. When she found what he had written, she looked back at him. Her expression was unreadable. "Good night," was all she said.

Shocked, he gritted his teeth. "What? I'm an open book. You know how I feel. Why is it so hard for you to tell me that you love me? Maybe you don't. We're going to settle this now—"

"Oh, we're going to settle this all right. Get out!" she screamed, pointing toward the door. "Or do you need for me to write it out for you?"

Storming to the door, Cameron gripped the doorknob. "Women . . ." he growled. Speechless, he walked out. With too much force, it slammed shut behind him.

A tear slid down Gabrielle's cheek. She was mortified when she saw her handbook of romance in Cameron's hands. In addition to her hopes and dreams, her insecurities and prayers to Jesus were written on those pages. Only three people knew about that book: her mother,

Denise, and Talise. And none of them had ever read it.

To ask him how much he had read would mean she would have to explain herself. With God, she never had to explain her thoughts. Jesus already knew she was afraid to love Cameron.

Chapter Thirty-One

*W*hat did I say?" Cameron asked his reflection in the mirror two days later. As he dressed for Sunday service, he was still perplexed. He hated when women got the last word. Before Gabrielle ordered him out, his plan was to walk out. She had some nerve.

On top of that, driving home that evening in a bad mood caused him to get a speeding ticket. It seemed like the weekend went downhill from there. With the ticket in his hand, he stormed through the front door of his extremely hot house—the thermostat read eighty-three degrees.

Not only was he sizzling mad, he was irked that he had to drive somewhere and buy a window air conditioner. Refusing to spend an uncomfortable night in extreme heat, a window unit would hold him until he could get a serviceman out the next morning. Of all times for his central air to break down, tomorrow was forecasted to be the hottest day of the summer.

The technician did arrive the following day, but it wasn't until ten at night. By that time, Cameron had already installed two units.

Gabrielle hadn't called or texted him and neither had he tried to reach her. As a matter of fact, she didn't even know he was planning to attend church. He tried to swear Ace to secrecy. However, his cousin quoted him not one, but two Scriptures about swearing: James 5:12 and Matthew 5:34.

"I give you my word, cuz. That has to be good enough," Ace had said. Then he added, "Good luck, because Talise told me that your woman was upset big time about something you did."

Frustrated, Cameron had thrown his arms up in the air, thinking, *How could I know? It was a raggedy, torn notebook.* "What did I really do anyway?" he asked aloud.

So, here he was tying his silk tie, getting ready to plead her forgiveness. He was going to surprise Gabrielle at the church she had attended faithfully since moving to St. Louis. He would eat humble pie. It seemed like yet again.

Of course, thinking it over for the millionth time, Cameron had to be honest with himself. He shouldn't have invaded her privacy. Besides, Drexel's words had come back to haunt him repeatedly. Gabrielle was causing him to jump through too many hoops.

Before he knew her, Cameron had already given up hard liquor. By her influence, he had added beer and wine to the do-not-consume list as well. Ever since they met, he had abstained from what he called lovemaking. Gabrielle called it an act of sin against the body and a one-way ticket to hell.

For her, he had rearranged his Sunday morning plan. It was too hot for golf that morning anyway. With a sneer, he wondered if that Sunday morning treat was going to be permanently taken away from him too. Deals were made on the golf course. For him, serious money was committed on behalf of his charities on the tee.

Satisfied with his appearance, Cameron walked out of his house but left his Bible. He went back outside. After retrieving it, he got behind the wheel. With a ticket in his wallet, he was careful to drive under the speed limit.

Arriving at Salvation Temple, admittedly, it had been a while since attending church was a part of his schedule. After he found a parking space, Cameron cleared the foyer with a purpose. He remembered where his brother and cousin sat and headed toward that section.

Cameron spotted Gabrielle first as he neared the family's pew. She wore a light purple dress with a hat practically smothering her head. "Excuse me." He climbed over Ace and kissed Talise. Frowning, Talise hesitated before creating an opening for him to sit next to Gabrielle, who was holding the baby and never glanced his way.

God had to be the orchestrator because, as he took his seat, Gabrielle stood up. The choir began singing a song that was upbeat but seemed to go on forever. Talise stood and took the baby from Gabrielle, so that she could be free to worship God. Others around them were doing the same, but Cameron remained seated and kept his eyes trained on her.

Finally, when Gabrielle reclaimed her seat, he tried to speak to her. Once again, timing wasn't on his side. She *shh*ed him, as the pastor stepped up to the podium.

"Praise the Lord, everybody," Elder Taylor greeted. "Thank you, choir, for that moving selection. And now, church, will you turn your Bibles to the book of Acts, chapter two. In verse forty, Peter is pleading with the crowd to be saved. What is so fascinating about this Scripture is that the men of God had to warn the people and beg them to be saved. With their God-given authority, they had to do everything in their power to get people to turn their lives around . . ."

Cameron was halfway listening. He wanted to hear the message, but his heart was heavy and aching to make things right with Gabrielle. "I'm sorry," he whispered.

She nodded her head without giving him a sideward glance.

"The apostle Paul also begged folks to give their bodies to God as a living sacrifice . . ." Elder Taylor continued.

"Can we talk after church? I really need you to forgive me."

"I do, Cameron," she lowered her voice. "But, we need to do some soul searching apart from each other."

Cameron blinked. Even strong men are weakened by rejection. Dressed in her classy hat, Gabrielle appeared regal and acted as if she barely noticed him. He started to get up right then and leave when suddenly the atmosphere around him seemed to tremble.

"Be still, and know that I am God; I will be exalted among the nations, I will be exalted in the earth." The voice of God carried Psalm 46:10 through the air.

He froze, feeling like a disobedient child being reprimanded. He had come to church with an attitude and was about to leave in the same condition. Closing his eyes, he tried to focus, but the preacher wasn't saying anything he hadn't heard before.

Stuck in an emotional limbo, Cameron dared not move until after the benediction. Without saying another word to Gabrielle or anyone else, he made a beeline for his car. Leaving, his current mood was worse than when he came.

Later that night in the coolness of his bedroom, Cameron recalled the experience at church. He doubted anyone else heard and felt what he had. Although he stayed to the end, his thoughts and heart were too tormented to get anything out of the sermon.

For years, Cameron had been reading his Bible and the words never changed. Neither had his understanding. Maybe he was suffering from a pre-midlife crisis. How could that be when he had everything going for him? For whatever reason, his confidence seemed to be crumbling.

Suddenly, a sense of defeat came over him. The feeling was foreign and highly distasteful. Driven to do something to combat his weakened state, one person came to mind. Cameron wasn't one to mince words or bite his tongue, yet he was about to do something unfathomable to him.

Getting up, he crossed the room to his dresser where his wallet rested and pulled out Philip's card. Tapping in the numbers, Cameron wasn't surprised when he got a voice mail greeting, but that didn't deter him. He left a simple message and hoped Gabrielle's brother would return his call sooner than later. At one in the morning to be exact, his cell phone chimed.

"Cameron, I'm sorry for the tardiness of the hour in returning your call. The healing service ran long, but it's God's timing, not mine. Is my sister all right?" His voice sounded commanding like it was when he preached during the revival meeting.

"Your sister is just as beautiful and sweet as ever. At least, that was before she threw me out of her apartment. She doesn't know I called you, and I'd rather that you not tell her."

Philip didn't respond right away. "Unless the Lord tells me otherwise, I can agree to that. Now how can I help you?"

"I believe our difference of opinions about God is standing in the way of Gabrielle trusting my genuine intentions concerning her." Cameron's assumption was really based on what he read in her notebook. "I don't like to discuss religion in a relationship, but it appears Gabrielle is forcing my hand."

Philip chuckled softly. "Good for her."

Cameron grunted. "Isn't a man of God supposed to be neutral?"

"I am. Please continue."

Cameron got comfortable on his bed. "She believes that salvation is a process. I don't. The Bible says if I believe, I'm saved. Period. End of story."

"Dying on the cross was a process. It could have been instantaneous by the power of God, but Jesus followed every detail. Salvation is about detail. Your heart, mind, and body have to be in sync. Otherwise, your salvation is not complete without it. The Bible lists everything we need to do to be completely saved. There are no dilutions or other recipes," Philip explained but not to Cameron's satisfaction.

"Complete? There are missing books of the Bible—the book of Nathan, the book of Shemaiah the prophet, the book of Iddo the seer, the book of Jehu . . ." Cameron was just warming up.

"John 21:25 lets us know that Jesus did so many miraculous things that *the whole world would not have room for the books that would be written.* In other words, God has given enough information for us to be completely saved. We don't need to load ourselves up with more than what we have. Many of us can't follow the instructions He's already given us. Trust me, God's burdens are lightweight compared to the yoke the world wants to put on us," Philip said quietly.

Cameron was ready to refute Philip, but the man struck a chord when he mentioned the yoke the world hangs around a man.

"When was the last time you prayed and asked God to evaluate your spiritual growth and give you a grade?" Philip asked.

"I've got this," Cameron said confidently.

"None of us have 'this.' The Bible says in 1 Corinthians 10:12 to be careful of falling. Especially if you think you're too tough to slip, I might add."

As weariness set in, Cameron wasn't up to decoding a parable. "I appreciate you taking the time to return my call." He yawned.

"Any time. God bless you." He paused before saying, "Cameron, between you and me, your solid ground is like quicksand. You're going down."

Chapter Thirty-Two

You're not the reason he was here, it's about Me, God had spoken firmly to Gabrielle while she sat in the pew.

Overcome with fear and shame, she repented on the spot. Instead of giving Jesus the praise for drawing Cameron to church, she had ignored his presence. Being too caught up in her acting role as the injured party, now Gabrielle felt foolish. When he left without saying goodbye, she didn't even try to stop him.

How could she call herself a Christian and hold a grudge? How could she love Cameron and not forgive him when he asked for forgiveness? All the hurt was because she wasn't comfortable enough with him to say the things she had written down and secretly tucked away.

Admittedly, she was insecure about loving Cameron. But should she give up on that love so quickly if he didn't pass the Jesus inspection? The love of her heart had to surrender to Christ on his own accord.

On Tuesday morning, with the self-inflicted torture too much to bear, Gabrielle swallowed her pride and texted Cameron: I'm sorry. Having so much more to say, she was still afraid to utter the words.

If you trust in Me, I will chase your fears away, God spoke comfort.

Gabrielle exhaled deeply and sent another text: I love you.

His response was immediate. I love you too, babe. I'm running late, but minutes away from your complex with a white rose.

She smiled. Before driving to Cameron's house for the Fourth of July celebration, she had no idea of the distance he drove several times a week to bring her a rose. The man practically backtracked when he lived minutes from his job. Traveling to her North County location and back to the Central West End was a long trip.

Thank you. I'll be here, she texted. While waiting in her car, Gabrielle scrutinized her makeup.

Minutes later, she looked up to see Cameron's Audi drive past the unmanned front gate. He stopped at the street ahead of Gabrielle's and chatted a moment with Talise's mother-in-law. Sandra was in her car getting ready to take off for work. She also lived in the complex.

Minutes later, Cameron headed in her direction and pulled his car beside hers. Shifting it into park, he got out and walked around to open her door. Extending his hand, she took it as he helped her out of the car. She stood in a daze. Wrapping his arms around her, she held on tight. Neither said a word. Reluctantly, Cameron finally set her free. After staring into her eyes, he handed her the rose and kissed her cheek.

"I've got to get to my office, baby. I love you."

"Thank you and I love you too," Gabrielle faintly whispered, as he slid behind the wheel.

"I knew before you told me." Cameron winked and drove off.

Sniffing the flower, Gabrielle grinned. Getting back inside, she buckled up and sighed a sigh of relief. They had survived their very first argument, and now they were back on track.

The remainder of the week was heavenly blissful, with Gabrielle freely expressing her love in texts and phone conversations.

One evening at his house, they had failed miserably when attempting to duplicate a Thai recipe. The culinary catastrophe ended with them ordering Chinese takeout.

After dinner, it was rather late so she didn't stay long. As she prepared to leave, Cameron insisted on trailing her home to ensure her safe arrival. There, in front of her building, they shared a loving embrace. Before going to bed that night, Gabrielle recorded his gentle stubbornness as a "wow" moment in her handbook.

However, the following Sunday, her spirit plummeted when Cameron didn't return to church. To her dismay, he had another legitimate excuse. His department was entertaining alumni and potential sponsors for the university that particular morning.

When service was over, Gabrielle hugged and kissed Talise's family before she headed to the parking lot.

"Oh, Gabrielle, I almost forgot. My mother-in-law said that she spoke to Cameron this week. I'm so glad things have turned around for you two." Talise beamed. "Although I've mentioned to Sandra before that you two live in the same complex, she had forgotten until she saw Cameron in your neighborhood one morning. She asked for your number. I hope you don't mind that I gave it to her."

Waving her hand, Gabrielle shook her head. "Of course not, any woman who could befriend her son's pregnant ex-girlfriend has sound wisdom. I'm sure I can learn a lot from her."

"That's right. We were friends first. She's a tough act to follow and a gracious lady at that. Anyway, she'll probably call you soon."

A few evenings later, Gabrielle arrived home from work later than usual. Talise's mother-in-law was out walking her dog. Gabrielle honked and waved as she passed by. Instead of continuing the pathway back to her bungalow community, Sandra strolled toward the apartment area of the complex to greet Gabrielle.

When they met up, the two women hugged. "I've been meaning to call you," Sandra said.

"And I've been thinking about visiting."

"You look like you worked forty hours in one day," Sandra said with a concerned expression.

Gabrielle mustered a weak chuckle. "They definitely got their money's worth out of me today, and I make a lot of money." Activating her alarm, she bent and patted Sandra's pet. "If I could take a bath and go straight to bed, I would do just that. I'm too tired to eat, so you know that's bad."

Frowning, Sandra hesitated before responding. "I made plenty of dinner. Why don't you take your bath while I take this little beast back home? I'll bring you a plate in about thirty minutes," she said, poised to head home.

"Thank you. There's no way I'm going to turn down the blessing of free food." Gabrielle grinned. "I'll take a quick shower. How about twenty minutes? I'm in 2B."

"Deal." Sandra agreed with a cheerful laugh, as she let her dog gallop ahead of her.

Upstairs in her apartment, Gabrielle showered and changed in record time. The warm water gave her a renewed burst of energy. Several minutes went by when the intercom buzzed, and she hurried to answer it. With hunger pangs growing stronger by the minute, Gabrielle thought about the popular TV show *Man vs. Food*. "At this moment, the food has it," she joked to herself, referring to the ridiculous reality show where the host, Adam Richman, tries to digest more food than humanly possible.

She opened her apartment door to find Sandra bouncing up the two flights of stairs as though she was on a jog. They exchanged air kisses and Gabrielle accepted the food offering. Sandra complimented her apartment as Gabrielle showed her guest to the kitchen.

Once they were seated, she didn't waste any time uncovering the plate. There was more than enough slices of roast beef, mashed potatoes, and sweet peas. Her stomach growled.

"It appears I'm right on time," Sandra said, smiling.

After saying grace, Gabrielle dug in while Sandra watched her in amusement.

"So how are things between you and Cameron? We chatted briefly one day last week when I was on my way to work. Even though we're not blood relatives because I never married a Jamieson, I treat him like a son. I'm so glad he's attracted to a beautiful woman who loves the Lord."

Blushing, Gabrielle didn't answer immediately. "Actually, things are wonderful now. We're still working out the kinks in our relationship, but that man really loves me." She paused a moment and took a deep breath. "I think he may be the one. Maybe I've been unreasonable with some of my assumptions about him." Gabrielle slipped another helping of mashed potatoes in her mouth.

Sandra squinted. "Unreasonable? In what way?" She leaned back into her chair, braced to listen intently.

"Well, Cameron has been nothing but a perfect gentleman. He's really sweet. I've been the one stressing about throwing caution to the wind and letting things happen naturally between us. Minus sex, of course. Let me throw that out there. God knows our hearts and . . ." Gabrielle grappled to verbalize her thoughts.

Deciding to share openly, she continued. "We had a big fight. Rather, I yelled at him and ask him to leave. It seems like the only one God has a problem with is me and my treatment of Cameron. I guess the red flags I saw were a figment of my imagination."

"I see." Sandra nodded. "Gabrielle, you're a smart lady. Otherwise, you wouldn't be my granddaughter's godmother and Talise's good friend. But you're still a woman who is falling for a Jamieson, like I once did. Sometimes when we blink, we miss the red flags, so keep watching and praying."

Gabrielle rested her fork on the table. "What are you saying? Is there something I need to know? Is that why you wanted to call me?"

Sandra nodded.

"Okay," Gabrielle said slowly with an uneasy feeling coming over her. "Go on. You know Cameron better than I do."

"Don't be so quick to give the Lord a deadline and throw out the red flags. Be ready in season and out of season to answer to God for whatever decision you make in your heart before you allow it to happen. Ask yourself, are you really convinced of his commitment to his Christian walk?"

A small voice within Gabrielle responded no, especially after he was a no-show at church this past Sunday. Even if his excuse was legitimate. Personally, she had flat-out informed her colleagues that she could not work on Sundays because of church attendance. As a condition of employment, the board of directors could either take it or leave it. After assessing her résumé and qualifications, they gobbled up her offer.

"I'm saying this for a reason. Around the time he first started dating you, Talise mentioned that she hoped he would go to church more often. Now that he's fallen in love with you, Gabrielle, with gentleness and respect, persuade Cameron why Jesus should be his first love. You may be the person God is depending on to reach him and get the job done. Remember what the Scripture says, '*Always be prepared to give an answer to everyone who asks you to give the reason for the hope that you have.*'"

Gabrielle recognized 1 Peter 3, although the exact verse escaped her. She sighed and her eyes misted. "Now I feel like I need to go back to square one with Cameron and keep him at arm's length." She slumped in her chair.

Sandra reached across the table and patted her hand. "We can never go back, especially when someone has a piece of our heart. Take this as your mission from God. Cameron wants you, and a man has been known to lose his mind over a woman. In his case, he will gain a stronger walk with the Lord. Your assignment is to draw him closer to Christ."

"That's easier said than done," was Gabrielle's only response. If Philip's preaching didn't increase Cameron's appetite for the Lord, then she was clueless on how to do it. Yet, recalling Titus 2:4, Gabrielle couldn't disregard any of what this spiritually mature woman had just shared with her.

Before Sandra left, she prayed with Gabrielle that God would give her sound judgment with Cameron. Alone to release her emotions, Gabrielle had a good cry. Why had it seemed like her happiness was tangible when it was slowly disappearing before her eyes?

In her heart, Gabrielle knew God had sent Sandra with nourishing food to satisfy her hunger. Now, she also understood that Sandra had come with something even more meaningful. Her words of wisdom were like a spiritual dessert, reminding her that Christ's love was more valuable than the love of a good man.

"God, I've known Your love all my life. I'm asking You now for a good man, who puts You first, to love me."

—⁓—

Cameron had a hunch that something had spooked Gabrielle a few nights ago. When he asked her about it, she declined an explanation for her latest mood swing. She was withholding her feelings again. Why?

Considering how upset she had become after he read her notebook, he decided not to push her. One thing he had learned about Gabrielle Dupree, she was tough on the outside and tender on the inside. That's why his arms would always be open to cuddle her whenever she needed him.

On the other hand, Cameron was just as guilty of hiding things. He hadn't told her about his conversation with Philip. When the two men spoke, he discovered that Gabrielle's brother was an engaging partner, if he wanted to discuss ideology. Smiling, he thought of his own brother, Parke, who was always prepared for a spirited debate as well.

Recalling their talk, Philip's point of view had been sufficiently thought provoking. Plus, speaking with him privately was a matter of pride for Cameron. He found it more appealing to go through the back door when it came to the discussion of religion. There were no third party witnesses who would be aware of his doubts about God.

Tonight the conversation with Gabrielle was short and to the point. Cameron called to inform her of the news that he had booked their flights to Alabama. They were going to the Jamieson family reunion together. Before they said good night, Gabrielle had asked him to pray for her. Caught off guard by her request, Cameron recovered quickly and said, "Bless my sweetheart, Jesus."

Gabrielle seemed disappointed. "That's it?"

He had chuckled. Was she testing or teasing him? "That's all I've got in me right now, babe."

Evidently, that had been the wrong answer. Gabrielle disconnected without saying another word.

"What have I done now?" he asked himself in utter frustration. If only Cameron could take another peep inside her notebook—he'd be sure to find out.

*A*s the Labor Day weekend approached, Cameron's anticipation was building about meeting the Jamieson clan. He agreed with Denise that the Jemison-Van de Graaff Mansion in Tuscaloosa, Alabama, was the perfect setting for a grand get-together. A week before the trip, Cameron dabbled in a little historical research about the accomplishments and struggles of African-Americans in that particular Southern state.

In doing so, he came across an interesting piece of historic information. According to Cameron's research, the story recounted the life of one Horace King. As an enslaved human being in Alabama, Horace King was respected; but as a freed man, he was a force to be reckoned with. Horace constructed bridges and was a freemason, proving that African-Americans were worth more than a piece of paper. In fact, he represented a proud race of flesh and blood human beings—not currency to be exchanged, like a mere commodity.

Robert Jemison—a variation on the spelling of the Jamieson name—was touted as one of the state's largest slaveholders. Cameron found articles suggesting Robert passed legislation to secure Horace's freedom. As a result, after the death of his second slaveholder, Horace wouldn't be sold to pay off debts.

Cameron's research extended beyond the digging Denise had done. In this case, his diligent search found out that the practice of slavery had divided an ancestral household. Slaveholder Robert Jemison was a distant uncle of the Robert Jamieson who helped Cameron's family escape through the safe houses in Illinois used in the Underground Railroad.

Cameron speculated about whether the abolitionist Robert changed the spelling of his last name to distance himself from the slaveholder. Cameron also discovered one more interesting tidbit. Robert Jemison-Van de Graaff had an MIT connection as a research assistant. This was sure to be an eye-opening adventure.

On Friday after work, Cameron was hyped as he and Gabrielle boarded the plane for the hour-and-a-half flight to Birmingham.

Of course, he would have preferred to drive in the caravan with the other Jamiesons, albeit eight hours on the road. But the airline industry had spoiled Gabrielle, which prompted him to give up the road trip for the airstrip.

A few times, he thought Gabrielle was about to back out, but she assured him that she had no intention of doing so. Although they had kissed—actually hugged—and made up after their argument, Gabrielle seemed slightly withdrawn from him.

Then out of nowhere, she had begun the oddest requests for him to pray for her. Where did that come from?

"Consider it done, babe," Cameron replied with a smile.

After they settled in their seats and strapped on their belts, Cameron turned to Gabrielle who was glancing out of the window with a smile on her face.

The reflection of Gabrielle's smile was a display worthy of an encore—the faint dimple, a slight opening of her lips, and the twinkle in her eyes. It was sheer seduction. And Cameron had to force his mind to think pure thoughts, a worthy task that proved virtually impossible for him.

Preferring not to disturb her, Cameron simply catalogued the moment. She was classy in whatever she wore. On this particular day, it was a gray sundress and matching shawl. The look of strappy pewter sandals, boasting her shapely legs, were nearly driving him crazy.

Time and again, he had to catch himself from succumbing to naughty thoughts. Rebounding quickly, Cameron banished such taboo scenarios. Instead, he concentrated on what was safe: her graceful hands, luscious lips—scratch that—her gorgeous hair. He reached out and fingered a few strands, which drew her attention.

Facing him, her face glowed. "You enjoy checking me out," she teased.

He leaned closer and cooed, "And how do you know that, Miss Dupree?"

"I can feel your eyes fastened on me." As she met him halfway, Cameron puckered his lips, hopeful that a kiss was forthcoming.

"And you'd better not be undressing me either," she whispered, brushing closely but never touching his mouth. "I want us to date with Christian dignity. That's what I've been praying for—without ceasing." She emphasized the last two words.

Blinking, Cameron bowed his head. "You caught me, so I confess." He grinned, hoping to cast an innocent look. It didn't work.

"You know, the Bible says if your eyes offend you then pluck them out."

"Now you do know that's one of many things in the Bible that Christ didn't literally mean," he stated in a hushed voice.

"Wrong. Jesus is serious about us making it to heaven by any means necessary."

When she didn't appear amused, Cameron accepted that Gabrielle meant business. As a matter of fact, not long after they hugged to make up—instead of kissed—she seemed recharged on her religious kick.

However, he too had been giving the Scriptures more thought lately. Retreating from any additional Bible discussion, Cameron wasn't ready to reveal that he had called Philip for some clarification of God's Word.

"Yes, dear. Forgive me?"

"Seven times seventy." When she didn't blink, Cameron challenged her in a staring dual. When his nostrils flared, Gabrielle giggled and lost.

Taking her hand in his, he massaged her slender fingers. "I won." Cameron winked. "So what was on your mind earlier? When you have that faraway look in your eyes, I know you're thinking about something significant."

"Remember the last time we flew together, and your seat mate—"

Cameron grunted. "That type of woman I would dare not bring home to Charlotte Jamieson. You've already met my mom, so no other woman need to try to apply for that position."

Toying with her ring finger, Cameron wondered what size she would wear if he were to slip a ring on it. The bigger question was how to actually get her to the wedding altar. That is, without her thinking she needed to get him to the prayer altar first. It was no secret between them that she thought he was lacking something major in the spiritual department.

"Thanks for coming along, especially after you told me about your rough week."

"I had decided to be a reunion crasher long before you and Denise double-teamed me, but you're welcome anyway. Besides, I'm excited about seeing my girl." She paused and sighed. "As for work, the honeymoon period is definitely over. Chaos is out of the gate, and my job is to rope in the bulls."

He listened, but his mind was elsewhere. Reflecting on their journey, he was now ready. They first met back in March. They started dating in St. Louis—somewhat in Boston. Then, when Gabrielle relocated, he stepped up his game. Now, six months later on their way to Tuscaloosa via Birmingham, Cameron was prepared to pop the question.

Suddenly, he wished they were en route to a secret destination for an exotic honeymoon. Before the weekend came to an end, Cameron planned to convince Gabrielle why she fit not only into his life, but also into the rich Jamieson history.

Chapter Thirty-Four

*O*nce she felt reassured that Cameron's lust had dissipated, Gabrielle captured the way he lovingly looked into her eyes. God knew he was the one she desired. Now she just hoped her prayers would be answered. Was he the one God had chosen for her? The uncertainty of it all caused her to refrain from dwelling on that thought any longer.

When they landed about an hour later, Gabrielle thrived on Cameron's possessive touches—holding her hand, encircling her waist to keep her close, and whispering soothing thoughts in her ear. Adding to that, he refused to let her carry anything.

Gabrielle felt cherished, adored, and . . . cheated. The man whom she loved refused to put more energy into making room in his life for Christ. No, she wouldn't allow that concern to plague her this weekend. She took her burden to the Lord and left it in His lap.

While Cameron stood at the car rental counter in the airport, Gabrielle texted Denise to let her know they had landed and would be there soon. Taking a nearby seat, she admired how God had formed Cameron perfectly in every way.

She was still amazed at how she fell for a bald-headed man. As if he sensed her attention, Cameron glanced over his shoulder and winked. Caught in the act, she blushed. Well, at least she could say she wasn't lusting; she was only giving the Lord His kudos.

Ten minutes later, he programmed the GPS and they were on I-20, heading toward downtown Tuscaloosa. Gabrielle suddenly remembered that she didn't give God thanks. Bowing her head, she said a silent prayer of thanksgiving for their safe travel. When she opened her eyes, Cameron was watching her. "What?"

He lifted a brow. "I thought you were about to take a nap on me."

Scrunching her nose, she grinned. "Nope. I was thanking God for allowing us to arrive safely."

Cameron nodded. "Yes. Amen. Still, I don't want you to get any ideas about a snooze. We're only about an hour away."

"Get real. Denise says we're closer than that." Almost instantly, she yawned and they both laughed. Gabrielle guessed he was thinking about the last time they traveled together for the short ride from Boston to Hartford.

"It's okay, baby. As long as you stay in your seat belt, you can snuggle next to me. I won't complain."

Gabrielle did just that. A few minutes later, she couldn't help herself as her lids fluttered and sleep succumbed her. Then, all too soon, he was nudging her awake. Blinking, she sat up and noted her surroundings. "How far are we from the hotel?"

"Not far," he replied.

Taking in the surroundings, something caught her eye. "Jameson Hotel, without the 'i'? Your family even has a hotel chain?" Gabrielle squinted. "Hmm. I'm surprised Denise didn't book the gathering there," she commented, finger-combing her hair.

"Me too, but the Courtyard by Marriott has roomy suites, so you'll get no complaints from me."

"Good, since I'm sharing a room with Denise's sister," she

announced. Gabrielle might have agreed to fly in with Cameron, but there was no way her reputation would be tarnished with any inkling that they might stay together. And she told Denise as much.

They pulled into the parking lot and observed several groups making their way to the hotel entrance—Blacks and Whites. "Do you recognize anybody?" she asked.

"I don't, but that's the fun of a reunion."

After Cameron located a parking space, hand in hand they walked toward the lobby. About that time, Denise was coming outside. It wasn't long before she spotted Gabrielle and made a beeline to her. Thrilled to see each other again, they hugged and kissed and hugged a second time.

Cameron cleared his throat. "I thought family was supposed to be first," he teased.

Denise obliged and then excitedly gave them a rundown of the next day's activities. While Cameron's full attention was with his cousin, Gabrielle relieved him of her small piece of luggage. Brushing a kiss on his cheek, she walked away to check in. While still in close range, Gabrielle heard Denise say, "You'd better take care of my girl."

Cameron responded, "I love her."

I love you too, she said silently, *and I'm scared to death we might not be equally yoked. Then it's over.*

—⁓—

Very early the next morning, Cameron and his brothers reported downstairs to help Denise sort through the welcome packets and pass out Jamieson Family Reunion T-shirts. Under the guise of assisting, Cameron was searching for Gabrielle's packet. Once he found it, he slipped an envelope inside. As far as he was concerned, his mission was complete.

The hotel was teeming with folks in all shapes, sizes, and colors who could be blood-related to him. Any other time, Cameron would be thrilled to be surrounded by family. But at this time, unsurprisingly to those closest to him, he craved a moment of privacy.

Since his heart wasn't in it anyway, Parke and Malcolm took pity on him. Relinquished of his duties, his mind was on one person alone. Finding a comfortable spot for them, he stared at the bank of elevators. Frowning, Cameron stood and checked his watch, wondering what was taking Gabrielle so long. He was about to reach for his cell phone when he was suddenly blinded by a set of sweet-smelling hands that fumbled to cover his eyes. Gabrielle. How did he miss her?

Placing his hands on top, he guided the owner around to face him. Just as he prepared to deliver a kiss, he realized the face didn't even come close to resembling his Gabrielle. The woman was pretty, inches shorter, and happened to be the one he had chatted with through Skype.

"Hi, cousin. I'm Queen Jamieson from Oklahoma. Finally, we get a chance to meet," she said proudly.

As soon as Queen reached out to hug him, Cameron saw Gabrielle bouncing carefree down the stairs. Immediately, he poised to take flight, practically dragging his cousin along with him.

"Ah, me too. Let me get back with you," he uttered. With no further hesitation, he rushed away.

By now, she had made it to the reunion table. Someone had given Gabrielle her envelope, and she was holding it in her hand. When they made eye contact, she waited for him to come to her. He was less than three feet away when one of his little nephews came running toward him and grabbed him about the knees. The small boy intercepted the path, and he wasn't pleased about it.

"Go find your dad," he said, without identifying which child it was. Finally, he made it to her and lifted Gabrielle up with a crushing hug, then placed her back on her feet.

"It takes a special woman to put up with a Jamieson man. I love you." She recited the words from the note tucked inside her packet, then mouthed in return, "I love you too."

Before they could engage in an intimate conversation, the sound of Denise's voice called for the group's attention.

"Okay, everyone. I'm so excited that you've all come. Our transportation will be here in thirty minutes, so please make sure you eat from the buffet before we head out. We have more than one hundred and twenty Jamieson family members here. There's lots to do! So stay tuned, we'll talk more when we get to the Jemison Mansion."

Cameron reached for Gabrielle's hand and led her to the dining room. Taking her order, he had her find a cozy corner while he went to prepare their plates.

Once seated at the table, he took her hand. Her love seemed to empower him, as he bowed his head and prayed, "Jesus, I do thank You for the safe journey with my lady. Thank You for blessing our food and for the family I have yet to meet. I also thank You that I am growing in You, in Jesus' Name. Amen."

A shocked look appeared on her face.

Cameron smirked. "Close your gorgeous mouth, sweetheart, before I feed you your breakfast."

"You know I love to hear a man pray. Thank you," she said slightly above a whisper. Her eyes were misty.

"You act like you've never heard me pray. After all, you've been requesting a lot of prayer lately." Without skipping a beat, he changed the subject. "So what do you want to do today?" He asked while smothering his bagel with cream cheese.

"It's your family reunion, remember? That's why we're here."

Cameron shrugged nonchalantly. "I guess so." Glancing around, he noticed his niece and nephews had found children about their ages. "With so many Jamiesons here, I doubt I'd be missed. So you and I can go sightseeing—"

"You've been touting this Jamieson dynasty ever since I met you. Now I'm curious to see what all the hype is about."

"Well, shut my mouth."

Fifteen minutes later, Denise announced there were two buses outside and that it was time to load up. Disposing of their trash, everyone gathered their cameras and things and boarded the transportation for the short ride. Since they were only going several blocks away, Cameron thought the bus was unnecessary. But when they arrived, he realized the house consumed most of the property, which left very little room for parking. The three-story mansion was huge and breathtaking.

Once the group got off the buses, Denise and Queen gathered them around. A jubilant Denise remained the spokesperson. "I'm so glad that you all responded to the phone calls, tweets, Facebook requests, and even snail mail to represent our ancestors here today. My siblings and I poured over many court documents and stayed up long hours doing research on the web. We also requested death and birth certificates to learn more about our family tree. I was truly inspired by an article I found on accessible-archives.com."

She began reading from an index card. "A Reverend W. S. Johnson wrote in the *Christian Recorder,* which is supposedly the oldest existing African-American periodical today. Reverend Johnson reported about the reunion of ex-slaves throughout the South on August 3, 1893. That was thirty years after slavery, and loved ones were still searching for those who were sold away."

Pausing a moment, she added her own words. "Now, more than a hundred years later, none of us are enslaved. As my good friend Gabrielle would say, Jesus made us free." She grinned and waited while "Amens" made their way through the crowd before continuing.

"Anyway, we're all connected by a prince who was captured in Africa, kidnapped to America, and escaped to freedom. No one knows more and can speak so eloquently about our heritage than our cousin, Cameron Jamieson, who I will now ask to come and give us a brief account of our history. It's all in his head."

A wave of laughter spread throughout the group. Nudging him, Gabrielle teased, "Go on. Dazzle your audience."

Cameron didn't budge. "Although I love to talk about the Jamiesons, I wasn't expecting to be on the program. I planned to share every moment today with you."

"Oh well, duty calls, Professor Jamieson." Shrugging, Gabrielle began clapping, which ignited a round of applause.

Reluctantly, Cameron made his way through the gathering to the front and accepted the microphone from Denise. "Your timing is terrible. My older brother is just as capable," he mumbled.

"But you're cuter than your brothers." Denise batted her eyes, trying to butter him up.

"You've got that right." Cameron cleared his throat and surveyed those in attendance. White faces, Black faces, and blends of color in between all stared back at him. Old timers, toddlers, and teenagers represented the multi generations.

"My tenth great-grandfather, Paki Kokumuo Jaja, was the firstborn son of King Seif and Princess Adaeze," he began. "He was twenty years old when he and his entourage were attacked. Tall, healthy, fearless, and good-looking, Paki was sold at the highest bid of $275 to wealthy slave owner, Jethro Turner, in front of Sinner's Hotel in Maryland. The slaveholder's only daughter, Elaine, became his common-law wife as they escaped, becoming fugitives."

Cameron paused and eyed the spot where he left Gabrielle standing. Talise and Ace were by her side. Satisfied that she wasn't alone, he continued. "They had five sons who lived. My tenth grandfather, Parker, was the eldest. Descendants kept the name until after slavery when the 'r' was eliminated to symbolize enslavement was removed from society—or so he thought. We have researched King Seif's tribe and roots as well as Jethro's family."

Denise stepped to his side and swiped the microphone. "I told you his mind is endless with knowledge about our heritage." She fumbled with a few index cards before reading from one. "Paki's brothers were Aasim, Fabunni, Sarda, and Orma. My family members are descendants of the youngest brother, Orma, who actually sold himself into slavery for the woman he loved, but I'll talk about that last."

Squinting, Denise glanced through the crowd. "Are there any descendants of Fabunni here today? If so, please come forward and introduce yourself and family."

After tracking a couple of censuses, Cameron discovered that Fabunni was the fairest of the bunch, and his descendants were routinely classified or passed as White. Before a hand went up, Cameron had already pinpointed them.

By all outward appearances, they were the only Whites in the group. From their appearance, he guessed they were probably the politicians he'd heard about or from some other part of the elite society. On the other hand, the Black Jamiesons, including himself, weren't hurting financially either. A tall, slender man with sandy-brown hair and green eyes made his way to the front. His proud walk mimicked Cameron's.

Taking the man's presence as a cue to return to Gabrielle's side, Cameron slipped away. When he rejoined her, she wrapped her arms around his waist and leaned on him for support. He relished in the moment of being missed.

A strong voice commanded everyone's attention. "My name is Hugh Jamison Jr., spelled without the 'e'. My wife and children are here, along with two of my brothers. We came purely out of curiosity. We are aware that our distant grandfather, Jethro Turner, was one of the largest slaveholders, like Robert Jemison."

Cameron couldn't tell if he was indifferent to that fact or embarrassed. He would withhold judgment until Hugh finished. When a breeze stirred Gabrielle's hair near his nose, he planted a kiss on the top of her head, which earned him a squeeze.

"We were able to find a picture of Elaine as a teenager in a newspaper article that reported her kidnapping." He cleared his throat. "Or escape. That's where the trail ended. I don't know if it was my great-great-great grandfather's intention to hide the fact that we have Black blood or not, but we grew up as privileged Whites. I regret to say that he enslaved African-Americans. We didn't know that our freedom came by chance, while many of our cousins couldn't buy their freedom." Hugh sighed and bowed his head. "I'm sorry."

Denise and others nearby embraced Hugh. The moment was surreal as everyone reflected on what Hugh had said.

"*My people are destroyed from the lack of knowledge—*Hosea 4:6," Gabrielle whispered.

Cameron held his breath and didn't respond to his woman's comment. She amazed and sometimes annoyed him when she applied a biblical context to what was happening in everyday life. However, this time he agreed with her. If those who appeared White knew that African blood ran through their veins, perhaps they could have made a difference and lessened the sufferings of their African descendants.

Once Hugh composed himself, he headed back in the direction of his family. Some in the crowd delayed him with handshakes and hugs.

Next, Denise asked for any descendants of the second oldest brother, Aasim. Two elderly gentlemen with blue-black skin and a head full of bristled gray hair made their way through the crowd. Both were on canes, but when one of them took the microphone, he stood erect.

"My name is Theodore Franklin Jamieson, with the 'e.' I'm eighty-seven years old, and here is my baby brother, Jess. He doesn't have a middle name. He's eighty-three. It's just the two of us now. The others have all died off. My papa never talked too much about his papa except he was a runaway from the law. I married three times and outlived all of them wives. I got all my teeth and hair, and I can drive if anybody wants to be wife number four."

Snickering echoed through the crowd. Grandma BB who rode with Parke stood nearby. Cameron heard her mumble, "Don't look at me. I've got my own hair and teeth too. I'm a mean momma behind the wheel. I don't need a chauffeur like *Driving Miss Daisy.*"

Shhh, someone hushed her. Cameron and Gabrielle exchanged grins.

Denise was the last to talk about her eleventh great-grandfather, Orma. He sold himself into slavery to be with Sashe, who was enslaved. She also mentioned there were rotten apples in the family tree, including her father, Samuel.

"But I do thank God for the siblings my dad left behind. There were eleven of us. Two are now deceased, which is why I was in a hurry to meet you all."

Cameron braced himself for Gabrielle's Bible footnote. When not even a sigh came, he said, "Tomorrow's not promised." Evidently, she was too slow to call it.

"Something like that. Proverbs 27:1."

He groaned first, laughed under his breath, and then squeezed her tight. "Woman, you are not only too smart for your own good, but you have me beat."

She looked up into his eyes. Then, closing her own, she offered her cheek for a kiss. He didn't disappoint, although he would have preferred her lips. "I'm proud of you too. The gifts that God has given you have wooed me."

"Finally." Cameron said with a grin. "It only took me how many months to accomplish that feat?"

Playfully punching him in the stomach, he grabbed her hand and redirected his attention to Denise.

"There are nine of us remaining, and we're a force to be reckoned with," Denise continued. "My siblings are Mayson, Jayson, Benjamin, Lacey, Zaki, Kidd, Ace, and Queen. Will my brothers and sisters join me up front now, please?"

Immediately, Cameron zeroed in on Kidd. His stance was defiant with his arms folded and face expressionless. Would his cousin comply? Kidd confessed that he was happy with his walk with Jesus, but it took his wife to quote numerous Scriptures about loving thy neighbor, enemies, and brothers to get him there. He stipulated that he would not be pushed on others for fake smiles and handshakes. Kidd would have the last word on whom he would embrace and how he would interact with his half siblings.

To Cameron, it didn't matter that he and Ace were products of an illegitimate affair. Cameron loved and embraced them in the same way he was sure other family members would.

"Unfortunately, there is one missing link, the descendants of Sarda. Before we take our tour throughout the house, I want us to promise ourselves to make an effort to bring them into the fold," Denise requested.

While her siblings obeyed her summons, many nodded and a chorus of "Amens" and "yeahs" floated through the crowd. Kidd walked boldly to the front with Ace trailing. Although he stood among his siblings, Kidd's expression remained stoic. Immediately, he folded his arms. After a brief applause, Denise thanked her brothers and sisters and the family started to migrate toward the mansion.

"Denise really outdid herself," Gabrielle said, "and it all started because of her quest for family unity. Maybe I need to talk to my parents, especially my dad, about our New Orleans roots."

"Is there a Bible verse you want to cap off your statement," he joked, towering over her.

"You know me so well. I want to date you with Christian dignity. Recalling Scriptures around you is my defense mechanism to keep me from falling victim to your charm. However, just so I don't disappoint you," she stopped and grinned, "during Denise's inspiring presentation, I thought about the great gathering of the saints in the rapture."

Cameron grimaced while Gabrielle finished her thought. "You can look up the passage for yourself. The bottom line is I want us, not just me, to be included in that great day. Heaven is a one-time shot, Cameron. I don't dare miss it."

"We're in this together, babe. I just don't think about Jesus 24/7.

If I had to have a one-track mind, it would definitely be on you. My spiritual readiness is intact."

"When I said that I loved you, I meant it. But here's the footnote you wanted. I love God more, and I will walk away if I have to."

The assault on his ego was swift. He looked at Gabrielle as if his eyes were crossed. "What? Just like that?" He snapped his fingers.

Standing her ground, she nodded slowly. Struggling to confirm her words, Gabrielle whispered as a tear escaped, "Just like that."

Chapter Thirty-Five

*G*abrielle had to make Cameron believe her about the importance of her whole armor of salvation. She desperately wanted them to be in one accord with their faith. Hugs, kisses, and saying "I love you" couldn't compromise her conviction. She could thank Sandra for reminding her of that.

Still struggling to keep her emotions in check, she was reminded of the saying, "You'd better stand for something, or you'll fall for anything." Unfortunately, she couldn't bear to see the hurt her warning had inflicted.

If it didn't involve her cousin, Denise would probably say about the situation, "He'll get over it."

As she blended in with the group entering the mansion, Gabrielle hoped so.

Stately long windows framing both sides of the massive front door were showcased by even taller archways that embellished the seemingly endless wraparound porch. Numerous tables and chair groupings were dotted everywhere, reminding Gabrielle of a shaded outdoor sidewalk café.

Clearing the doorway and stepping into a foyer the size of two rooms, Gabrielle was in awe. The home had twenty-six rooms, according to their tour guide. Putting it all into perspective, she considered that the average house has six to eight rooms. Ten to twelve were pure luxury. Her parents were affluent, and they had a five-bedroom/eleven-room house.

An elaborate stairwell climbed the left side of the lobby and began winding its way up as it crossed the upper floor. The guide continued her spiel, "One writer reported this mansion has more than fifteen-thousand-four hundred square feet. We haven't taken the time to measure it."

The woman chuckled to herself and then snapped back into her professional mode when no one else laughed. "It's now listed on the national historic registry. The Jemison-Van de Graaff Mansion is often rented out for functions like fashion shows, bridal parties, weddings . . ."

Weddings. The interior design was stunning. Gabrielle could easily imagine it as an excellent backdrop for memorable romantic photographs. She would love to get married in a nostalgic place such as this. Sadly, she would probably never see inside this mansion again if Cameron Jamieson wasn't going to be her groom. Her heart was breaking over the uncertainty of whether his pride would let him surrender completely to Jesus.

Unfortunately, he hid behind one Scripture that says if a person believes on the Lord Jesus Christ, he shall be saved. Yet he ignored the ones that teach about righteous living, presenting his body as a living sacrifice holy to God, and God resisting the prideful.

"Hey, are you okay?" Talise asked, as she scooted next to her.

Gabrielle nodded. If she spoke, she might bawl. Evidently, Talise wasn't convinced as she wrapped her arm around Gabrielle's shoulder.

"I don't know what happened between you and Cameron, but something did. One minute I glanced at you two lovebirds whispering sweet nothings to each other. The next moment, you left Cameron standing alone. Since I love both of you, it's hard to take sides, but I have no problem jumping allegiance as I see fit."

Gabrielle chuckled. "You married a Jamieson and you've become a traitor."

"Nah. You know we'll always be close. You were there for me and your loyalty forged our friendship forever."

"I don't want to burden you." She sniffed.

"You're kidding me, right?" Talise gave her a dumbfounded expression.

"I broke Cameron's heart, and then mine crumbled. Although I can't choose who I love, I will give him up for Christ. I know He can recycle a person's way of thinking and give him back to me in mint condition."

Looping their arms together, the two fell in step as they trailed along with the group. Their guide was explaining the Italian influence on the architecture.

"It took three years to finish this masterpiece, which began in 1859. This mansion was considered the most elaborate great house in the state of Alabama before the Civil War. It was almost destroyed before it ended. Rumor has it, Senator Robert Jemison fled to a swamp near his plantation and hid from the Yankees," their guide stated. "But back to the house. He spared no expense, incorporating the latest technology like flushing toilets, copper bathtubs—"

"What about the African-Americans he enslaved?" an unidentified Jamieson asked, interrupting her.

"Senator Jemison owned eight to ten slaves who managed this house. He also owned at least seven other plantations with more than four hundred slaves," she said. "Here's another piece of gossip. A tale is still believed today that an underground tunnel exists where slaves escaped. It was actually a deep well used for cooling purposes to preserve food before modern refrigeration was even heard of."

"You know," Talise whispered, distracting Gabrielle, "I've grown since God saved me last year. You would be proud. I believe the Lord

266

is telling me to tell you to be still. He knows His plans to prosper you, to give you hope and a future." She paused and then smiled. "You know where that came from in the Bible, don't you?"

Gabrielle nodded and wasn't going to say, but Talise continued to press her. "Jeremiah 29:11."

Pumping her fist as a form of victory celebration, Talise was about to steer Gabrielle in another direction when they bumped into someone. Turning around, a handsome guy, wearing a family reunion T-shirt, gave them a cocky grin.

"Please tell me you two aren't related to me," he flirted.

"Sorry. You missed your chance." Talise stated. "I'm a Jamieson, my baby's a Jamieson, and so is my husband." She stuck out her hand and nearly blinded him with her rock.

He looked to Gabrielle for her to show or tell. Shrugging, she began to explain that she was a guest. "I'm not a Jamieson—"

At that instant, muscular arms snaked around her waist. Cameron answered for her. "She's definitely taken, trust me." He dismissed the man and turned to Talise. "Your husband is coming right behind me to claim his package." Then he ushered Gabrielle away from the crowd.

Rubbing his jaw, Gabrielle stared into his eyes. "I'm sorry if I hurt you."

"I can bounce back, baby. I'd rather take the blow than you, because I'll seriously hurt somebody if they mess over you. I'm not losing you by any means necessary."

—⟋〰—

Yeah, Cameron had rebounded all right. That was after the shock wore off. When his brothers approached him and advised they were taking their brood to the children's museum later, they must have sensed something wasn't right. He lied that he was fine.

Cameron never had a reason to fib to his brothers, except now. He had to save face after losing his heart. They had trapped him into a yes-or-no answer until he told them what happened, just to get rid of them.

Hours later, back in his hotel room, he was exhausted after a day at the mansion. Cameron stared at the Gideon Bible on the nightstand. The voice in his head wasn't Gabrielle's, but something Parke had said a while back.

"You think you have everything and are in need of nothing. In actuality, you are poor, naked, and disgusting," his brother had said. Then Parke told him to check the book of Revelation for himself.

Cameron had read chapter three and verse seventeen, but the passage didn't seem to apply to him. In theory, he knew the Bible basics. If he wanted to discuss specific principles, there was always Gabrielle's brother Philip. The evangelist had been engaging, but Cameron could hold his own. He just wasn't convinced there was more to salvation.

Closing his eyes, he prayed. "Lord, I'm clueless to what Gabrielle wants from me. Help me to convince her that You sent her the best man . . ."

—⁓—

The weekend ended on a jovial note among the Jamiesons, except for Cameron. If any other woman was putting him through this nonsense, he would have walked. God help him because Gabrielle was forever testing him.

Cameron gave her his word that he would make attending church with her a priority. That was easier said than done. On the second Sunday in a row, he struggled to get into the message. By the third Sunday, his relationship with Gabrielle was strained.

One night, he was unable to shake his bad mood until finally he placed another call to Philip. Disappointed, but not surprised, that he had to leave a message, he did and waited.

When Philip called back, Cameron hurried through the pleasantries. "I love your sister. I want to marry her, but Jesus is tearing us apart, not bringing us together."

When Cameron finished venting, Philip's first comment was simply, "Hmm."

"If the Lord is pulling you two apart, then it's for a good reason. What seems to be the sticking point?"

That was the million dollar question. "We seem to have a difference of opinion about the definition of being heaven-bound." What was it about Philip that made him comfortable with sharing the details of his conversations with Gabrielle?

"You've come to me just as Nicodemus approached Jesus with a perplexing question. Despite his high IQ and status as a member of the Jewish ruling council, he couldn't comprehend God's complete, simple plan for salvation. In John 3:3–5, Jesus told him no one can enter the kingdom of God unless he is born of the water and spirit. Have you done that?"

"I didn't think that was necessary if I accepted Christ and believed on Him that I'm saved."

"Among other things, the Bible is God's instruction in righteousness. I think we both can agree on that, but I would encourage you to complete your course work with Jesus. Are you attending church with my sister?"

"Some, but I just can't get into the preaching," Cameron admitted with a deep grunt. "I can't focus. Maybe I needed to be under a tent," he said off-handedly.

"I'm back stateside now to hold a weekend revival in Miami."

It was just a joke, but Cameron gave it some real consideration. Maybe a change of environment might be good for him. Coming to a decision, he asked Philip for the times and location. "I'll book my flight. Again, please don't share this information with Gabrielle . . . I don't want to come across as weak."

"If only you would allow yourself to be weak, because that is when we are the strongest in the Lord," Philip counseled and then gave him the information. "I look forward to seeing you, but let's do some prep work before you come. It's repenting time. Confess your faults to God, the sins you've committed with your body and in your mind. God is a rewarder of those who diligently seek Him."

Philip seemed to command his soul's attention through the phone, causing Cameron to shut out everything around him. As he listened to the man of God pray, a tear escaped from Cameron's eye for the first time in recent memory.

Something was wrong. Jamieson men did not cry. They were equipped to lead the world. Ever since he was a boy, he was drilled to have pride in himself. Now Philip was asking him to turn over his driver's seat to Jesus and allow Him to direct his path.

Another tear escaped, as Philip prayed for him to have the faith to trust and believe not just handpicked Scriptures, but the whole counsel of God. When they ended the call, Cameron's face was wet. The floodgate had opened.

You say I am rich. I have everything I want. I don't need a thing, and you don't realize that you're wretched and miserable and poor and blind and naked.

Cameron blinked. It wasn't Philip's voice this time. It shook with the authority of God. Was Jesus condemning him? That's when Cameron heard his own soul cry out, "Lord, save me."

Chapter Thirty-Six

*G*abrielle hadn't spoken with Cameron much in the past week. It was time to accept that she and Cameron had drifted apart. Talise's mother-in-law had been right. There were still red flags. Yet she had to give Cameron credit for trying. After their last conversation at the family reunion, he had attended church but only seemed to suffer through it for her sake.

Sniffling, Gabrielle dabbed her nose and finished her morning prayer. Getting up from her knees, she took a deep breath to gather her emotions. As she walked into the bathroom and studied her reflection in the mirror, she whispered, "Lost love."

"Oh that men would give thanks and praise unto Me for My unfailing love and wondrous deeds," God spoke from Psalm 107:15.

Gabrielle nodded and closed her eyes. "Yes, Lord, in good times and sad times, I will praise Your name," she uttered, trying to let the words settle in her heart.

As she gathered mental strength, Gabrielle showered and began to praise Him for all He had done. She thanked Him for her family, health, job, safe travel to foreign countries over the years, and the love of a good man. The more she praised Him, the anointing fell. When the presence of the Lord descended, she worshiped Him in words and song.

After her shower, not only did her body feel clean, but her soul felt clean. With a ravishing appetite, she went into the kitchen. Suddenly, her phone rang. It was only seven thirty.

Checking the ID, it was her mother. She frowned. An early call could mean something was wrong. "Hello," she answered tentatively. "Mom, is everything okay?"

"That's why I was calling. I was sitting here reading my Bible, and God placed you on my heart. Are you okay, sweetie?"

How was she to answer that? If she said no, then her fellowship with God earlier would be in vain. But a yes response felt like a half truth. "I had church this morning with Jesus. I've been bummed lately about Cameron, and God wanted me to praise Him."

With her phone anchored between her shoulder and ear, Gabrielle opened the refrigerator door and grabbed some eggs to make an omelet. She smiled, thinking about how her mother stuffed her omelets with two kinds of cheese and Italian sausage, but she didn't have those ingredients.

"How do you know God is a healer unless you're sick? How do you know God has the answer unless you have a problem? How do you know God is a way maker unless there's no way out?" Veronica began to sing the lyrics to a song. Gabrielle was convinced God had given it especially to her mother when she was a child.

Closing her eyes, Gabrielle listened as tears fell. "Thank you, Momma."

"Love is a good thing, sweetie. God has Cameron in your life for a reason. Maybe it was never about you, but Jesus was working on him. Remember, God has a blessing with your name on it. Trust Him for the gift."

Gabrielle nodded. Soon the conversation turned to what she was mixing into her omelet, how her job was going, and the big case over which Drexel was presiding.

"I sure miss the airlines, when you could jump on the plane and come home just about any time."

"Me too."

"But that won't keep me from my baby. Your dad and I can drive down, so can Drexel, and you know Dashan won't want to be left out."

Gabrielle imagined how nice it would be to see them again. "Sounds like fun, but hold off for now. I may be jetting off to the Philippines soon because of some restructuring at that office. I'll know after a conference call this morning."

"Will do. While you're over there, bring home one of those hot Filipino men."

"Right." Gabrielle laughed at her mother's nonsense. "I can't handle the men here. What makes you think I can handle one over there?"

"Honey, you've been handling men all your life."

"Yeah, and you see what that's gotten me—a man with common sense, but no God sense," Gabrielle griped, as they said their goodbyes. Immediately, remembering her prayer time with Jesus, she repented of her complaining.

"Okay, God. Let me rephrase that. I don't want to be a nun."

—⚏—

Cameron headed to the airport straight from his office. He had to agree with Gabrielle about her brother. There was something special about the evangelist. Philip truly had a gift if he could get Cameron on a plane to attend church.

The man of God had opened Cameron's eyes to see that his life in Christ was deficient. Yes, Cameron already believed that God raised His Son, Jesus, from the dead, he believed in the Name of Jesus for his salvation, and he believed the Bible. The only thing left to fulfill was Acts 2:38. He was not ready to fully surrender his life to Christ.

Once he was settled in his seat on the plane, a woman made herself comfortable and sat next to him. Instantly, he thought about Gabrielle. At this point in his life, despite all his worldly possessions, he had nothing to offer her.

The more his seatmate tried to engage him in idle conversation, the more he pulled his mind toward Jesus. He had fought hard not to lust after his woman, he wasn't about to lust over a stranger. At times like this, he wanted a ring on Gabrielle's finger and his too. More than anything, Cameron wanted them to belong to each other.

It had been a while since he'd visited Miami. Years ago, he attended the National Society for Black Engineers conference. The thought never once crossed his mind that he would return later for a tent revival service.

After landing, he located the ground transportation area to pick up his rental car. Programming the GPS, Cameron headed toward downtown Miami where his hotel on Biscayne was located. It was literally across the street from Bayfront Park where the revival would begin soon. He checked his watch—only an hour and a half to spare.

In spite of cutting it close, he was determined to be in attendance. Noting the many other nearby attractions, his immediate focus was on the revival. Nothing could distract him from it. Whatever confidence Gabrielle had in the Lord, Cameron wanted it also.

He checked in, showered in record time, and dressed for Miami's eighty-degree, late September weather. Crossing Biscayne Boulevard, Cameron headed to the park where men and women were passing out flyers. Many wore T-shirts declaring *Jesus Is Coming Back—Be Ready*. He accepted a flyer, which invited the public to the Tina Hills Pavilion where the honorable Evangelist Philip Dupree would preach the uncensored Word of God.

Instead of a large white tent, the organizers had constructed a covered platform. A crowd was already gravitating toward the music. As though a magnet pulled him by a force greater than him, Cameron strolled through the crowd. Any other time, he would have been content sitting in the back. But not now. Cameron spied an empty chair near the front between two wide-hipped women.

Glancing around for other options, there weren't any. Taking a deep breath, Cameron proceeded ahead. He was already out of his comfort zone. The pair seemed more than eager to shift their bottoms to make room for him. Seconds later, he was sandwiched in between. Evidently, the Lord had a sense of humor because Cameron wouldn't be able to escape if he wanted to.

With his eyes closed, he didn't want anything to distract him while he meditated on everything Philip had said the other night. When the music softened, a young man invited anyone who had something good to say about the Lord to stand and share it with the crowd. One after another, people testified about healings, drug deliverance, homes for homeless families, and so on.

Suddenly, Cameron felt ashamed that he had no ready testimony about what God had done for him. Jesus had blessed him with good health and a good life. As he continued to listen, one man boasted of how he had everything his heart desired, but he didn't have Jesus.

"I was miserable without Jesus. Friends, women, and money could no longer satisfy the hunger in my life," the older man said to the audience. "But one day, I found a Bible someone left on a table in a restaurant. I picked it up and began to read it. The next thing I knew, a woman came back to get her Bible. When she saw tears streaming from my eyes, God let her know His Word was to be shared. She told me that I could have it."

He pumped a worn Bible in the air. "This is more valuable than my Lexus, my ten-room home, or the hundred-dollar bills I used to carry in my wallet just because." When the man started dancing, others rejoiced with him. Even Cameron got on his feet and clapped along with those who shouted, "Praise Jesus!"

The testimonies continued, further convicting Cameron that he had shunned God without even knowing it. Soon enough, Philip came to the stage and asked everyone to stand.

"This is the day the Lord has made, let us rejoice!" he shouted. "If we fail to praise Him, the Bible says the Lord who created the wind, sea, and mountains will command the rocks to rise up and praise Him. Praise Jesus!" he instructed the crowd. More dancing, rejoicing, and talking to Jesus followed.

Finally, Philip regained the attention of the crowd, which had grown to a huge number.

"If you have your Bibles in hand, go with me to Galatians 5:19–21, and I'll begin reading, *'The acts of the sinful nature are obvious: sexual immorality, impurity and debauchery; idolatry and witchcraft; hatred, discord, jealousy, fits of rage, selfish ambition, dissensions, factions and envy; drunkenness, orgies, and the like. I warn you, as I did before, that those who live like this will not inherit the kingdom of God.'*"

He closed his Bible. "That sounds scary, doesn't it? And you should be scared if your lifestyle is listed among them. When is the last time you thought, read, or heard anyone preaching about hell?"

Cameron had to think. He couldn't recall.

"If I don't preach it, if it's not discussed over the water cooler, or even if you choose to never think about it—that doesn't mean hell isn't ready and waiting for its next victim. Don't let it be you. Just say no to the devil!"

For the next hour, with a captivated audience, Philip broke down the process of what it takes to be completely saved.

Finally, he ended with, "Come today and get your sins washed away. The blood of Jesus, without detergent or bleach, will wash you clean . . . won't you come?"

Despite the tight fit between the two ladies, Cameron leaped from his seat. Accepting the call, he was ready to experience his Nicodemus moment.

Chapter Thirty-Seven

*G*abrielle received the news secondhand before Sunday's church service. Talise via Ace told her that Cameron was out of town, and he didn't offer any clues about his destination.

She had digested that tidbit with sorrow, despite the morning sermon about "Casting our cares on Jesus because He cares for us."

As a couple, she was used to being privy to the details—both small and important—in Cameron's life. Gabrielle told herself it didn't matter anymore. She was packing for her own trip—a daylong flight to the Philippines. Unfortunately, her trip was a job-related one to put out fires and stabilize her staff.

Monday morning, she boarded the American Airlines plane for Chicago. It was her first of two stops, which would add up to a twenty-five-hour flight to Manila. At least, she had a two-and-a-half-hour layover where she could have breakfast with her parents.

They were waiting for her by the baggage claim area. After hugs and kisses, the Duprees whisked their daughter away to Yia Yia's Pancake House for some special Belgian waffles. Once they were seated and had placed their orders, Veronica made her concerns known.

"Are you sure you'll be okay? I read that it's monsoon season this time of year."

"I know." Gabrielle nodded. "You would think the company could have launched a new product line and handled restructuring another time of year. I won't be there long, so I'm sure I'll be fine."

Her father drummed his fingers on the table. "Still no word from Cameron, huh? I'm disappointed, but relieved that it's over if he wasn't going to do the right thing."

Now Gabrielle wished she hadn't told her mother about the ultimatum she gave Cameron. And he did try, so she couldn't fault him for that. It was as if he was allergic to the walls of the church building.

"Bernard, don't go worrying her about him before she gets on that plane, or it will ruin her flight," her mother scolded him.

"It's all right. This too shall pass. I will praise God anyway, Daddy."

"That's a good attitude," her father said, as their food was served. Knowing they had to get her back to the airport in time for her flight, he requested the check upfront.

Although breakfast was abbreviated, she enjoyed her meal and gave her parents tight hugs when they dropped her back off at O'Hare Airport.

Breezing through the security checkpoint, she had one hour to spare before arriving at the terminal gate. Gabrielle spent some time browsing in the airport gift shop.

Once aboard the Korean Air jetliner, she settled in for the thirteen-hour flight to Seoul. Then she would change planes for another four-hour flight to Manila. Sadly, there weren't enough movies to watch or books to read to keep her mind off Cameron. The only option she had left was to put on her headset and hope for sleep.

Awhile later, she stirred from her nap. To utilize the time, she pulled out her dictionary and brushed up on her Spanish. Then, out of sheer curiosity, Gabrielle tried her hand at Filipino, although English was widely spoken. Somehow, her mind kept drifting back to Cameron.

The next day, the plane finally touched down in the Philippines. After retrieving her luggage, she boarded the shuttle to her hotel suite five miles away in Makati.

Nodding to a few weary-looking passengers, Gabrielle was now wide awake. Jet lag hadn't kicked in yet. She was still operating on Central Standard Time not Greenwich mean time. Glancing out the window, she could see downtown in the distance. Called the City of Skyscrapers, this enchanting place would be her home for the next six days.

Finally checked in, Gabrielle used her international calling card to let her parents know she had arrived and was in her hotel suite. She chatted with her mother, who cautioned her to be careful and do plenty of shopping. When she disconnected, Gabrielle indulged in a hot bath, which didn't do anything to make her sleepy.

Grabbing her laptop to check her email, she was online when an unexpected Skype call came through. Her heart skipped a beat when she recognized Cameron's number. They had barely spoken the previous week, and now he wanted her attention.

She couldn't deal with him at the moment. Gabrielle was there to do a stellar job. As her first overseas trip for the company, she planned to prove why she deserved the salary they paid her. Opting to focus on the task ahead of her, she courageously rejected his call when she wanted to talk to him so badly.

On Wednesday morning, she woke sluggishly. A shower and some food helped her get her bearings. Gabrielle then left the hotel and walked with a purpose into the Rockwell Center to the satellite office. Expecting to meet with three shifts, she prayed her sleep would hold off for the time being.

Later that evening, Gabrielle barely made it back to her suite. There she collapsed, designer suit and all, into the bed. At three in the morning Manila time, starvation gripped her, and she was wide awake. After ordering room service, Gabrielle checked her email. She thought about

Cameron and her refusal to accept his Skype and fired off a quick email to him.

Hi Cameron, I'm in the Philippines on business, she wrote and then hesitated. She didn't want to play a round of tit-for-tat with him. Cameron didn't let her know he was going out of town and that's why he didn't know she was in Manila. Actually, Gabrielle wanted to say, I miss you, I love you. But what was the use? Staring at the words already typed, she left it at that and pushed Send.

Five minutes later, he emailed her back. Hey babe, I'm in a meeting. Be safe. I am so much in love with you. C.

That's right. St. Louis was thirteen hours behind her. Gabrielle's eyes teared at his declaration. Unfortunately, their love couldn't keep them together. Clearing her head, Gabrielle turned her attention toward work and reviewed her game plan to boost employee morale. She didn't have to be featured on the popular CBS show *Undercover Boss* to listen to her staff's concerns and recommendations.

A computer tone alerted her to an email. It was from Cameron. She opened it and read aloud. I'm sorry, sweetheart, that I couldn't give you the attention you deserved earlier. I wanted to share some great news with you. Then I learned you're a big ocean away from me. But don't think I won't cross it. When are you coming back home? Anyway, I went to church on Sunday and fulfilled my Nicodemus walk. Jesus completely saved me.

Her mind raced. Ace said Cameron was out of town. Cameron went to church? Gabrielle had so many questions that she forgot to praise God for what He had done.

"My angels rejoice over one sinner who repents," God spoke from Luke 15:10.

Ashamed, Gabrielle repented immediately. "Lord, forgive me for judging him. I know You chasten those you love. Thank You for loving Cameron enough to save him."

She then emailed Cameron back. Hallelujah! I'm excited with

you, honey. I miss you too. Gabrielle wanted to question his whereabouts but held her tongue and fingers.

His response came quickly. You know this is not going to work for me. We're going to have to Skype, but I'll have to wait until after I get home from work. I have too much activity going on in the department today. I want to see you. Will you still be awake? C

She could feel his excitement and typed: There is a thirteen-hour time difference between us. St. Louis is behind Manila. Four P.M. your time is already the next day for me. Okay, but I can't guarantee how I'll look without my beauty sleep when you see me.

Gabrielle logged off and set her alarm. There was no way she was going to miss his Skype, but she also needed to get a power nap for the next day at the headquarters.

The next thing she knew, her phone alarm frightened her awake. Gabrielle didn't even realize she had fallen into a deep sleep. Getting up, she hurried into the bathroom and washed her face, brushed her teeth, and put on light makeup, hoping to hide the bags under her eyes.

Signing on to her computer, she waited for the connection. At exactly 3:59, Cameron signed in. She laughed. *Some things never change,* she thought, remembering he had never been late for one of their dates.

When his face came into clear view on her monitor, she sighed. *Lord, he is so sweet and handsome. I praise You for giving him a testimony of Your goodness.*

Reaching out, Cameron touched the screen as if his hand could penetrate it and touch her. "You are so beautiful. I love you."

"I love you too." Her eyes blurred and it wasn't because she was half awake.

Linking his fingers, he sat straighter, as if he had prepared a speech. "Where do I begin?" He paused and squinted closer to her monitor. "Did I tell you how pretty you are?"

When she nodded, Cameron continued, "I've been in contact with Philip."

Gabrielle's mouth dropped open. "What? Philip? When . . ."

"This past weekend in Miami, I attended one of his revivals. Philip opened my eyes to things that I've been missing for years in the Bible."

She had hoped to hear those words from his mouth, and they finally came while she was thousands of miles away.

"Baby, don't cry," Cameron said, reaching out to the monitor again. Shaking her head, she whispered, "I won't," as the tears fell.

"It's okay because one night after talking to Philip, God started speaking to me. I cried for the first time since . . . since . . . I don't know, maybe grade school. But I truly repented."

So her brother had reached him. Thank You, Jesus. She dabbed her eyes with her fingers. Needing a tissue, she didn't want to leave the computer to get some from the bathroom.

"Anyway I flew to Miami where Philip was conducting another outdoor revival. That place on the beach was nothing like the tent meeting in Forest Park. He had been counseling me, and last Friday, I made up my mind. I went all the way with Jesus. My family, especially my brothers and cousins couldn't believe it. Once the shock wore off, let me just say we had a Holy Ghost party."

Bawling by now, Gabrielle got up and retrieved the entire box of tissue from the bathroom. Momentarily forgetting about Cameron, she wiped her face and then lifted her hands in praise. Then she mingled talking to God with singing a victory song.

Hearing Cameron praying in the background caused her to compose herself. When he finished, she smiled. "Come here." Gabrielle urged him closer to the monitor. When he did, she smacked a kiss on the screen. He returned the favor and they laughed.

"You know that's not going to do it for me either," he said with a smirk.

Her heart was filled with so much joy, she giggled. "It better not."

"So am I forgiven for everything that I did wrong in our relationship?"

"I don't remember a thing." Gabrielle smiled before they signed off.

Chapter Thirty-Eight

*C*ameron's life would never be the same, and he thanked Jesus for that. But, at that moment, the love of his life was missing, and he couldn't bear it. With thousands of miles separating them, it left him no choice but to go and get his woman.

Gabrielle told him that she was counting the days until she left the country on Sunday night. After assuring her that he would pick her up at the airport, Cameron came to his senses. That was too long for him to wait. He would have to work on mastering patience at another time.

Without balking at the cost, he booked an afternoon flight the next day to Manila. Next, he picked up the phone and called Philip. When he answered, Cameron greeted him with a resounding, "Praise the Name of Jesus!"

"Well, Brother Cameron, I'm rejoicing with you."

"I would like to speak with your parents. Do you mind giving me their phone number?"

"I was wondering when you would need that. Sure, and congratulations." Philip recited the number and then listened patiently as Cameron shared the awesomeness of God in his life.

Before calling the Duprees, Cameron prayed. Gabrielle's mother answered the phone.

"Good evening, Mrs. Dupree. This is Cameron Jamieson, and I would like to speak with your husband."

There was a slight hesitation before she responded, "It's about time you called, Cameron, and congratulations. My son gave us your salvation report. Praise the Lord! Hold on, I'll get my husband." Muffling the phone, she called for Bernard. "Pick up the phone, dear."

When he came on the line, Cameron invited Gabrielle's mother to stay on. "Mr. and Mrs. Dupree, I want to thank you for having such an incredible daughter. I have been blessed to be a man whom Jesus saved and filled with fire and a desire to walk with Him until the day I die. I need Gabrielle to walk with me, and so I'm requesting your blessings for me to ask for her hand in marriage."

Although Cameron held his breath, he had Jesus on his side. He never had a problem with her parents, just the judge. That would soon change too.

Mr. Dupree cleared his throat but didn't respond right away. "I appreciate you coming to me in a respectful manner concerning my baby girl. I praise God that you surrendered and my daughter remained steadfast."

Patience turned into impatience as Cameron waited for the man to say yea or nay. He held in his sigh and continued to listen to Gabrielle's father's stipulations on how to treat her. That's where he needed no guidance. He truly loved her.

"So I consent to you asking my daughter. Her answer is up to her," Mr. Dupree said, granting permission.

When they disconnected, Cameron had a pounding headache. As he went into the kitchen, he prepared a light snack. He had to go ring shopping before he boarded that plane. There was no way the university would see him the next day. When Tiffany & Co. opened the next morning, he would be their first customer, and he wouldn't leave until

284

he had an engagement ring wrapped inside Tiffany's trademark little blue box.

———ɯ———

When Cameron landed in Manila, feeling drugged and seeing double, he was certain his eyes were bloodshot. That was the longest flight of his life! He needed rest, a hot shower, and Gabrielle. At the moment, she had precedence over everything else. First, he thanked Jesus for safe travels over the airways and waterways.

It took him this long in life, but he could now say with confidence that God had written his name in the Book of Life. He didn't need Gabrielle to point out that Scripture in Revelation.

Mrs. Dupree gave him the name of the hotel where Gabrielle was staying. Her father advised him it wouldn't look right for him to stay at the same hotel, urging him to strongly consider making his accommodations somewhere else. Not to give the appearance of wrongdoing, he cited 1 Thessalonians 5:22.

With his carry-on roller in one hand, Cameron patted the Lucida one-carat diamond ring in his pocket before popping a breath mint into his mouth. He would have to do something about his bloodshot eyes later because he wasn't making another stop. He was on a mission.

Grabbing a taxi, he headed straight to Gabrielle's hotel. He couldn't believe the traffic on a Saturday afternoon. "And people call New York the City That Never Sleeps," he mumbled under his breath, as the driver sped in the direction of towering skyscrapers.

After paying the cabbie, he strolled into the Best Western. The lobby was impressive without an overkill of luxury. He went to the desk for a house phone to call her room.

After three rings, she answered drowsily, like he felt.

"Hi, babe."

"Cameron, hi." She suddenly came alive. "Why are you calling me on the hotel line instead of my cell phone? You're spending way too much money on calls when I'll be home soon."

"Not soon enough." He snickered. "It's already cost me." The last-minute trip was thousands of dollars—let alone the cost of her ring—but he couldn't put a price on love. "What are you doing?"

"Lying here with my eyes closed, dreaming about seeing you soon. I really miss you."

"Good. How much?"

"I see your arrogance hasn't left you. What do you mean how much?"

Cameron had enough of this teasing. "Baby, I missed you more. Come down to the lobby and find out. You have ten minutes." *Click.* If he didn't give her a time limit, she would be all night. Anything longer than that, he might be snoring in the lobby. Going to the bank of elevators, he leaned against the wall, crossed his arms, and waited.

When the doors to one elevator opened, Gabrielle rushed out, looking around frantically. She screamed when she saw him before almost barreling him over with hugs. Laughing, he enjoyed the feel of just holding her. He didn't release her until she squirmed.

Stepping out of his embrace, Gabrielle blinked rapidly as if she still didn't believe it. "You came all this way for me?" She was delirious. "I told you I would be home the day after tomorrow . . ."

"Patience is a virtue. I don't have it yet." He kissed her nose then tugged her toward the lobby in a secluded corner for privacy. When she sat, Cameron joined her and clasped her hands in his. Then he brought both up to his lips and kissed them.

"First of all, haven't you ever heard Diana Ross sing, 'Ain't No Mountain High Enough'? In this case, I couldn't swim across the ocean, so I flew."

Again, she almost barreled him over in a gripping hug. He laughed until he had to detangle her arm from around his neck so he could breathe. Then she smacked tiny kisses on his lips.

"I guess you're happy to see me."

"Do I have to cry to prove it?" She scrunched her nose then hugged him again and again. Again, he had to loosen her hold to get air.

He stared at the love of his life as he slid to one knee. Gabrielle gasped, watching his every movement.

"Before God sent His angel—you—to me, I thought I was all that. My parents drilled into my head to be self-assured, which I translated into being self-sufficient, but you proved me wrong. I am nothing without God, and I'm lifeless without you in my life."

Cameron waited while she wiped at her tears.

"Your father and your mother have given me their blessings. So has Philip. I haven't spoken with Dashan or checked in with Drexel, but the judge will have to deal with me if you consent to be my wife. I love you, Gabrielle. You've fit into my puzzle and become my better half. Will you marry me?"

"Yes," she whispered, but Cameron shook his head.

"I need a resounding yes, like folks shout Amen in church."

She flew off the sofa into his arms again, cutting off his airway. Very loudly, she screamed "Yes!" in his ear, causing a ringing sensation. Now he was hearing echoes.

When he pulled out the ring box, Gabrielle sucked in her breath. "You went to Tiffany's?"

He nodded and opened the box. After Cameron steadied Gabrielle's hand, he slipped the platinum ring on her finger. It was a perfect fit—just like she was in his life.

Six months later

*G*abrielle Jamieson had no complaints after exchanging vows with Cameron at the Jemison-Van de Graaff Mansion in Tuscaloosa. Her wedding day was better than she could have ever imagined. In the morning, she and her husband would fly off for their weeklong honeymoon in Brazil.

As the moonlight stirred Gabrielle from her peaceful slumber, she smiled and fluttered her lids. Once she opened her eyes, she stared at her sleeping husband and admired his handsomeness. Carefully, she slipped out of bed. She didn't want to leave her husband's protective arms. But she was filled with so much joy that she couldn't sleep. She had to write down her emotions.

God had blessed her—really—more abundantly than she could have ever hoped for. She walked through the rooms of their luxury hotel suite in search of her carry-on and fumbled inside for her tattered handbook of romance.

Staring at the notebook decorated with flowers, this would probably be her last entry in it. After all, she had met and married the man of her dreams. Fairy tales do come true, and she didn't need a fairy godmother when Jesus was her Godfather. Cradling the notebook, she sat at the desk and turned on the lamp. After a moment of deep concentration, finally, she scribbled, "The end. Happily Ever After!"

Suddenly her husband snuck up behind her. Wrapping his arms around her neck, Cameron leaned over and coaxed her for a kiss. While he distracted her, he plucked the pen from her fingers. Turning to the last page of her handbook of romance, he put a line through her note and wrote, "The Beginning of Our Bliss, in Jesus' Name. Amen."

"Come back to bed, babe," he whispered.

At the sound of his words, the Lord brought her verse 22 of Ephesians 5, *"Wives, submit yourselves to your own husbands as you do to the Lord."*

Smiling, she thought, *Jesus, I can do that.*

Then she recalled the twenty-fifth verse in chapter five: *"Husbands, love your wives, just as Christ loved the church and gave himself up for her."*

She was sure Cameron wouldn't have a problem fulfilling that command either.

Giggling, Gabrielle stood and took her husband's hand. Following his lead, she replied, "Yes, dear."

BOOK CLUB QUESTIONS

1. When Cameron asked Gabrielle about her interest in her family roots, she responded that she was satisfied with what she already knew. What is your interest in your roots?

2. Are you content with your spiritual level? What is your interest in knowing more about Jesus, or are you satisfied with what you know already about the Bible?

3. Did Gabrielle have a real reason to keep Cameron at arm's length because he didn't measure up to her level of faith?

4. Discuss Gabrielle's constant prayer to Jesus not to fall when she took the leap of faith to date Cameron.

5. Was Cameron justified in missing Sunday services by volunteering his time to help others?

6. How did you view Sandra's talk with Gabrielle? What about the advice from Gabrielle's mother and friends, Denise and Talise?

7. Cameron based his salvation on one Scripture. Discuss if that is enough.

8. Who was your favorite character and why?

9. When was the last time you attended a tent revival? What was your impression?

10. What did you think about Gabrielle's handbook of romance? Have you ever physically or mentally kept record of what you want in a man, and did you get exactly what you wanted?

Look for more stories in the Jamieson Legacy.
Please visit www.patsimmons.net

For the wisdom of this world is foolishness in God's sight.
As it is written: "He catches the wise in their craftiness."
—1 Corinthians 3:19:

To the many bloggers who have given me space to talk about my Jamieson men; the radio hosts who invited me on their shows; and many readers who sent me emails and posted reviews, I do not take your kindness and the opportunities lightly. May God bless you for blessing me.

To the military facilities across the country that have welcomed me to their facilities—thank you. I salute our active/retiree military service men and women who have become fans. Thank you for your support and service.

Shout out to my Guilty fan club captains, thanks for keeping me, my mind, and fingers lifted up in prayer.

Special thanks to Ian Crawford at the Jemison Mansion in Alabama who allowed my Jamiesons to host their first fictional family reunion.

To the staff at Lift Every Voice Books/Moody, God has really blessed me through you.

Happy Birthday to my agent Amanda Luedeke with the MacGregor Literary Agency. Thanks for representing me!

Shout out to my travel agent and GPS guided chauffeur, my husband, Kerry, for his support with my schemes during the past twenty-nine years; my son and daughter, Jared and Simi.

To the descendants of Minerva Jordan Wade; Marshall Cole and Laura Brown; Joseph and Nellie Palmer Wafford Brown; Thomas Carter and Love Ann Shepard; Ned and Priscilla Brownlee; John Wilkinson and Artie Jamison/Charlotte Jamison, and others who were tracked down on the 1800s censuses and other documents; and my in-laws: Simmons, Sinkfield, Croft, Sturdivant, Strickland, Downers . . . and the list goes on.

ABOUT THE AUTHOR

*P*at Simmons considers herself a self-proclaimed genealogy sleuth. She is passionate about researching her ancestors, then casting them in starring roles in her novels. She has been a genealogy enthusiast since her great-grandmother died at the young age of ninety-seven years. Pat enjoys weaving African-American history and local history into contemporary stories.

She describes her Christian walk as an amazing, unforgettable, life-altering experience. She is a baptized believer, who is always willing to share her testimony about God's goodness. She believes God is the true Author who advances her stories.

Pat has a B.S. in mass communications from Emerson College in Boston, MA. She has worked in various media positions in radio, television, and print for more than twenty years. Currently, she oversees the media publicity for the annual RT Booklovers Conventions. She has been a guest on several media outlets, including radio, television, newspapers, and blog radio.

She is the award-winning author of *Talk to Me*, ranked #14 of Top Books in 2008 that Changed Lives by *Black Pearls Magazine;* she also received the Katherine D. Jones Award for Grace and Humility from the Romance Slam Jam committee in 2008. Pat is best known for her Guilty series: *Guilty of Love, Not Guilty of Love,* and *Still Guilty*, which was voted the Best Inspirational Romance for 2010. *Crowning Glory,* was voted the Best Inspirational Romance for 2011 by the RSJ committee.

The Guilty series continued with the Jamieson legacy. *Guilty by Association* (2012) and *The Guilt Trip* (2012). Completing this recent trilogy is *Free from Guilt* (2012). Expect more from the Jamiesons in 2013.

Pat Simmons has converted her sofa-strapped, sports-fanatical husband into an amateur travel agent, untrained bodyguard, and GPS-guided chauffeur. They have a son and daughter.

HERE IS MY PATERNAL GRANDMOTHER JESSIE BROWN WADE COLE ATKINS'S FAMILY TREE:

Jessie was a twin to Louis Wade. They were the third generation of twins.

Jessie's mother was Minerva Brown (my great-grandmother). She was born in Arkansas in 1891 and died in 1988 in St. Louis.

Jessie's father was Odell Wade (my great-grandfather). He was born in Arkansas in 1888 and died in 1972 in St. Louis.

Minerva had twin brothers: Ellis (who lived to be 100 years old) and Louis. Minerva's mother was Nellie Palmer (my great-great grandmother was a twin to Solomon). Both were born in Arkansas in 1874. Nellie's mother was Minerva Palmer born 1848 in Arkansas. Yes, I also have three generations of Minervas in my family.

Minerva's father was Joseph Brown. I am still researching his side. With a last name of Brown, it's not easy.

Odell's mother was Callie Young Lowe (my great-great grandmother and of the Choctaw tribe). She was born in Arkansas.

Odell's father was Winston Wade (my great-great grandfather) was born in Tennessee in 1856. His date of death is unknown.

Winston's mother was Manurva (my great-great-great grandfather). She was born in North Carolina in 1822 or 1828.

Winston's father is unknown, but his father was born in Virginia.

Manurva's father was possibly Jacob Jordan (if so, my fourth great grandfather). He was born in 1801.

Whew! That's all, folks.

THE JAMIESON LEGACY SERIES

978-0-8024-0368-1   978-0-8024-0380-3   978-0-8024-0389-6

The Jamieson Family Legacy series follows the lives of the two Jamieson brothers in Boston—Kidd and Ace—and their cousin Cameron from St. Louis. Kidd, the older brother, struggles with anger and resentment toward his father who abandoned their family (*Guilty by Association*). Ace, on the other hand, is a "chip off the old block." When it comes to women, he's just like his father (*Guilt Trip*). Cameron, their highly educated cousin, thinks the key to saving his family is getting them to recognize and embrace their royal lineage (*Free from Guilt*). These three men will be challenged to accept that the past and present are both in God's hand. Without Him, they can't move toward their future blessings.

Also available as an eBook

L E V B®
LIFT EVERY VOICE BOOKS

lifteveryvoicebooks.com

THE LAST WOMAN STANDING

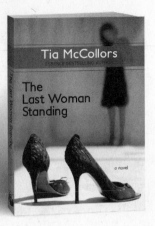

After ten years of marriage, Ace and Lynette Bowers ended their marriage. Four years later, it seems as though their love never ended. Sheila Rushmore is Ace's current girlfriend and a woman who is used to getting what she wants—except Ace's commitment to marriage. When Sheila realizes Lynette may be the cause, she launches a plan to play the hand of God, instead of allowing God to bring the love they all desire.

978-0-8024-9863-2

STEPPIN' INTO THE GOOD LIFE

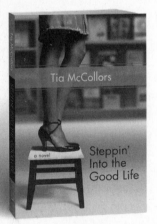

Sheila Rushmore thought she'd be the last woman standing when it was time to fight for her man. Instead Ace, her boyfriend of two years, chose to reunite with his ex-wife, leaving Sheila emotionally devastated. Now, a year later, Sheila moves forward determined to be a better woman—a woman of faith. But now that she's decided to live for God, things will get easier. Right? At least that's what Sheila thinks…

978-0-8024-6291-6

Also available as an eBook

LEVB®
LIFT EVERY VOICE BOOKS

lifteveryvoicebooks.com

LIVING IN THE PINK

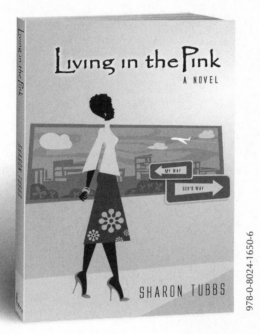

978-0-8024-1650-6

Sister Pinky, Camille, Corrine and Chandra used to "live in the pink" but now they see the pink life for what it is—holding on to the scarlet stain of sin instead of striving to become pure. In this playful and exciting book of short stories, we learn how to pursue the Greatest of Lovers instead of lesser lovers whose promises don't last.

Also available as an eBook

L E V B®
LIFT EVERY VOICE BOOKS

lifteveryvoicebooks.com

LIFT EVERY VOICE BOOKS

Lift every voice and sing
Till earth and heaven ring,
Ring with the harmonies of Liberty;
Let our rejoicing rise
High as the listening skies,
Let it resound loud as the rolling sea.
Sing a song full of the faith that the dark past has taught us,
Sing a song full of the hope that the present has brought us,
Facing the rising sun of our new day begun
Let us march on till victory is won.

The "Black National Anthem," written by James Weldon Johnson in 1900, captures the essence of Lift Every Voice Books. Lift Every Voice Books is an imprint of Moody Publishers that celebrates a rich culture and great heritage of faith, based on the foundation of eternal truth—God's Word. We endeavor to restore the fabric of the African-American soul and reclaim the indomitable spirit that kept our forefathers true to God in spite of insurmountable odds.

We are Lift Every Voice Books—Christ-centered books and resources for restoring the African-American soul.

For more information on other books and products written and produced from a biblical perspective, go to www.lifteveryvoicebooks.com or write to:

Lift Every Voice Books
820 N. LaSalle Boulevard
Chicago, IL 60610
www.lifteveryvoicebooks.com